CANVASBACK COVE

LYNN STEWART

GROOVE CITY
PUBLISHING

For Sweet Petunia

"Most of the time, a kid doesn't think about what he's doing or why. This is the privilege of childhood."

— ROBERT FULGHUM

1

There was no wind. Zip. Nada. Zilch. Nothing. Landon Shultz glanced at the instrument panel on his father's towboat. According to *Little Jo* (aptly named for his mother, who had been a scant five-foot-tall), the wind was blowing out of the south at three miles per hour. Impossible. If the instrument could capture negative wind speed, today's would be off the charts.

He felt the hair at the back of his neck with one hand and wiped the sweat building there with the other. *Damn, it's hot out here.* Thank God for *Little Jo's* diesel engine; she generated her own wind motoring across the waveless Chesapeake Bay. He mindlessly twisted his hair into a man bun and secured it with Susan's hair tie. He sighed with relief as the boat-generated wind evaporated the sweat.

Man bun. Landon had never even heard that term until his friend Susan mentioned it this morning. As a Navy SEAL, his hair was usually buzzed high and tight. His team had just completed a covert mission (they needed to blend into society and not look like Navy SEALS) when the shit hit the fan with his son's mother. Landon didn't bother getting a haircut. Instead, he submitted the request for emergency leave and was out of there as fast as he could pack two duffle bags and secure a flight home.

Earlier this morning, he had been sitting in his father's kitchen scrolling through lists of all-day preschools in Coronado when Susan handed him a cup of coffee and chided him for how scruffy he looked.

"You need a man bun," she said, pulling the hair tie out of her own "messy bun" (another term he had recently learned). She twisted the back of his almost shoulder-length hair and regarded him as an artist might do after slathering the final brushstrokes on what was sure to be a masterpiece. She put her hands on his shoulders just as Willie ran through the kitchen, arms outstretched, plastic salad bowl on his head like a helmet, singing *Na Na Na Na Na Na Na Na Na Na Na Na Batman!* The little guy stopped at the table and grabbed a handful of dry Cheerios and two chunks of a donut off his Batman plate and was back in the family room in a flash, where *Baby Shark* streamed on YouTube.

"Don't you think you're letting him watch too much TV," Susan said, giving Landon's shoulders a little squeeze. She sat down and shot him that scrunched-up eye look. Her light-brown hair, now falling loose around her face without the hair tie, looked freshly highlighted, although Susan would never admit to coloring her hair. She claimed the sun bleached it.

Landon craned his neck and peered into the family room at Willie, who was on the floor pushing his plastic Batmobile around in circles. Susan stared at him with a raised eyebrow. She looked cute today. He should be falling all over her, but he just couldn't. She kissed him last week after making dinner at her house while Landon's dad babysat Willie. He didn't feel a spark but kissed her back anyway, trying to get into it, trying to appreciate this woman who had swooped in to help him with his son. He hadn't really needed the help, but there she was, just like she had swooped in to comfort him after the accident, the summer before their senior year. She'd aged well in the twenty years since then, but...no spark. If he could turn back time and erase last week's kiss, he would do so in a heartbeat.

He got up and turned off the TV, which had quickly gone from background noise to a sensory overload. Landon had bought the smart TV for his dad shortly after arriving home, promising to have movie nights with popcorn and Coke (like they always did when he was growing up). Like a crafty salesman, Landon promised his dad hours upon hours of streaming everything about NASCAR. Landon hated NASCAR but watched it with his dad anyway because that's what good sons did. Right? His father scoffed at the idea. Didn't like the "monstrosity" hanging above the fireplace. And went into a too-long diatribe about supporting the local channels and watching the damned car races live.

"Susan, he's three. He'll be fine." Landon felt guilty for his less than pleasant tone. "Sorry. It's just that, well, he's three. I survived watching cartoons. All. The. Time. Erin used to come over, and we'd watch...*Scooby-Doo*...never mind." He shoved Erin down into the safe he kept locked up deep inside of him. "Thank you for being so good with Willie. He's going to hate it when we go back to Coronado next month."

"So don't go back. You've been in the Navy, what, twenty years? Why don't you retire? Move back here. Help your dad run his business." As if sensing Landon's displeasure with the direction of the conversation, Susan changed course. "I could fly out to see Willie, spend a week during winter and spring breaks. And then, of course, there's summer when I'm not teaching." She twirled her hair into a braid and grabbed for the hair tie that lived perpetually around her wrist. But alas, the hair tie was holding Landon's man bun in place; she released her hair and looked at him expectantly. "I could come down to give you a break, you know, watch Willie while you hit the bars with your buddies."

Landon extended an olive branch in the form of the hair tie. He shook the man bun loose, imagining that he looked a lot like Shaggy from his favorite Saturday morning cartoon. Shaggy. *Scooby-Doo*. Erin. The safe in his heart threatened to pop open. He imagined himself wrapping a thick, metal chain around it, then securing it with an indestructible padlock. He swallowed the key. Susan waved off hair tie, motioning for him to keep it. And as far as her comment about him retiring from the Navy to help his dad run the boatyard was concerned, well, that was none of her damned business.

Landon hadn't planned on spending the whole month at home. But his dad's dockhand was nursing a broken ankle, leaving the elder Shultz to run his small boatyard alone. It had been, what, all of two weeks? He was going absolutely stir crazy and questioned the logic of having taken emergency leave. He loved the Navy, loved being a SEAL, and enjoyed Coronado well enough. But he especially loved the excitement of his deployments—the fear and uncertainty—even if it meant being away from Willie for long stretches.

His relationship with Willie's mother had gone south, pretty much the minute the little meatball was born. The Navy doctor had eventually diagnosed postpartum depression. He prescribed a litany of medications which seemed to help. For a while, anyway. Landon wasn't surprised when she dropped the bomb that she needed a break. Nor was he surprised a few weeks later when she stumbled through a haphazardly prepared speech of being too young to be tied down, not maternal enough, not cut out for nurturing. Landon had listened, nodded, agreed, and generally accepted that this meant he was about to become a single parent. At the end of the conversation, she kissed Willie on the top of his head and practically ran out the door. And, well, that was the end of that.

Landon had hardened his heart a long time before but had allowed himself to grow comfortable playing house. However, it was telling that he wasn't terribly upset when she left. Not to mention being incredibly grateful that he hadn't married her when she got pregnant. Raising Willie alone would be a logistical nightmare, for sure. But he had a good support network on the base. One way or another, he and Willie would survive. His commanding officer wasn't as confident, though, and insisted that Landon take thirty days of emergency leave, more if he needed it.

On summer break from teaching, Susan turned out to be a godsend, telling Landon she'd help him with Willie. He was amazed at how quickly he got used to having her around; she frequently dropped everything to come over and watch Willie on a moment's notice. Other times, she found excuses to pop over. This morning it was fresh donuts from the corner bakery, which he thanked her for but summarily declined. His phone buzzed.

"Hi, Dad. Yep. Let me check." He set the phone on the table and looked at Susan. "There's a sailboat heading to Canvasback Cove from Baltimore. No wind. Broken motor. Needs a tow." He peered into the family room where Willie had abandoned his Batmobile and was curled up on the couch, asleep. "Can you stay with him? Otherwise, I can take him with me."

"Don't be silly. How long will you be gone?" She looked at her watch. "I need to be home at three to help my mom in the restaurant."

"Either my dad or I will be back way before then." He picked up the phone. "Sure, Dad. I'll head up the bay."

As *Little Jo* came abreast of Poplar Island, Landon scanned the horizon for a stationary sailboat—the object of today's mission. Sailboats were useless, in his humble opinion; if you couldn't sail them because the wind refused to blow, what good were they? Today, there was a paucity of sailboats, so the immobile, drifting, listless boat should be easy to find.

Soon, *Little Jo* was making her way under the four-mile-long Chesapeake Bay Bridge and passing several fishing boats anchored near the pilings, the fishermen taking advantage of the structure's shade. Landon cringed at the sound of cars, trucks, and campers on the bridge speeding over the expansion plates. The traffic caused the bridge to vibrate, creating an ominous echo that hovered around the pilings—the low moan from the souls of the people who had jumped or fell to their deaths.

Landon reached up and yanked the man bun loose and gripped the helm as tightly as he could—anything to get his hands to stop shaking. The shade from the bridge brought the temperature down several degrees. Shivering, he revved up the engine. The faster he could get to the other side, back into the blinding sun, the better. *Little Jo* complied, spitting him out like a rat who had suddenly made it all the way through a cold, dark drainpipe. The sun engulfed his body like a snuggly, warm blanket. He slowed *Little Jo* and let her idle while taking several, deliberately deep breaths. Loosening his grip on the helm, he let his hands fall as he plopped into the captain's chair. The sun wasn't warming him fast enough; he brought his legs to his chest, wrapping his arms around them, willing his body to stop shaking.

Landon didn't often think about that period, twenty years before, when he had seriously contemplated jumping off this bridge. Back then, he imaged standing on the girder, raising his arms—middle finger on each hand pointing toward Heaven—and yelling FUCK YOU at the top of his lungs before diving head-first off the tallest part of the bridge span. He had spent many sleepless nights considering ending his life and reviewing his options. The obvious choice, of course, was his hunting rifle. His initial plan had been to drive out to Erin's house and give her the letter he had spent the better part of his senior year writing. A final apology for what had happened that summer was the crux of the letter. After eleven pages, he had finally run out of ways to say *I'm sorry for ruining your life.* And then, a twelfth page, the page where he laid out his feelings for her, all raw and jumbled and complicated.

Landon apologized profusely right after the accident happened. And in the ambulance on the way to the hospital, too—*I'm so sorry, Erin, God, I'm sorry.* An obsessive mantra meant to comfort him as much as it had been to apologize to her. Thinking back, it was astonishing that the paramedics let him ride in the ambulance with her. The fact that the EMT on duty that night kept two boats at his father's marina might have had something to do with it. Even crazier was that the two sets of parents piled into Landon's dad's Suburban as if they were heading to Junior's for half-priced beer and oyster night instead of chasing an ambulance carrying Erin.

He apologized hundreds of times in the hospital, mainly to the waiting room walls. By the time Erin was sentient and on enough pain medication to quell her hysteria, she told everyone within earshot that she didn't want to see him. Her younger brother became the gatekeeper of her hospital room, a sorry-ass sentinel, straight-backed and poker-faced, a Buckingham Palace guard wannabe.

His calls went unanswered in the days and weeks that followed, even after everything had calmed down and Erin was no longer in danger of dying. Showing up at her house was a nonstarter; there was no way in hell the Conrads were going to let Landon within five hundred feet of their daughter.

"Teenaged stupidity is all," he heard his mother say on the phone, he supposed, with Erin's mom. "It's not like he did it on purpose." His mother held the receiver away from her ear, releasing a barrage of incomprehensible high-pitched sounds into the air. Landon shimmied his back closer to the wall and tiptoed a few feet around the corner into the family room, making sure his mother couldn't see him. "I know, I know. Look, Lydia (confirmation that his mom was, indeed, talking to Erin's mom), we've been friends for how long? Twenty-five years? He didn't mean to do it. My Landon is a good kid. You know this! You're his Godmother, for Heaven's sake!"

His mother slammed the phone into its cradle so hard that Landon jumped and ran out the back door. He made up his mind then; he would shoot himself in the woods, but not the woods near Erin's house. He would deliver the letter first and then drive deep into the country and do it in the woods far from Canvasback Cove.

Plan in place, he drove down the Conrad's long, gravel driveway. Nickelback's *How You Remind Me* blared from his truck's CD player on a continuous loop—all the way from his house, six miles away. He turned down the volume right before turning left onto the driveway. He wanted to hear the gravel crunching under his wheels. Without the music, the crunching echoed through his truck, and he panicked, thinking the Buckingham Palace guards would hear the truck approaching and pepper him with bullets. *So be it,* he thought. *Let them shoot me. At least that will save my parents the agony of their only child committing suicide.* But then the letter might get covered with blood, rendering it unreadable. He caressed the envelope on the seat next to him, his hunting rifle holding it down like a paperweight. His logic was simple: Erin wouldn't read the letter if he handed it to her alive. But if she found it after he was dead, she would have no choice but to read it.

He pulled off onto the dirt parking pad between Erin's house and her dad's workshop—an old barn that Landon and his dad had helped Mr. Conrad build. He turned off the engine and sat, thinking about Mr. Conrad's stockpile of fireworks. Landon longed for a magic wand to reverse the plan that had cost Erin her leg and had cost him Erin. She had been apprehensive of taking the fireworks, but he assured her it would be okay and that her dad wouldn't miss two Roman candles and a bottle rocket.

Landon took a deep breath and tucked the envelope into his back pocket, carefully opening the door to avoid sound and sliding out of the truck. He quietly made his way to the edge of the property, where Erin's treehouse overlooked the creek like a lonesome castle on top of a mountain. He climbed the wooden pegs nailed to the tree, pushed open the little door, and found the loose floorboard. He lifted it high enough to regard its contents—the *Scrabble* set they had spent hours playing two days before the accident. He lifted it out and caressed the faux velvet bag, letting his thumb and forefinger pretend they were rubbing Erin's hand. He loosened the drawstring and let the tiles tumble out. He mindlessly shuffled them around on the floor, then plucked seven tiles out of the pile and turned them over, hopeful for any word that might give him a sign. He wasn't exactly sure what kind of sign he was lookin for. Maybe letters that spelled L-I-F-E (a sign that he shouldn't follow through with his plan). Or D-E-A-T-H (a sign that he should). Alas, no such words appeared. Just a sad combination of useless tiles: W, X, E, J, L, Q, C. He swept the tiles back into the bag and placed the *Scrabble* set under the loose floorboard with his forearm. He put his letter on top and wiggled the floorboard back in place. Feeling the permanence of his status as persona non grata at the Conrad residence, he scooted across the floor on his butt until his back was against the wall. He glanced around Erin's treehouse—

their treehouse—and nearly choked on his despair. He had helped her decorate it with four oversized floor pillows, a lantern, and a pile of her favorite books. On the far wall were her cross-country medals, hanging from a deer antler he had found in the woods. The scene was too much. He drew his knees to his chest and wrapped his arms tightly around them. And then he sobbed. Big, heavy sobs. All the groans he'd been two shocked to let out in the days and weeks after the accident.

Landon had no idea how long he had been sitting in the treehouse against the wall. At some point, the waning sunlight or the sound of the mockingbird that liked to sing at dusk alerted him that he'd better get out of dodge, lest the Conrads have him arrested for trespassing. He took a shallow, shaky breath and tried to stand, but his legs felt too weak. He tried again, but that time an invisible force helped him up, assisted him down the pegs, and led him back to his truck. He climbed in, turned on the ignition, and inched away from the barn. Soon he was back on the gravel driveway, and instead of turning left to head into the woods to shoot himself, he turned right and headed home.

"WHAT'S WITH THE BEATLES' hair?" Landon's father had said, looking him up and down in silent disapproval when he picked him up from the airport two weeks ago. Willie had been sound asleep in Landon's arms, his head cocked at an odd angle and dangling over Landon's shoulder, his skinny legs wrapped part of the way around his waist.

"Since when do SEALs go around looking like beatniks?" His father wouldn't let it go.

That was the whole point of the hair—to make us look like beatniks, Landon thought but didn't say. He didn't want to wake Willie; he just wanted to get in the air-conditioned car and pretend to sleep. *Beatnick.* Who talked like that anymore?

Landon slowly became aware of *Little Jo* rocking, ever so slightly. A fishing boat had plodded by, leaving just enough of a wake to gently shake him out of his ruminating. Suddenly blazingly hot, he grabbed his hair, desperate to get it off his neck.

"It's called a topknot, not a man bun," Susan had corrected this morning when his first attempt had his hair gathered on his head like a crown. "There is a distinct difference." She then showed him how to do a proper man bun.

Topknot. Man bun. Landon didn't care. The sun was hot, he was sweating profusely, and he just needed his damned hair off his neck. He made a mental note to shave his head later today. Damned Susan. He didn't want to string her along, but she was so helpful with Willie. There was only so much his dad could do alone. Landon made another mental note: this one to sit down with his dad and discuss possibly selling the boatyard and marina. It wasn't like they were raking in the bucks—quite the contrary. Boaters preferred keeping their boats at the yacht club or the municipal marina, not a dingy marina in the country with four slips, only two places within walking distance for dinner or drinks, or a dusty boatyard where the owner promised to get to the work when he could. It was a wonder his dad had any customers at all. And those who came and tie up for the night received a coupon for Conrad's on the Bay—the B&B Erin's parents had opened a decade ago. One more feeble attempt over the years to show support for the huge gulf that had grown and continues to grow between the two families.

He pulled a bottle of water out of the cooler and poured it over his head and shoulders, shuddering as it dripped down his bare chest. *Time to get serious*, he thought, putting *Little Jo* in gear and making way toward the coordinates his father had given him. Naval Academy grads, he figured. Probably rented the boat. Or perhaps a family from inland, somewhere in Maryland or Virginia, with the notion of how fun it would be to rent a sailboat and head toward the sleepy town of Canvasback Cove. Or a group of experienced sailors out of Baltimore who had too much to drink.

Landon spotted a sailboat just sitting, gently rocking in the still air. He idled *Little Jo's* engine and went into the cabin for his binoculars. The photo of his parents taped to the bulkhead next to the instrument panel haunted—his mother standing on the shore, maybe, ten years ago? It was the last time he was home, which turned out to be the last time he would see his mother alive; she'd had a fatal heart attack the next day. The people of Canvasback Cove rallied around his dad, dropping off casserole after casserole. Susan and her mother showed up and made sure the house stayed clean, graciously accepting the hashes, soups, and stews on the bereaved widower's behalf, rearranging the fridge to make room. They ensured the coffee pot was perpetually filled and invited anyone who dropped by the house for a cup.

He considered—more than considered—hopping in his truck and driving to the Conrads's house to tell them his mother had died. Because, indeed, they did not know. Because if they knew, they would have at least send a card. Stopping by would have been better. But as far as Landon was concerned, sending a card was a no-brainer. They couldn't possibly still hold a grudge against his family for the accident, could they? He had stopped trying to contact Erin years before. After his first major deployment, he'd tried, in earnest, to get in touch with her. He gave up when it became apparent she wanted nothing to do with him. His parents had been innocent—collateral damage to his stupidity. To this day, he doesn't understand the Conrad's vitriol, their inability to forgive, and their unwillingness to move on. His mom had been best friends with Erin's mom for, what, a million years? Practically sisters! The accident had happened, what, a decade before? Erin had survived! Not only that, but aside from the tiny inconvenience of losing her leg, she was thriving and living in Baltimore, happy as a clam. But Canvasback Cove was a small town; surely the Conrads knew about his mother's death. Landon had held out hope that they (and Erin, too) would come to the wake (the local funeral home made his mother look beautiful in the blue dress his dad had insisted she be buried in).

In the end, the Conrads didn't come. Okay, maybe the wake was a bit too personal. He'd hoped they (and Erin, too) would attend the memorial service. They could slip in and out without so much as a hastily uttered, *I'm sorry for your loss.* They didn't come to that either.

Maybe stopping by the cemetery for the burial later that afternoon was all they could handle. He stood tall next to his father, his military bearing on full display while he discretely scanned the mourners circled—several rings deep—at the grave. Nope. No Conrad's. He shifted his gaze to the horizon, thinking they (and Erin, too) might drive by, slow their car down, say a silent prayer, then quickly drive away. He didn't even know what kind of car they had. Nor did it matter; nobody drove by. It irritated him that the Conrads didn't bother to attend the service. To his knowledge, not even a card to his dad.

Landon's chest tightened, thinking about those days. He grabbed the binoculars from the shelf above the photo and climbed out of the cabin, back out into the blinding sun. The stagnant air (hotter than hell) felt like a blast from an ice-cold air conditioner, contrasting with the sauna below deck. He squinted, shading his eyes with his free hand, blinking furiously. *Damn. How long was I down there?* When his eyes finally adjusted, he noticed that the sailboat he had seen earlier appeared to be moving, inching along the exceedingly flat water, struggling downwind under a barely filled, ugly white spinnaker.

Not many boats out today, he thought, as he again checked his father's coordinates. True, today was smack-dab in the middle of the workweek. But it was August; there should be at least a handful of boats out here. Besides the fisherman huddling under the bridge, the Chesapeake Bay was pretty much empty.

Landon pulled out his phone and glanced at the bars in the upper left-hand corner. Not an excellent signal, but enough to make a call. He dialed the number scribbled above the coordinates and waited as it rang. And rang. And rang. He sighed, wondering what to do next. Call his dad, he supposed. Worst case, the sailor no longer needed a tow; best case, he had gotten away from Susan for a few hours. Being out on the water today, in the heat and sun, was truly a pain in the ass. But it got him away from Susan. He tossed the guilty thought from his mind and let it land in the bay, where it floated next to *Little Jo* before getting nabbed by a hungry fish.

He liked Susan well enough, he supposed. He touched the puff of hair on top of his head. *And she taught me how to wear my hair off my neck.* Susan was good company. Truly. They had a lot of laughs. And enjoyed the same shows on TV, mainly *Game of Thrones* and reruns of *The Office.* She was good with his son, too. Surprisingly, Willie hadn't asked for his mother since they'd flown East. Landon figured it was only a matter of time before he needed to spin the truth into a tale a little kid could absorb without feeling like it was his fault his mother had left him. But—and this was a big one—he didn't want Susan following him back to Coronado in a few weeks. Nor did he want her to visit. He needed to double down his efforts to avoid sending mixed signals. He'd be her hometown friend. Nothing more.

Landon picked up his phone to try again, but it buzzed just before he was about to press the button to place a call.

"Shultz Towing. Yep. Hang on." Landon set his phone down and peered through the binoculars. The sailboat with the ugly white spinnaker. "Yep. I see you. Hang tight. I'll be there in about five minutes."

2

With so little wind, the smell of diesel exhaust from the blown riser threatened to choke Erin Conrad as she trimmed the spinnaker with one hand and pushed the spinnaker pole farther out with her other hand. *The towboat, thank God*, she thought.

The murmur of her rescuer's motor danced across the waveless water. Squinting into the sun, she made out the vessel's shape. If he were still alive, her father would never let her hear the end of this—calling for a tow—and would have teased her incessantly, in good humor at first. As a friendly critique of her sailing skills and how she should have been able to make the boat sail, given enough tenacity. Lack of wind be damned, her father, through the tiniest of sail trims and tweaks, would have had them ooching along, making slow, steady progress. On windless days on the Chesapeake, her father sent her to the bow pulpit to look for cat's paws—those tiny little ripples that appear out of nowhere on even the calmest water. *Meow*, he would say if he sensed her mind drifting or noticed her staring into space. *Find the wind. Find the cat's paws.* And if like today, the cat's paws simply did not exist, he would hand her a pair of binoculars and say, as playfully as he could, *meow*.

"There it is!" Erin's boyfriend, Wes, stood up in the cockpit, waving his arms a bit too frantically. "Over here! Over here!"

"There what is, where?" Erin scanned the horizon, realizing Wes was pointing at the towboat. She was hot, frustrated, and missing her dad. *We've moved about thirty feet in the last hour*, she thought. Surely her dad would understand. For an experienced sailor, calling a towboat was a last resort. Technically, she didn't call for the tow; Wes did. God, she missed her dad. "Wes, calm down! You're acting like we're floating in the middle of the ocean on a raft, surrounded by sharks. Release the spinnaker halyard."

Wes stared at her like she was speaking a foreign language. Her patience was wearing thin; she had to remind herself that Wes was inexperienced. She took a deep breath, knowing herself well enough to realize she was being unnecessarily harsh. Blame it on the sun. Blame it on Wes, forgetting to bring sandwiches like they'd discussed yesterday. Thank God she'd had the forethought to pack a small cooler with a few extra water bottles.

Wes grabbed one of the lines—the wrong one, of course—and held it up for her to see. "Okay, so not this one." He lifted another. "Nope, not this one either?" He laughed. "Which one?"

"The one with the green and white stripes," she said, softening at the sound of his laughter. "Just lift it out of the jam cleat." With the halyard running free, Erin pulled the spinnaker down and onto the deck, careful not to let it fall into the water. She bunched it up and dragged it to the cockpit.

"Sorry about that, babe." Wes reached into the cabin and pulled out a canvas bag. "I'll stuff the sail in here and put it away; it's the least I could do."

"Not that bag," Erin said, her patience and tenderness toward him returning. "I'll be right back. She hobbled back onto the foredeck and unclipped the spinnaker bag from the bowsprit. She noticed another sailboat in the distance...sailing. The cat's paws crept toward her, taunting, reminding her that the afternoon sea breeze would fill in if she just waited. She imagined her dad, larger than life, sitting on an Adirondack chair in Heaven, taking deep breaths and exhaling in enormous, billowing blows. Sending an army of cats to dance across the water and leave their paw prints for her to follow. *Thank you, Dad, but you're too late. The motor is dead, and we'd never make it to Canvasback Cove before dusk. You wouldn't want us out here without an engine, right? You wouldn't want us floating along in the dark, right? Wes did the sensible thing by calling for a tow. You would have liked him, Dad. He's a cardiologist at Johns Hopkins.* Erin's breath caught in her throat. *You would have liked him.*

She held onto the lifeline and cautiously headed back to the cockpit. The stump below her knee ached a deep, unrelenting throb, radiating up into her hamstring. She had described the pain to her massage therapist as sciatic nerve pain, but not precisely sciatic nerve pain; the damned pain was difficult to describe. She removed Doris—her prosthetic—and set her on the deck next to the companionway hatch. She kneaded her leg, pressing her fingers into the flesh as hard as possible. Surprisingly enough, the calf on her good leg was calm today. Her surgeon had issued a stern warning twenty years ago: no more running. It was a miracle that she could even walk, let alone run. According to her surgeon, if she took up running again, she could damage her good leg and someday need a wheelchair. Well, it's been twenty years since the accident, and she and Doris have been running (jogging, more realistically) for ten years. She supposed her surgeon had never heard of Paralympic runners and their blades. She didn't use blades—Doris did just fine with a running shoe over her metal toes.

She unhooked the spinnaker sheet shackles from the sail and folded it like her father had taught her so long ago, holding the head in the middle and bringing the starboard and port tacks up to greet it. She stuffed the whole thing into the bag and threaded the Velcro tab through the holes to keep the clews in place. Sure, she could have just rolled it into a tight ball and packed it in the bag, but she wanted to leave the boat in better condition than when she rented it. True, the rental company gave her a boat with a bum motor, but as a sailor, she didn't feel justified not tidying up. She expected some sort of compensation for the motor failure, though.

Erin put her leg on the settee and rubbed, just like her massage therapist instructed. She was trying to take a homeopathic approach to manage her pain rather than give in to her doctor's recommendation that he prescribe pain pills. There was no way she wanted to go down the narcotic path. No way in hell. She lived in Baltimore and saw what opioid addiction did to so many people. Plus, she had first-hand knowledge from watching how easily her brother had become addicted after surgery for a complicated knee injury. Sandy's dependence scared him (and the whole family) to death, and he got help. Thankfully, no lasting ill effects and no relapses. So, as far as Erin was concerned, prescription pain pills were off the table.

On the other hand, Ibuprofen could sometimes be a godsend; she had no trouble popping an Advil here and there. In fact, Advil sounded heavenly right about now. She pulled two gelcaps out of her pocket and swallowed them without water.

She continued massaging her leg, pressing her thumbs into the pressure points, wincing in pain when she pushed too hard. On a work-related call, Wes, who was in the cabin, used terms like *myocardial*, *stenosis*, and *pericardial*—the dead giveaway that someone, somewhere, needed him. How often had he left her sitting in a restaurant by herself, his expensive meal getting cold while she waited, only for him to return and say he was needed at the hospital? There's not much chance of that happening in the middle of the Chesapeake Bay. The thought of Wes being trapped with her made her momentarily forget the pain in her leg. She stuck her head through the companionway hatch and blew him a kiss. He held a finger to his lips and shook his head as he muttered *pulmonary*, *ventricular*, and *acute* into the phone. Suddenly her leg pain surged with a vengeance, throbbing in lockstep with Wes's words.

"You've been running again, haven't you?" Her mother had recently asked during their twice-weekly FaceTime call. Erin vowed, then and there, to keep her pain management journey to herself. She could hide it easily enough, walking on Doris without a limp and mindful of where and how she sat. "Well? Have you been running? You know what the doctor said about running." Over the years, Erin had become quite an expert at ignoring her mother's annoying, if well-intentioned, questions. She changed the subject to more practical matters, like when she and Wes were planning to arrive. "I can't wait to meet him! Do you want to, you know—"

"Sleep in the same bed?" Erin laughed. "Yes, Mom. Unless that would upset your Puritan sensibilities."

"Poppycock!" Erin's mother swatted at the screen with a dishcloth. "See you next Wednesday, then? I'll put you and Wesley in the Great Blue Heron Room."

"We're staying on the boat, Mom. I already told you that."

"The room will be so much more comfortable."

"I rented a thirty-five-foot sloop. It will be nice. Anyway, need to go. See you soon." Erin had blushed at the thought of her mother offering to prepare a special room for her and Wes (the Great Blue Heron room was the B&B's bridal suite). She was under no illusions that her mother knew she was sexually active. She was thirty-seven-years-old, for crying out loud. On the downhill slope to forty. *Over the Hill.*

She remembered when her father turned forty, a million years ago, and they threw him a surprise party. She and her mother had spent much of the afternoon decorating the house with black balloons printed ominously with *Over the Hill.* She was twelve and, at the appointed time, was huddled in the middle of the family room with her brother Sandy, both sets of grandparents, her best friend Landon, Landon's parents, and what had seemed like a million of her parents' friends.

He's pulling into the driveway, the lookout by the door shouted. The house went dark, and a series of *shushes* and *be quiets* ensued. And in her complete and utter excitement (it had been her first surprise party), she grabbed Landon's hand and squeezed.

Erin pushed the memory of Landon away, wondering if Wes

would throw her an *Over the Hill* surprise party on her fortieth birth-day. Her mother had no such fanfare when she turned forty a few years later. But on her sixtieth, her father pulled out all stops and bought her a defunct, dilapidated house a few miles from their home. The six-bedroom house overlooking the Chesapeake Bay was at the end of a two-mile gravel driveway behind a grove of bald cypress trees. Erin's mother had lusted after that property for as long as she could remember. Once a year or so, she would declare that the old place would make a great B&B and that someday, she would buy it. Never mind that it would take years to get it into useable shape or that the property alone was worth a fortune. Let's not forget the tiny problem that it wasn't for sale. Or that her mother hated cooking. Erin supposed a variety of cereal and fruit counted as breakfast. *Let's just drive out there and walk around*, she would say, and the family would pile in the car, stop at the gate, then walk right through. How often had her mother tried prying the side door open, oblivious that the house, as unlikely as it seemed, could be wired with a security system?

Erin and Landon sometimes hiked to the old house, where she always declared that she would write a novel set in that house one day. A thriller or a murder mystery. No, a romance. No, maybe a family drama. Yes! A family drama with a little bit of romance and a little bit of murder. Landon laughed and told her that anything she wrote would be a best seller.

When Erin's dad bought the property, it had been deteriorating for nearly twenty years, to the point where it was almost beyond repair. When they finally had the key and Erin got to see the inside for the first time, she thought, *this isn't so bad.* It took her parents (no longer young and spry) almost three years to renovate it. That first summer, they reserved all the rooms for extended family—the first official Conrad family camp was born. This year—the fifth—would be the first without her dad. This was also the first year she was bringing a boyfriend. God, she wished her father could meet Wes. She wondered what he would think of her getting involved with a cardiologist.

"I HAVE good news and bad news," Wes said, fanning himself with a chart of the Chesapeake as he emerged from the cabin. "The good news is, my patient with the mass of infection in her heart, the one I told you about at dinner the other night, is finally cleared for surgery."

"That's wonderful!" Erin shielded her eyes from the sun and scanned the horizon for the towboat. "Hey, didn't you say the tow was on its way? I thought I heard him earlier, but now I'm not sure."

Wes shrugged. "That's the bad news. I mean, not about the tow. He should be here soon, I think." He looked at his watch. "He told me he would be here in five minutes, and it's only been five. Shouldn't be too long now." Wes pointed across the bow. "I think that's him, way over there."

Erin's leg was on fire; the Advil she swallowed was taking longer to spring into action than she would like. She shifted her position on the bench and reminded herself that everything takes longer on the water. The horizon was deceiving; what looked near might be quite far. "What's the bad news?"

"The bad news is..." He climbed out of the cabin and sidled next to her on the settee, drenched in sweat. "The bad news is—"

"Come on, out with it!" She frowned, remembering their dinner date at Dino's a few weeks ago when he returned after a fifteen-minute phone call declaring that he had good and bad news as he did just a minute ago. She braced herself.

"Surgery is the day after tomorrow."

"But we'll be in Canvasback Cove the day after tomorrow."

"My hands are tied."

"Can't someone else perform the surgery?"

"Babe, this case is...." He put his arm around her. "...this case is different. I've been working on this case for the past couple of months." He pulled her closer, but she stiffened and pulled away. "Come on, Erin. My patient is relying on me." He released his arm, letting his hand hit the settee on the way down; a flourish as if to say *enough is enough.* "I don't expect you to understand. You spend your days writing jingles for—"

"Jingles? Is that what you think I do? And if I did, there's nothing wrong with writing jingles! It takes a lot of talent to write a good jingle! I wish I was an Oscar Myer Weiner, for starters. Oh, and then there's Lucky Charms. They're magically delicious. Ah, and my personal favorite: Where's the beef?" She looked at him, raging, incredulous, and hurt that he minimized her work. "I write back cover blurbs for books. I write the synopsis that pops up when you look at a book on Amazon. I write ad copy for writers." She scrunched up her nose. "I'm tired of you making me feel bad about myself because I'm not a highfalutin doctor."

"Now, that's not true." He scooted closer to her. "I'm sorry, Babe. I'm stressed, is all. I have a ton of prep to do ahead of this surgery. Plus, I need to make sure I'm good and rested." He shook his head. "The sun and heat aren't helping. We should have driven. I could have just left you at your mom's and been halfway back to Baltimore by now."

She softened, feeling guilty for pressuring him to agree to her romantic dream of sailing across the Chesapeake to the B&B. He had shot back with a litany of reasons her idea was crazy, but, in the end, he went along with it because he loved her. How could she stay mad at him for that?

"You weren't even born when those jingles were popular." "A good jingle is timeless. But...I don't write jingles!" She stood. The faint smell of diesel was a harbinger of joy. "It's the towboat! Look, port side, right off the beam."

Wes shrugged. "I'll never understand sailing lingo." He waved his arms as if the towboat driver couldn't find them otherwise. "Over here! Over here!"

Mortified, Erin begged him to quiet down. "You're tagging yourself as inexperienced."

"I am inexperienced."

"Please, let me do all the talking." Erin stood and smoothed her tee shirt, bracing herself for a round of explanations and assuring the towboat driver that she was an experienced sailor.

"WES RUBIN?" A voice billowed into the cockpit from the towboat, which was now idling next to them. Erin recalled a family trip to England. They visited Stonehenge and marveled at the unanswered questions. Erin parked herself on a bench overlooking a hayfield while her parents went into the gift shop for souvenirs. Lambs wandered aimlessly, bleating, crying, looking for their mothers like toddlers lost in a crowded department store. The ewes zigzagged through the field until, like magnets, each found their baby. Erin remembered being fascinated that a ewe could pick out her baby in a sea of hundreds of identical lambs just by its voice.

"Yes, I'm Wes." He jumped up, extended his hand over the lifeline, and shook the towboat driver's hand. "Wes Rubin. Yes, I'm the person who called you. I found you on Google. Engine trouble. No wind. Need to get back to Baltimore ASAP."

So much for Wes letting her do all the talking. Feeling very much like a lost lamb, Erin studied the towboat driver. His voice—at once familiar and strange—was incongruent with the person behind the helm. The sun, ten times brighter than it had been a minute before, made her eyes water, despite the sunglasses. She shaded her eyes with her hand, wishing she hadn't forgotten to pack a ball cap. Barely aware of her surroundings, she overlaid the driver's voice—shouting instructions at Wes—with the voice in her head; the voice she buried a hundred years ago (or so it felt). The voice that still occasionally haunted her dreams.

The sailboat heeled, snapping Erin back into reality. The towboat was now at the bow, the driver dancing around on his foredeck.

"Hold onto this," the driver said as he flipped Wes a rope, then gracefully hopped from the bow of his boat to the bow of the rental, taking the rope out of Wes's tight grip and tying the towline to the foredeck cleat. Wes, who all day had been afraid to leave the safety of the cockpit (as if he could possibly fall off an unmoving thirty-five-foot sailboat on water that was as still as a stagnant pond), leaned against the mast watching the towboat driver do his thing.

With Wes's back turned to her, Erin couldn't hear everything he said, but certain words were hard to miss, such as *surgeon* and *they need me, right away*. The tenderness she had felt for him a little while ago evaporated at his blatant sense of self-importance. She took a deep breath and reminded herself that Wes was a good man. He loved her. She loved him. He would meet her family this week! She hung onto the promise of family camp and showing Wes around her hometown. As much as she tried, right now, at this moment of intense heat, humidity, sun, and hunger, she simply couldn't force excitement into her heart. Or was her increasingly hostile mood merely a case of past meeting present? Erin stared at the towboat driver, the past twenty years threatening to suffocate her.

3

"All I'm saying is, if you need to head back to Baltimore, you're better off sailing." Landon pointed at the wind direction indicator at the top of the mast. "The wind is filling in from the northeast. Your boat is, what, thirty-five feet? It will be a broad reach, pretty much all the way there. You could easily do ten to twelve, whereas with the tow, we're talking eight or nine." Landon didn't like this guy, this Wes Rubin, who seemed to think he was the only cardiologist on this side of the Bay Bridge who could perform surgery.

"It's not my boat." Wes crossed his arms over his chest. "Confession. I don't even like the water. I agreed to this to appease my girlfriend."

"Girlfriend?" Landon didn't remember seeing anyone else onboard. He turned toward the cockpit, but it was empty. "So, you're telling me your girlfriend is the experienced mariner, not you?" He didn't wait for a response. "Well, I'm going to need to talk to her."

"Right. Of course. Right." Wes sprang into action and gingerly made his way to the rear of the boat, gripping the lifeline. Landon suppressed a laugh. He didn't like it that he felt so judgmental toward this dweeb, a guy he didn't know and would likely never see again in his life. Unless, of course, he ever needed heart surgery. "Babe, get up here. The tow guy wants to talk to you."

The dweeb disappeared into the cabin. Landon tapped his foot, waiting for something to happen. He'd be happy if these folks decided to sail back to Baltimore. Susan texted him three times in the last hour, asking when he thought he would be back. Willie, apparently, was being...well...a three-year-old.

Put him down for a nap. He's probably over tired, Landon texted back.

Susan replied with a wink emoji. And then: *Probably overstimulated from too much TV this morning.*

Landon would be so happy with not having to tow these clowns that he'd send them on their way free of charge and worry about his dad's wrath later.

4

Erin found a microfiber cloth and wet one corner of it with her sweat. God, it was hot down here. But there was no way —no way!—she was going back up there. She used the wet corner of the microfiber cloth to wipe the filthy porthole, a gunky brown film making way to tinted plexiglass. *There. That's better.* She could finally see outside and made a mental note to complain to the boat rental company. In fact, she had a litany of complaints, not the least of which was the defunct motor. She tilted her head and followed Wes's sneakers up his skinny white legs, to his beige Land's End shorts, his Heart Health Awareness Half Marathon tee shirt, his long, sinewy arms, all the way up to his head, covered in a floppy fishing hat with sunglasses that were a bit small for his angular face. His jaw was set and his lips a straight line; she knew he was chewing his teeth, even though she couldn't see the telltale, rhythmic bulging of his cheeks. She could tell he was mad, annoyed, and clearly unhappy with what the towboat driver was saying.

She wiped the endless sweat from her face using the clean end of the cloth. It dripped into her eyes as fast as she could wipe it away. She blinked several times, then dug her fingers into both eyes to try to ease the burning. Sunscreen and sweat were a dangerous combination. Fixating on the bare chest next to Wes, she attempted to overlay the voice she had heard a few minutes before with a midsection that appeared rippled enough to create dents on your cheek if you ever had the good fortune to fall asleep wrapped in his arms. How many times had she imagined falling asleep just like that? Only his chest had been soft then, or at least that was how she had imagined it. The summer before senior year, he still had a layer of baby fat around his belly.

She let her eyes fall onto the older Landon, standing on the other side of this flimsy plexiglass porthole. She remembered her dad's *Beach Boys* music, a frequent companion in his workshop. Other music too, but the *Beach Boys* was one of the soundtracks of her childhood. In fact, she had an entire playlist in her online music library titled "Dad's Music."

She wished she could say there had been no clear demarcation point when Landon Shultz went from being her best friend to someone she thought about day and night. She wished she could say it was more like the proverbial lobster in a pot of water, the heat turning up so gradually that the unsuspecting lobster didn't realize the water was boiling. But it hadn't been like that at all. It was more like Dorothy in the *Wizard of Oz*—one moment, she was living a boring life in shades of black and white, and the next moment she was swallowed up in a world of vivid color.

She and Landon had been in the workshop, helping her dad sand the new table he had built for their kitchen (she didn't recall anything wrong with their old kitchen table, just that her mom had wanted a bigger one). Standing side-by-side, arms practically touching, the *Beach Boys* billowing, a song came on about being older and how nice it would be to say goodnight and sleep together. She had been old enough then to understand the concept of sex and how babies were made. But she was still too young, too naive to truly understand what it meant to sleep with a man. And until she'd heard that song, she had never thought about spending her entire life with someone.

A flood of strange, physical sensations made her feel self conscious. She stopped sanding and moved a few inches away from Landon.

Erin continued staring out the porthole, which was now thick with fog. She wiped the condensation away with the cloth and panicked when the towboat driver shifted his position and moved out of her sightline. She instinctively moved forward to the next porthole, then stopped herself. It couldn't possibly be Landon. Just someone with a similar voice. Her Landon didn't have muscles like that. And the hair! Her Landon would never have hair long enough to wear bunched up on the top of his head. But wait, look at how he waved his hands around as he talked. Her Landon—the Landon she knew way back when, before the accident—spoke with his hands too. She swallowed her thoughts. *Her Landon.* He had never been her Landon. He could have been, maybe. But not after what happened, what he did, what his actions had cost her.

"Yo, Babe!"

Erin jumped, hitting her forehead on the bulkhead above the porthole.

"Babe, where have you been?" Wes was crouched in the companionway. "The tow guy wants to talk to you."

"You scared me half to death!"

"Why are you down here? It's like three hundred degrees. Come on. I need to get back to Baltimore. We're wasting time." He held out his hand, but she didn't budge. "Babe. Why are you acting like this?"

"Acting like what?" She rubbed her forehead. "You made me hurt myself."

"I did no such thing." He let more of his body hang into the cabin. "Please? I'm not sure what's going on, but I need to get to Baltimore. My patient's life depends on it."

"Your patient will be fine whether you get back an hour or two hours from now."

Wes retreated into the cockpit, then turned back and shouted into the cabin. "The guy wants to talk to you, Erin. Now."

"Fine!" She took a deep breath and convinced herself that the guy with the pecks was not Landon. And if the guy with the pecks was

Landon? She reminded herself of what he did to her. She reminded herself of her anger and hurt feelings. In a fit of pique, she stomped up the ladder using just her good leg, then stomped right back down while Wes looked on in horror. "Tell him to put a shirt on, then I'll come up."

5

L andon's eyes widened when he heard the pompous cardiologist call for Erin. Quite a coincidence since he'd thought about Erin Conrad more during the past few hours than he ever allowed himself to over the past two decades. The Bay Bridge had been triggering. Too triggering. Driving over, it never was, probably because a road was just a road to Landon. But for some reason, motoring underneath it today, imagining his younger self diving off, doing a cannonball, or simply jumping feet first with his arms held tightly against his sides...well...he couldn't keep his safe locked. The damned thing wanted to open.

Okay, so he had been thinking about Erin. It's like that phenomenon...it has a name; he'd just read about it in the paper a few days ago. Before coming home two weeks ago, Landon didn't remember the last time he'd sat down and read an actual newspaper. The article was about the brain, about how, for example, you're in the market for a black Honda Civic, and suddenly, every other car you see on the highway is a black Honda Civic. Such it was with the name Erin, he supposed. He wondered how many women named Erin he would encounter in the next few weeks.

"My girlfriend wants you to put a shirt on," the cardiologist said, emerging from the cabin drenched in sweat. "She's being a pain in the ass, and I'm not sure why." He shrugged. "Maybe the heat is getting to her."

"Unbelievable," Landon muttered under his breath. He grabbed the towline and pulled *Little Jo* closer to the sailboat. He could hear the cardiologist yell at him to be careful. Landon ignored him and jumped over the lifeline and onto *Little Jo*, almost wishing he would fall and break an arm or something just so he could continue to be pissed off at this guy. Landon didn't like this guy for reasons he couldn't quite articulate. Too damned pompous. Yeah, that was the reason. The guy was utterly full of himself.

He picked up his phone and texted Susan. *I'm sorry, it's going to be a while. These people are assholes. I'll tell you about it later.*

He texted his dad, too (at least his dad was technologically savvy enough to text). *Rescue mission taking longer than expected. Difficult people, long story. I'd be grateful if you could relieve Susan. She needs to go home at three. I'll buy you a beer later.*

As grateful as he had been to get away from Susan today, he suddenly wished he was home, kicking back on the couch with her —ideally while Willie napped—watching mindless TV and just, well, just existing. The concept of just existing often got a bad rap, particularly in Landon's circles. In the Navy, you were constantly striving, constantly doing whatever was necessary to better your chances of promotions (medals were nice too). He had made Chief Petty Officer earlier than many of his shipmates. And he was on a fast track to becoming a Senior Chief. Landon was not one to sit still for too long. He needed motion, an occasional adrenaline rush, and to feel like he was making a difference. But everyone needed an ounce or two of just existing, right? Every now and then? Once in a blue moon? Well, he certainly did. And he felt no guilt for wanting to mindlessly channel surf. Susan had given him a baby jogger— borrowed from a friend—but Landon didn't even want to do that. Too much effort. During his time at home, he was determined to just help his dad, bond with Willie, and get his head screwed on straight so he could return to Coronado with a fresh perspective. Oh, and he was determined to start showing Susan how much he appreciated her help.

Landon put on his shirt and hopped back on the sailboat with renewed determination to convince these people to sail back to Baltimore. He'd sweeten the deal by telling them he wouldn't charge them for his time. He would impress the pompous cardiologist with his knowledge of all thing's mariner, explaining that the square root of the waterline length gives you the theoretical hull speed of a boat in the displacement mode, which was precisely why it made more sense to sail back to Baltimore than for him to tow them.

6

Erin scrambled around the cabin for a disguise. Not that Landon would recognize her; she suspected he wouldn't. She recognized his voice, though, didn't she? And the way his hands moved in concert with his words. Still, the towboat driver's hair was anything but Landon's hair. Plus, she knew he was a Navy SEAL. How did she know this? Her friend (sort-of) Susan made sure she knew. She remembered being shocked to hear Landon had become a SEAL. Based solely on what she had seen in the movie *GI Jane*, she didn't think Landon had the gumption; the Landon she knew would never have made it through the first day. He had obviously changed.

Since high school, Erin had only seen Susan a handful of times, but they had become online friends when Facebook was new. Erin made a mental note to curate her Facebook friend list. Or, better yet, get off the platform entirely. She'd be lying if she said she never searched for Landon. She supposed, as a SEAL, it was safer to not get entangled with social media. She had a short list of people she occasionally searched for on Google, Landon being somewhere toward the top. Either he had no electronic footprints, or they were invisible. Susan ensured she knew the latest Landon news, even though Erin repeatedly told her she wasn't interested in such knowledge. Susan let it slip out that Landon had a serious girlfriend. And then, later, a son. She blocked Susan for a while but couldn't bring herself to unfriend her. She sighed, confident that the man on the deck talking to Wes was not Landon. As a Navy SEAL, he wouldn't have hair like that.

Still, there was something hauntingly familiar about this man's voice. She remembered the Stonehenge lambs again. She peeked out the porthole but couldn't see his face well enough through his sunglasses and the shadow from his ball cap. Sunglasses. Ball cap. She didn't have a ball cap but had sunglasses, so that was, at least, the start of a disguise. Plus, she'd been wearing her hair short for many years now; it had hung straight and scraggly down the middle of her back in high school, worn in a haphazard braid most of the time to keep it contained for running. It had never occurred to her to just wear it short.

Not until she entered the corporate world and didn't want to look like she had just rolled out of bed. Not that the company she'd worked for nearly all this time was "corporate" in the traditional sense. It really wasn't. The company was considered small and was founded by two sisters and had grown to about thirty employees. By publishing house standards, it was minuscule. She loved her role as lead back-cover copy editor. Loved coming up with catchy blurbs, especially for novels. She had three underlings, one of whom was a rising star when it came to writing blurbs for self-help books (Erin hated those). Watching her younger colleagues grow and develop gave her a sense of maternal-like pride. She kept a file on her computer containing pages and pages of ideas for her own novel, collecting ideas like someone might collect seashells or ceramic elephants. She had so many ideas—many good ones—that she could easily write twenty books. She was often inspired to turn one of her ideas into a catchy back cover blurb. The problem was that she had all these ideas and even pages of various and sundry blurbs and synopses but never wrote even one sentence toward developing them into books. And she wasn't entirely sure why.

The rental sailboat was well stocked with towels, bedding, dishes, and even a Tupperware bowl containing coffee and loose tea (a can of peanuts or a few granola bars might have been nice). She fished through the cabin, flinging dishtowels every which way, not knowing exactly what she was looking for but figuring that she would know it the moment she saw it. She stood in the middle of the cabin, panting, hotter than hell, sweating so profusely that her tee shirt was soaked. She was about to give up on disguising herself and just go outside and meet her fate when she remembered one drawer under the bed in the V-birth. She shuffled toward the extreme forward end of the hull and opened the drawer. And as if a genie had popped out of a bottle to grant her three wishes, she found a colorful cotton garment folded in thirds and tucked in the far corner of the drawer. She lifted it out and opened it, watching in amazement as it exhaled and expanded—like one of those mattresses that arrive at your doorstep in a box much smaller than a mattress should come in—into an over-sized, floppy sun hat. If biblical Joseph had a technicolor dream coat, she had just stumbled upon its complimentary hat. She smiled and put it on. No way Landon (if the guy who had come to rescue them was even Landon) would recognize her now.

She considered changing her shirt—she had packed enough to get her through the week without doing laundry—but didn't want to soil a fresh shirt unnecessarily. She was wearing a modest bikini top under her tee shirt, which happened to be cobalt blue; there was no chance of her looking like she was in a wet tee shirt contest (plus, she had no boobs to speak of...). She put on the hat, adjusted her sunglasses, and, using her arms to pull and compensate for having no leg below her left knee, stumbled out of the cabin.

7

"Hello? You wanted to see me?" A skinny woman in an enormous hat emerged from the cabin and cleared her throat.

"Babe, why are you talking like that?" Wes said.

"Talking like what?" The woman grabbed both sides of the humongous brim and pulled the hat down over her ears. "You can tow us back to Baltimore, right?"

"Stop it with the voice, Erin! I don't know why you're fooling around, but I need to get home, cleaned up, and to the hospital ASAP." The dweeb cardiologist appeared to be losing patience.

"I'm not fooling around." She cleared her throat again. "I have a tickle."

Landon needed to take charge of the situation and quickly. The clock was ticking, and he wanted to be out of here. Maybe tonight, he would select a movie for him and his dad to watch. He let go of any consideration that this skinny Erin standing before him was the skinny Erin of his past.

"Ma'am, I explained to your boyfriend that, given the wind has filled in significantly, you might be able to sail back to Baltimore."

"No!" The cardiologist stomped his feet. "I hired you to tow us. Now! Please."

"How about this," the skinny woman said to her boyfriend. "You could ride on the towboat with him back to Baltimore, and I'll continue on to Canvasback Cove."

"By yourself?" Wes took her hands. "Babe, I don't know about that. I was figuring we'd go back together, and we could drive to your mother's house tomorrow or the day after that."

"Then I'd miss half the week at family camp." The skinny woman's voice sounded more normal, like...she glanced at Landon and cleared her throat (this woman seemed to do that a lot)...the Erin from his past. "I wanted to be there the week, and I don't want to waste my vacation." The strange, deep voice was back.

Family camp. He couldn't recall any kind of camp in Canvasback Cove. Granted, he hadn't been home in years and didn't keep up on all the town's events and happenings. But it was a small town, and he thinks Susan might have mentioned something. Landon searched the far recesses of his brain and came up blank. *Family camp. Family camp. Family camp. Family camp!* Mrs. Conrad's B&B. *Holy shit.* Susan had said something about Jim Scully looking for someone to ferry guests from the B&B to St. Michael's and Oxford. Susan had called it a "family camp." Landon was only half paying attention, which was typical when he was with Susan. But he recalled it now—in technicolor and living sound, as his dad liked to say. Jim Scully was Lydia Conrad's brother, Erin's uncle.

Landon took a deep breath and tried to swallow his shock. Without being obvious, he let his eyes rest on her tee shirt—an obvious sign that he had initially missed. *Georgetown University Cross Country.* He couldn't believe she still had that shirt. She had planned a double major in English and psychology. He found a way to buy her a Georgetown tee shirt online and gave it to her to celebrate her scholarship.

Landon's eyes left the tee shirt and traveled the length of her long legs, formerly sinewy from running, now thin and lacking muscle tone. He kept his eyes moving until he found what he was looking for

—her prosthetic. *Oh my God*. How had he not noticed the artificial limb before now? He fumbled for the mast and wrapped his arm around it, fearful he might pass out. After a few seconds and three deep breaths, he spoke.

"Doc, let me take you to Baltimore." He looked at Erin, doing his level best to feign neutral, non-recognition. "The wind is filling in from the northeast at five, gusting to eight." He turned to Wes. "I suggest your girlfriend..." He stopped talking and scratched his head, making a show of not knowing her name. He looked at Erin. "We haven't been properly introduced." He extended his hand. "I'm Landon. Landon Shultz."

"I'm Erin." She did a lousy job of disguising her voice. Oscar nominee, she was not. She took his hand, and Landon's heart stopped. The electricity in her touch startled him--it was at the same time as warm and familiar as an old blanket and as new and exciting as a new car, bright and shiny.

"Erin." He held her hand a fraction of a second longer than necessary. He opened his fingers and let her hand drop. He knew she was an experienced sailor and would have no problem handling the vessel alone. It appeared to be a standard cruiser with a roller furling headsail. He played along, though, for effect. "So, I trust you know how to sail."

Erin rolled her eyes. "I got this far, didn't I?" The artificial voice was gone. "Look, I'm not sure what Wes told you when he called, but we departed the Lighthouse Marina in Baltimore this morning. We motored out of the harbor and down the Patapsco River, under the Key Bridge. I hoisted the sails and had a nice tailwind for about three hours before the wind slowly died. I figured I'd motor-sail for a bit. The engine ran great for about thirty minutes, then...poof."

"Poof?"

"Yes. Poof." Erin opened her eyes wide and used her hands to depict something going *poof*. "So, yes, I know how to sail."

Bright sun shining in Erin's brown eyes rendered them translucent, with tiny flecks of yellow shimmering like the sun-kissed ripples on the water. The yellow pepper of her eyes was invisible unless the sun shone on them at just the right angle. He had always considered himself one of the privileged few who ever noticed. He didn't remember exactly what he wanted to say to her the night of the accident, but he was sure he would have mentioned the yellow pepper. He peered at the dweeb cardiologist over the top of his sunglasses. *I'll bet he never noticed her eye-pepper.* Despite the heat, Landon shivered. He took a deep breath and continued pretending to not know her.

"Unless the wind dies again, and I don't think it will, I figure you'll arrive in the channel at Canvasback Cove around six or six-thirty. This time of year, you'll still have plenty of daylight."

"Oh, for God's sake!" Wes moved toward Landon, who took a step backward. "Can we stop talking about daylight and focus here? I'm a cardiologist and have an emergency at John's Hopkins." He turned to Erin. "I'm about to jump off this damned boat and swim back to Baltimore."

"Good luck with that," Erin said, barely audible. And for some reason, it made Landon smile.

"Babe." Wes pressed his fingers into his eyes as if seriously considering swimming. "This isn't funny."

"Nobody is laughing." Erin shook her head. "Look, I get that you're needed at the hospital." She sighed. "Mr. Shultz here will take you back, and his deadrise should get you there in two hours. I'll go down below and get your bag."

"No, no." He seemed to soften. "Keep it here. I'll drive down in a few days. This way, I don't have to shlep it around." He patted the back pocket of his shorts. "I have my wallet and my phone; that's all I need."

Landon looked at Erin. "By the time you get to Canvasback Cove, the tide will be ripping through the channel to the drawbridge. Without a motor, you won't be able to navigate the tight space. Just drop anchor outside the channel and wait for me. I'll tow you into the channel and to the boatyard."

"I don't know about this," Wes said. "I just don't know. I really think you should come with me."

"Look, I may catch her on my way back to Canvasback Cove and make sure she's okay." Landon wasn't ready to let on that he knew. Yet, he found it impossible that Erin didn't recognize him. Maybe she did. Perhaps that was the bit with the bad hat, the disguised voice. All he knew was that he wouldn't be the first one to break the ice. Nope. Twenty years was a long time. A very long time. He reminded himself that Erin had cut off all communication with him. She had every right, he supposed. After all, she lost her leg because of him. And her scholarship. And her ability to do the one thing she loved more than anything else in the world—even more than she loved sailing: running. He had robbed her of her identity.

"It's a good idea, Wes. It will take twice as long to get to Baltimore with a thirty-five-foot sailboat in tow." She put her arm around him. "I know what I'm doing. Don't worry, I'll be fine."

8

Landon. *So, it's really you,* she thought, dumbstruck. She cleared her throat and let her eyes scan the towboat, the same old deadrise of many childhood memories, going with Landon and his dad to pick up stranded boaters. They took the deadrise fishing, too. Never particularly good at fishing, there was the one time she caught a large rockfish. She had been what, all of eight or nine years old? Landon's dad snapped a photo of her holding the fish like a winner at the White Marlin Open. She wondered whatever happened to that photo. The old towboat was painted blue now and sported the name *Little Jo* (it had formerly simply said, in big, red, block letters: *Shultz Towing.*

Erin felt like her leg might buckle under the weight of seeing Landon. She looked at the towboat again: *Little Jo.* Yep. The name on the deadrise said it all. *Little Jo.* She should have known. A few years ago, Erin's mom had called her, sobbing hysterically, that Joelle Shultz had died. Best friends since college, they had found themselves at an impossible impasse after, as her parents frequently reminded her, their son blew her leg off. As angry as Erin had been at the time, she knew, in her heart of hearts, that Landon didn't deliberately blow her leg off. Yes, she knew this, but she still, feeding off her parents' vitriol, concluded that Landon wasn't worthy of her time. If she really allowed herself to think about it deeply, she had felt Landon pulling away, ever so subtly, in the weeks leading up to the accident, when Susan had been fawning over him when they performed in *Once Upon a Mattress* together that year.

For that matter, Erin had no interest in musical theater; neither did Landon, but Susan had convinced him it would look good on college applications, showing him as a well-rounded student. But even if Erin had wanted to participate, she was hopelessly devoted to running, and rehearsals would have conflicted with track practice. If she wanted Georgetown to take her seriously as a runner, she needed to be the best of the best.

When summer rolled around, and the accolades of the play were long behind them, Susan—the nerve of her—took a job at the tiny bait and tackle shop in Landon's dad's boatyard. And then Landon—the nerve of him—invited Susan to stop by for the Fourth of July fireworks. At Erin's house!

"She can watch the town fireworks on Saturday," Erin had said.

"But she'll be in Annapolis at her grandmother's."

"How can you invite someone to something my family is hosting?" Erin wasn't buying Landon's lame excuse.

"Susan is your friend too. Nearly everyone in Canvasback Cove comes to your place for fireworks."

So, yeah, Erin had been primed to be angry at Landon. The night of the fireworks, when Landon pulled her aside and said he wanted to show her something...well...she had been hopeful. Susan was nowhere in sight. She had no idea what Landon had up his sleeve, but whatever it was, it was for her alone, not Susan. Apprehensive when he took her into her dad's workshop and stole a few fireworks from his stash, she went along with it, but something had raised her hackles. Landon raced her to the water, something they always used to do as kids; he always lost. But Susan was sitting on the grass when they got to the water. Livid, Erin started to leave, but Landon begged her to stay.

"Just ignore her," he had said. "She's so far away, she probably can't even see us."

"If we can see her, she could see us." Erin started walking up the hill, back to the house. And in a moment of stupidity, she relented and turned around.

ERIN PUSHED THE MEMORY AWAY, mystified that Wes had called Shultz Towing instead of the number on the dog-eared and faded TowBoatUS card she had given him. She carried the stupid card in her wallet like a talisman. It had been her father's card. He had purchased annual memberships the year after the accident rather than rely on the Shultz family's towing services. He even started taking his boats quite a way down the Choptank River to a boatyard in Cambridge rather than have Ed Shultz work on them.

Little Jo. She couldn't believe it. Couldn't believe the guy with the long hair and pecks standing on this good-for-nothing sailboat rental was Landon. She had been in Costa Rica attending her best friend's wedding the week they had his mom's funeral. She remembered calling home to make one final plea to her parents to attend. Or, at the very least, pay their respects. *We'll think about it*, is what her mother had finally said, complete and utter defeat in her voice. Erin had kept her expectations low. Very low. But hopeful. At least a glimmer of hope. Okay, not even a trace. In the end, her parents fled to Brooklyn to see an art exhibit by an artist her mother had "discovered," saying it was now or never because the show was closing later that week and that they would send flowers and a card. *Bullshit* is what Erin remembered thinking about the exhibit and the flowers.

She knew her parents would regret their decision to flee, especially her mother, but never circled back to talk about it. The Shultz family was as taboo a topic as decapitating a kitten. But, as much as she didn't desire to see Landon, she would have gone to the funeral if she hadn't been in Costa Rica. Hell, she might have even given her regrets to the bride and booked a flight home had it not been for the

little complication of being the *maid of honor*. Joelle Shultz had been
like a second mother to her. At least in the "before" times.

"I'm sorry about your mom." She studied her shoes as she said it--
an old pair of docksiders she'd had forever. In the earlier hullabaloo
with Wes, she somehow managed to shimmy her stump back into
Doris without being obvious. She cautiously looked up to gauge
Landon's reaction and read his eyes. A split-second look passed
between them; one she couldn't put her finger on. Recognition, of
course (she suspected her foolish attempt at disguising herself had
been for not), but something else. Anger? Sadness? Disgust? Resigna-
tion? Regret? She simply couldn't tell. And just as quickly as the look
came, Landon nodded and turned away.

"You know each other?" Wes draped his arm around her and
pulled her close.

"A long time ago," she said, gradually returning to reality. She
stretched and made herself as tall as she could to reach Wes's head
and whisper, *I love you*, into his ear.

"I love you too," he said a little too loudly, likely for Landon's
benefit. A few days ago, Erin might have been flattered by this
gesture, and this slight posturing might have signified a step closer to
the demarcation of a more permanent relationship. Today, it was like
Wes was peeing on the bushes, and she didn't like the smell of pee.

Wes followed Landon through the cockpit and onto *Little Jo*. She
stood at the helm and watched them motor away, Wes waving wildly
like he was departing for a long journey across the Atlantic. Landon's
jaw was set, his eyes focused on the horizon.

9

———

Landon let the boat-generated wind whip his face and scatter his hair hither and yon. The man bun broke free as he glanced at the dweeb cardiologist sitting with his back toward Landon, gripping the sides of the settee and watching Erin and her rented sailboat get smaller and smaller on the horizon until they curved toward the left and Erin was no longer visible. His mind swirled in a sea of thoughts—a million thoughts per second—swirling and swirling and swirling. He needed to put this in a box (his fireproof, indestructible safe had been blasted open when he realized he'd been standing two feet away from Erin) and focus. The dweeb cardiologist had tried to engage him in harmless banter, mostly about himself and his life-saving surgeries. *Pompous ass*, Landon thought. After nodding, grunting, and making other gestures to convey that he was not interested in talking, the dweeb cardiologist shut up.

"So, how do you know Erin?" Wes came to the surface, yelling above the drone of the engine and the song of the wind.

Landon pretended not to hear.

"How long?"

Can't this bastard take a hint? Landon rolled his eyes. "We've known each other since we were kids."

"Fine. But that's not what I was asking." Wes let go of the bench long enough to tamp down his hat, which looked like it could blow away at any moment. "How much longer until we get there?"

The harbor was in full view, albeit still quite a distance away. "Twenty minutes, at the most."

"Erin never mentioned you," Wes said.

"We haven't talked in a long time."

"How long?"

"Twenty years."

"Why so long?"

Clearly, the dweeb cardiologist wasn't about to let this go. Landon didn't want to talk about it, so he changed the subject. "Hey, you mind taking the wheel for a minute?"

Wes cautiously stood up and made his way to the helm. "Do you think that's safe?"

Landon lowered the motor's speed. "See that building on the horizon? The tallest one? Just point at that."

He stepped aside to make room for the dweeb. The only problem was that this guy wasn't a dweeb. Tall and fit. Legs were a little too skinny and a little too hairy, in Landon's opinion. He studied the guy's forearms: thick, but not too thick; muscular, but not too muscular. He remembered Erin describing her favorite male body part to Susan during biology class: Forearms. Forearms! *I love forearms, she had said.* He had never looked at forearms the same way since then, always wondering if his measured up. The cardiologist had pretty good forearms. But, like his legs, a little too hairy.

The dweeb wasn't really a dweeb in other ways, too, like putting his dislike of the water aside to sail across the Chesapeake with Erin. And he was giving up part of his vacation for a worthy cause. Sure, he was a pompous ass, but didn't he earn the right? He was a cardiologist, after all. Someone who fixes hearts. Landon wondered if this non-dweeb could fix his.

"What if I run into something."

Landon swirled his head to the left and right. He twisted his body and looked over his shoulder to see behind him. "Like what? There's nothing out here to hit. Just point at the building. You'll be fine."

Wes took a deep breath and exhaled loud enough for Landon to hear over the motor and wind. He wedged his body between the helm and captain's chair and gripped the wheel, looking at Landon for approval. Landon, certainly no judge on whether a man's face was handsome or not (he had a pretty good idea of ugly, though), looked into the cardiologists' eyes. Blue. Bright blue. Almost turquoise. He thought about his own battleship-gray eyes. Hazel was what Erin had once called his eyes. Hazel. Wasn't that an old-fashioned woman's name? Landon preferred battleship gray. Stone cold when he needed his eyes to be. He thought about Coronado, his quasi-home, his team, wondering what he was missing.

Wes, still gripping the wheel and staring at Landon, shrugged. "Am I going the right way?"

Thank God this journey is almost over, Landon thought. "Do you still see the building?" Landon waited for affirmative acknowledgment; Wes gave him three quick little nods. "Just point the bow at the building. I need to make a call. I promise to be back in a minute or two. Long before we need to do any kind of fancy navigating." Landon brushed a handful of wind-tangled and salt-encrusted hair out of his eyes and left Wes to drive *Little Jo*.

He made his way forward and into the tiny pilot house to call Susan. He pressed the button and waited for her to pick up; it eventually rolled to voicemail. "Hey, long story, but I picked up this couple. The guy is a doctor and got called back to the city. Taking him back there now. The wind filled in, so Erin...um...so, his girlfriend is sailing to the island. After I drop the doctor off, I'm going to head back. I told the girlfriend to drop anchor outside the channel. The sailboat has a broken motor, so I will need to tow her from there to the boatyard. Anyway, I was thinking about getting together for dinner, maybe just us, without Willie, but I don't know. Depends on my dad. I'll call you when I have a better idea of when I'll be done with this mess."

He called his dad next. He and Willie were at Charlie Brown's eating chicken nuggets; Susan had gone home to help her mother. Landon was equally relieved that Susan would likely be unable to break away to hang out. He wasn't even sure why he said what he said in his voicemail. He didn't want to hang with Susan tonight, not if he were honest with himself. And, holy fuck, he didn't mean to mention Erin, but it just flew out of his mouth. He thought back to his words and consoled himself by remembering that he'd said her name fast, then quickly backtracked and referred to her from that point forward as the generic "girlfriend." He doubted the name would even register in Susan's brain, particularly given the length and wordiness of the message. What did it matter, anyway? Erin would only be home for a few days. A week maybe. Right? Honestly, he didn't know, and he didn't care. Erin had a boyfriend—a cardiologist!—after all. And he had a sort of thing going with Susan. Didn't he?

He closed his eyes and thought about how Susan's hair framed her face this morning and how much Willie liked her. Maybe he should give Susan more of a chance. Not that he needed a romance to complicate the rest of his emergency leave. But it couldn't hurt, could it? Could a spark ignite in a few weeks? He smiled, unsure. He didn't want to make any promises, but he committed, then and there, to at least keep an open mind toward Susan.

10

Erin entered the channel into Canvasback Cove ahead of schedule. Or at least ahead of her self-imposed schedule. As she headed south, the wind had filled in even more; she had a beautiful tailwind and could broad reach on just the jib and mainsail. She could have tried putting up the spinnaker, but that had been hard enough in the light wind earlier, with Wes helping her (to the degree that he was able; in some ways, he had been more of a hindrance than a help). The sailboat hummed along at eight knots—an easy sail that gave her plenty of time to not think about Landon.

To her surprise, not thinking about him was easier than she expected. She held onto the last thread of her anger, which had faded dramatically over the past two decades. She even thought she had made peace with her fate long ago. Seriously, did she really need to run cross country at Georgetown? Did she even need to run cross country at all? She didn't need to be on a cross-country team to get a good education. In fact, she got a good enough education at Chesapeake College. Did she even need a second leg? Two legs were highly overrated. And what did it matter that she spent her college years living with her parents?

So, she missed the typical college experience, big deal. She liked her life. If she had gone to Georgetown, well, maybe she wouldn't be writing back cover blurbs at a boutique company in Baltimore. She loved the company and loved the job. Oh, and if she didn't get the job at the boutique company in Baltimore, she would never have been standing in line at Sam's Deli picking up lunch for a brainstorming session with her boss. And if she hadn't been standing in line at Sam's Deli, she would never have met Wes, who had been standing behind her and making no attempt to hide his annoyance that she couldn't make up her mind between pastrami on rye or turkey on wheat.

"I completely forgot whether my boss wants pastrami or turkey," she turned around and told him. "I didn't write it down, thinking I'd remember. Andrea always gets ham and provolone, but she said she wanted something different today. And the 'something different' was so out of character for her that I just knew I wouldn't forget. I should call her." She shrugged and punched a button on her phone. She looked up. "Not answering."

"Can I jump in ahead of you then?" He started to step around her, but she blocked him. "Come on. I'm in a terrible hurry."

"Your time is somehow more valuable than mine?" She turned back to the woman behind the counter. "Let's add a pastrami on rye and a turkey on wheat to my order." She smiled her most smug and sarcastic smile at the impatient dude behind her. "Oh, and throw in a ham on provolone too, just for fun." She turned to the dude. "If I completely messed up the order, at least I can offer my boss something I know she likes."

"Just for fun? You're holding me up 'just for fun' while my patients languish in the hospital." He crossed his arms over his chest.

"So, you're a doctor, then?"

He puffed out his chest. "I'm a cardiologist."

"I was under the impression that doctors never eat, let alone stand in line at a deli for lunch." Erin shook her head, unimpressed. She had noticed his unusually blue eyes, though. And his forearms weren't too bad, either.

She stepped aside to let the "cardiologist" have his turn at the counter. "You should try the knish. They make the best knish here."

Walking back to her building, Erin laughed at the strange encounter with the handsome doctor, if a bit arrogant and entitled.

THE TIDE WAS GOING OUT, just as predicted. The guy at the marina in Baltimore who rented the sailboat to Erin said *Jolly Good Day* draws about four-and-a-half feet. That should certainly give her enough clearance to navigate the channel. She had heard from Wes a little while ago—he was on the ground in Baltimore. She relaxed and called her mother, giving her the CliffsNotes version of what had happened. She left out the part about their knight in shining armor being Landon Shultz. The one and only Landon Shultz. The Landon Shultz she had once quietly and secretly loved. The Landon Shultz who ruined her life.

She flung that last thought away—about Landon ruining her life. She reminded herself of all the good that had happened because of and in spite of her injury. In the months after the accident, she had to be deliberate in choosing to visualize the silver lining. It was harder than hell, but she had managed to get quite good at it. But seeing Landon today dissolved the delicate stitches that held her broken heart together all this time. She didn't even realize, until today, that the stitches were so flimsy. She would have to talk to Wes about that. Maybe the excellent cardiologist could reinforce those old stitches.

She did a quick calculation from the time Wes called her, factoring in *Little Jo's* maximum boat speed. She was sure Landon would take his sweet time, smell the roses, and not be in a hurry to help her through the channel. She came up with the simple fact that she had no desire to sit in the channel and wait for him. By her calculations, he was at least an hour away; it would take her that long to get through the channel and to the pier at her mother's B&B. She would not let Landon drag her to his father's boatyard. No way in hell. She had let the guy at the marina in Baltimore talk her into buying a one-week insurance policy for the rental. Surely it covered a broken engine. The only problem would be getting the boat back to Baltimore next week. *At least I renewed Dad's BoatUS membership*, she thought.

Erin furled the jib—the wind and narrow channel demanded less power. She couldn't just plow through like a powerboat; she needed to navigate slowly and carefully, with just the mainsail. *Let me try the engine one more time*, she thought. If she could get it to run, even for a minute or two, she would be free and on the other side. She turned into the wind to slow the boat and tried the motor. Nothing. Not even the click-click-click of an engine trying and failing to turn over. Not even a puff of smoke. The thing was deader than dead.

She picked up her phone to call the drawbridge, wondering if Smokey Jones was on duty today. She made a mental note to pop over to his house this week and bring his wife some jalapeños from her mother's garden. Smokey's wife had an elaborate garden but insisted that Lydia Conrad's jalapeños were the spiciest in town. Erin told herself she would make a point to return home for the Pepper Festival at the end of the summer. She had missed it the last two years, although Smokey's wife had saved her a jar of her famed jalapeño jelly. Erin's mouth watered, thinking about the jelly spread like frosting over a block of sharp cheddar. She'd have to introduce Wes to the jelly and wondered why she hadn't yet.

She closed her phone without calling the drawbridge. The reality was beginning to sink in; there was no way she could sail through. Heading downwind, down current, it was just too risky. Not that she would get into trouble, it was simply that it would take her a long time to get through the bridge. Too long. The traffic would build up and down Moss Street. The locals would understand, especially the sailors among them. But the tourists would blare their horns and quite likely give Smokey the finger as they passed by the bridge tender's hut where he spent most of his days during summer. And while she knew Smokey would hold the bridge open for her, she didn't want to do that to him.

Shultz Boat Yard and Marina—the faded red letters emblazoned on a chipped and peeling wooden sign in the distance—taunted and beckoned. The last thing Erin wanted to do was run into Landon's dad. In fact, she would rather donate a kidney than admit defeat by tying up *Jolly Good Day* there. But what other choice did she have? Drop anchor and stay here all night? She supposed that was an option, but her location wasn't ideal for a lazy night under the stars. She wasn't even sure the battery on this less-than-stellar sailboat would work.

She turned into the wind again and crouched in the companionway hatch, reaching her arm around the instrument panel. Her fingers found what they were looking for, but she didn't want to just start pushing buttons—she might blow up the boat! Ha! That would solve all her problems. She used the upper body strength she had developed swimming (she couldn't run, not really; swimming filled in the gap rather nicely) and lowered herself into the cabin. She flipped the switch for the bow and stern lights and popped her head through the hatch to see if, at the very least, she had a mast light. No such luck. *Stupid boat.* She knew the rules by heart: a white, all-around masthead light with two-mile visibility. No way she could safely spend the night anchored. She shook her head and flipped the switch back, defeated and resolved.

Erin didn't need to look at the phone number painted on the Shultz Boat Yard and Marina sign; it was the same as when she and Landon were kids, and she knew it by heart. She called and was surprised when it rolled directly to voicemail. Fine. She loosely devised an alternative plan: she would jibe her way to the floating dock and sidle up beside it. Thank God it was Wednesday. The floating dock would be lined with boats if today had been a Friday or Saturday. Today, it was as if the dock had been waiting just for her.

Alternatively, she could do the practical thing and drop anchor. The tide was still relatively high, and the sun negated the need for a light. Her sensibilities begged her to wait for Landon to show up.

He would be able to help her inch the boat toward the marina and help guide her to the finger pier closest to the travel lift. Rarely practical and not much into sensibilities, Erin decided to proceed without assistance. She didn't want or need Landon's help. Plain and simple. She didn't want or need anything from him. Not now, not ever.

As LUCK WOULD HAVE IT, the wind died again. Not as abruptly as it had died earlier in the day. Earlier today, the wind had been a mouse innocently seeking a piece of cheese and getting decapitated by a spring-loaded trap—one minute there was wind, the next minute there was none. Wham! Lights out. The wind's recent death was more drawn out and subtle than earlier. Hanging on by a thread, the wind sputtered and heaved its final breaths, speaking the last words to impart wisdom or make amends. This time the mouse had bitten into a poison apple and was now hunched over and dragging its feet, tail between its legs, trying to find a quiet, out-of-the-way corner to curl up and die. The two deaths were different, but the result was the same—no wind.

Erin picked a spot on the horizon—the restaurant with the cobalt blue picnic tables, the one Susan's parents owned—and waited for the tables to grow bigger, for the RAR beer logos printed on the umbrellas to come into readable focus. She wondered what the Rupert's were calling the place now. They had changed the name thrice during Erin's childhood, morphing from Rupert's to R's Bar and Grille to R's Burgers. Ten years ago, they had changed it back to Rupert's. And a year after that, Rupert's Dockside Grille. At some point, Erin stopped paying attention.

Nearly a half-hour had gone by, and she was only close enough to see that Rupert's Dockside Grille had been distilled back into the stark Rupert's. Someone needed to seriously talk to those people about branding. The only aspect of their business that never changed was the mediocre burger recipe and the patio decor; the cobalt blue picnic tables and yellow umbrellas remained the only constant. Erin sniffed. The aroma of burgers hung in the air and called like a siren.

Great. Now Erin was thinking about burgers, fries, and...onions. Suddenly the faint hint of onions mingled with the stronger-by-the-second smell of burgers. Onion rings! Rupert's may not have the best burgers in town, but they certainly had the best onion rings. Her mouth watered—she was famished. Absolutely starving. She imagined her stomach eating its own walls; she was that hungry.

Maybe, after she tied up the boat, she would walk across the drawbridge and get an order of onion rings before heading home. An impulsive decision, yes, but impulsive decisions sometimes yielded more than piping hot onion rings. A month or so after her annoying encounter with the arrogant, in-a-rush cardiologist, she impulsively walked into Sam's deli. She had been walking to the post office to return a Land's End sweater she had ordered and immediately hated (it made her look like a clown) when the smell of potatoes and onions assaulted her. She hadn't planned on going into the deli for lunch; she had a perfectly good box of Stouffer's frozen macaroni and cheese in the office freezer and looked forward to eating at her desk and catching up on email. Like today, that day too had been a Wednesday.

Land's End package under her arm, Erin had pushed open the door to the deli and was practically knocked down by someone rushing out. Yep. The arrogant doctor. Did he bother to apologize? Of course not! *Arrogant bastard*. And that was the end of that. It wasn't until she stood in line, ordering a knish to go, that she realized someone was staring at her. The cardiologist. Yep. The cardiologist was sitting at a high-top table near the window. His dark hair, messy from the wind, made him look younger, humbler.

"Don't you have more important things to do? Like save lives?" she said as she walked by his table on her way to the door. She pushed the door open with her shoulder.

He took a sip of his Diet Coke. *Singing in the Rain* crackled from the speaker hanging from the far corner of the ceiling. "Can you sit for a minute?"

She looked at her watch and shrugged. "I guess." She set the package against the wall and climbed onto the empty chair, wondering what she was doing. "I only have a few minutes. I need to get back to work" She had more than a few minutes, a half-hour, but she didn't want him to know that. He could be a serial killer, for all she knew. She glanced at the John's Hopkins badge hanging from a lanyard around his neck and compared the laminated face with the face across the table. The laminated face seemed a little darker, the hair a little thinner. She squinted to get a better look. *Dr. Wesley Rubin. Department of Cardiology.* The serial killer could have easily accosted the actual Dr. Wesley Rubin, who was probably in a custodian's closet, bound and gagged.

"I tried the knish," he said. "You were right. It was excellent. Not as good as my mother's, though. But close." He smiled and extended his hand. "Wes. Wes Rubin."

She took one last look at the hospital badge. Both the photo and the natural face had almost translucent aquamarine eyes. She supposed the serial killer could have somehow altered the badge. Sharpies come in all sorts of obscure colors these days. A blue dot over each eye on the photo would do the trick. Presto! A nearly perfect likeness. She shook his hand, deciding that the natural face, with the actual eyes boring into her, was worth the risk. Serial killer or not, she was sucked into those eyes.

"Erin Conrad."

Wes nodded. "Erin." He let go of her hand. "I'm sorry I almost plowed you down earlier. I wasn't even in a hurry." He looked at the floor, then back at Erin. "I stopped in for 'breakfast' after a long night and morning at the hospital. "I just wanted to get home to..." His eyes danced, and his mouth broke into a toothy grin. "I had to poop." He laughed. "There. I said it. I had to poop."

Erin busted out laughing. This, she had not expected. "Let me guess. You don't like pooping in public restrooms."

"I don't know why, but my body shuts down in them."

"What do you do at work?" She leaned closer and lowered her

voice. "I don't poop at work either, by the way. But then again, I don't work crazy shifts."

"I'm usually so focused that my...um...plumbing goes into hibernation. There's a single-stall bathroom with a lock on the door, and it's in the orthopedic department on the sixth floor. Sometimes I sneak up there...if I can't wait."

Oh my God. This guy is a serial killer, and the actual cardiologist is locked in a hospital bathroom. She wondered why the serial killer would give her such an obvious clue. She was about to get up and leave but felt mesmerized by his eyes and the fact that they were sitting in a deli discussing...poop.

Erin chuckled at the memory, wishing Wes didn't get called back to Baltimore. She understood how critical this surgery was. Her chuckles suddenly turned sour. Well, weren't all his surgeries important? Resentment slowly crept in. She reminded herself that this surgery was a special case that almost couldn't happen because the girl was too sick. He had been talking about this patient for weeks—the unusual mass of infection in the girl's heart was just one in a series of complications from a years-old tick bite. Wes had described, in painful detail, the tragic vigil the family was keeping in the ICU waiting room.

Erin remembered being unexpectedly triggered by Wes' ICU recap, particularly his play-by-play of the grieving family. *The girl is hanging on by a thread,* he had said, crying into his hands one day—yep, at the deli over Diet Coke and knish. *She has her whole life ahead of her.* While Erin didn't remember her own family's vigil when she, too, had been hanging on by a thread, they didn't let her forget it, mainly when the name Landon Shultz came up. Her parents' vitriol toward Landon fed her hurt and anger toward him. Soon, his name was never mentioned at all. It had become taboo—a name you dared not say, lest you'd have to relive the whole damned tragedy, the long recovery, the slow progress to the new normal. Listening to Wes drone on about his patient caused Erin's sympathy to slowly morph into unjustified competitive feelings. She felt them bubbling around the edges, threatening to boil over.

What about me? She bit her tongue, desperately wanting to turn the discussion to her ordeal, two decades before, which she had described to him in painstaking detail early in their relationship. The only pieces she left out: her complicated feelings for Landon during the summer of the accident or the fact that they had been inseparable as children.

I was hanging on by a thread too, she had wanted to shout. Instead, she almost choked on her knish. She took that as a sign and let her brain settle back into performing the "good girlfriend" routine. So, she listened, sipping her Diet Coke, nodding where appropriate, shaking her head when he shook his head and patting his hand at perfectly choreographed intervals.

THE HIGH-PITCHED SOUND of an osprey interrupted her unproductive brooding. *Maverick*, she thought. She let her eyes follow him to his nest—a mansion he and his mate, Goose, had built on the platform that Smokey Jones had installed atop a piling near the mouth of the channel about ten years ago.

Maverick delivered a fish to his two babies, already full-grown but still happy to have their daddy bring them food. She would have to ask Smokey what he named the babies this year. The old drawbridge tender had long ago exhausted all the major and minor characters in his favorite movie, *Top Gun*. The only constants were Maverick and Goose.

Erin let her mind drift back to missing Wes. Of course, she was glad his patient had stabilized enough for surgery. Very glad. She just wished it had been last week. Or next week. Or even two days ago. She was anxious for her mom to meet him and had hoped they'd have a day or two alone with her before the rest of the family trickled in. She imagined sitting under the pergola with a glass of wine, laughing about that fateful Wednesday in the deli when she and Wes talked about poop. Perhaps they could go there for knish on their anniversary if they ever get married.

Suddenly quite wistful for him, she pulled out her phone and texted. *Miss you. Hope your surgery goes well. I'm rooting for you (and your patient). See you in a day or two. Love you.* She ended it with three heart emojis. She looked at her watch; another half-hour had gone by, and she had barely moved. Erin glanced at her depth sounder as she slowly approached the mouth of the channel. Dead. Of course. Should she have expected anything more from this sailboat? The guy who rented it to her didn't know yet, but she planned to bomb his website with bad reviews. She pushed the button on the instrument, jamming her finger into it with force, and she winced. Nothing. She took a deep breath. She knew these waters like she knew her own name. They were a part of her, embedded in her DNA. She also knew that there was a sandbar about a hundred yards in. Most of the time, the sandbar would not be an issue. But it could be a big issue at low tide for a sailboat that drew more than four feet.

Holding her breath as she entered the channel, she seriously considered dropping anchor to wait for Landon. The tide had gotten relatively low—too low for her comfort level. The sensible thing to do was to just sit tight and not try to navigate without a motor through a shallow, narrow channel. But her sensibilities had flown away the moment she saw Landon today. She needed to distance herself from him. The bigger the gap, the better.

Crap! Erin lurched forward as the keel hit bottom. The sandy, silty bottom felt solid today. At least it wasn't a granite ledge, like when her family had gone to New England to visit her dad's brother. They had been enjoying a pleasant sail when Uncle Hal hit a granite ledge outside the Block Island lighthouse. At six years old, Erin thought it was fun when the adults screamed, and the kids—her brother and several older cousins—all ended up in a pile on the deck, laughing.

The keel bounced off the bottom, slowing the sailboat's momentum. She regrouped and tried to steer away from the shoreline to what she thought was deeper water. The sandbar was longer and broader than she remembered, and as she turned the rudder, it slammed into the compacted silt.

She gripped the helm as the channel's current pinwheeled the boat off the sandbar. Completely turned around with no wind filling her sails, the boat plowed, bow-first between the pier and bulkhead. The sound of fiberglass grinding against wood was not a happy sound. Erin, and the boat, were screwed. She tried to use her weight to rock the boat, hoping to dislodge it. No such luck. The current held *Jolly Good Day* like a thumb pressed against a mouse's tail.

11

"Holy Crap! What the Fuck?" Landon had been watching Erin and the rented sailboat for the past hour, keeping a respectable distance, wondering what she would do next. *Stupid. Stupid. Stupid.* He should have just motored up to her well before the channel. *Stupid. Stupid. Stupid.* How could she be so... not stupid? He was the stupid one, the one who should have known better. No. How could she be so...maybe careless was a better word. She knew it was coming up on low tide. She knew about the sandbar. How often had his dad let them wade out on the sandbar when they were kids? Bunches. Closely supervised, of course. But bunches.

"You couldn't just wait, could you," he muttered. God, she was stubborn. She never waited, stayed put, or accepted help from anyone. Especially him. Even when they were on speaking terms, she always went her own way, always had to do things her way and herself.

"Dammit, Erin!" He pounded the helm, frustrated with himself for stalking her. Because that was what he had been doing for the past hour. Right? Stalking her? Almost like it was a test. Would she drop anchor and wait for him before trying to navigate the channel with no motor? He wasn't sure why he felt he needed to test her. He knew the answer—that she wouldn't wait. How many of his guys would have gotten killed during a mission if he had "tested" them? He shook his head, flinging the thought into the water. This situation —Erin's boat wedged against the piling—wasn't life or death. But it did involve a rented sailboat that now had a hell of a lot more damage than a busted motor. A hell of a lot more.

"She knows about the sandbar. Why did she have to try and go through the channel?" Landon wasn't sure why he was so upset about this. He took a deep breath, giving himself a few seconds to try and identify the underlying thought process causing him to be so upset. Erin was nobody to him. Maybe she had been a long time ago, but not anymore. As far as he was concerned, she was the one who "left" him, if he could even think of it that way, because they were never more than friends. Best friends. But friends, nonetheless. So, his being this upset that she didn't wait for him seemed out of synch with reality. Was it merely concern that she damaged a boat that wasn't hers? He thought about that for a split second. Nope. He didn't care. That was between Erin and the rental company. "If she thinks, even for a minute, that I'll tow her and the broken vessel back to Balti-more, she's crazy."

At least he could identify that he was upset instead of shoving it aside and letting it eat him alive, which was his default mode. In between deployments, when Willie was barely six months old, Landon had gone to a counseling session with Willie's mother. He didn't want to. Taylor was the one with the problem, not him. He understood postpartum depression well enough. He had even sympathized and accommodated. He lost count of the dark mornings he had slept on the couch with Willie perched on his chest, just to give Taylor a little more sleep. So, yeah, he didn't view himself as an insensitive jerk. But he had to draw the line somewhere, and he drew it when the topic of him joining her for a counseling session came up. *It's a chemical thing, treatable with well, chemicals*, he had told her. *What will your counselor say to me that I don't already know?* That, apparently, had not been the right thing to say. His commanding officer summoned him a few days later, ordering him to attend at least one session. Commander Diaz didn't suggest it, didn't request it, didn't even make it a condition of one thing or another. Nope. He ordered him to attend. Ordered! Landon's blood boiled, thinking about it.

He slowed the motor to just above idle and navigated *Little Jo* through the channel, careful to avoid the sandbar, pretty sure that the tide was low enough to cause him problems, even in a relatively flat-bottomed boat. He carefully pulled up next to the floating dock, turned off the engine, and jumped out, quickly tying the dock line to the bow. He jogged to the T-pier, where the rented sailboat was wedged against the piling. He assessed the damage without seeing it: dent and scratches in the fiberglass, maybe a hole, depending on what she hit. Oh, and the way the boat spun around like a whirligig, the rudder was probably damaged beyond repair. He sure hoped, for Erin's sake, that the boat was insured.

"Hey." Landon stood on the pier and shouted. "You okay?" No answer. "Erin?" He moved closer to the vessel, no longer feeling as tightly wound, as upset. He had attended four counseling sessions—three with Taylor and one by himself. He learned that stopping long enough to name the emotion sometimes helped bring him back to the present moment. Even better if he could spend a few minutes trying to identify the trigger. So, that's what he had learned in counseling—to name his emotions. In the end, Taylor still left, which was okay with him. If she didn't want Willie, then he didn't want her.

"I'm fine. I'm fine." Erin's head popped out of the companionway hatch, no longer adorned with a hat that was fifteen sizes too big for her. And as quickly as it had emerged, her head disappeared back into the depths of the boat.

The sun had settled behind the trees and wasn't the blinding light it had been earlier. Erin's sunglasses were on the top of her head, holding her short hair in place. There was a calmness about her, a sort of peace on her face that he found alluring and unsettling. She had probably just gotten off the phone with the dweeb cardiologist and was happy. Happy in love. Landon wasn't allowed to be on Facebook. Okay, that wasn't entirely true. It was strongly discouraged for a Navy SEAL doing black operations to be on social media sites. So, he never got an account. Taylor, however, practically lived on the platform.

"Isn't there someone you want to look up? See how they're doing?" Taylor shoved her iPad in his face. "Go ahead. I won't even ask to see, and I don't care if it's a girl or a guy."

Taylor wouldn't let it go, so he typed *Erin Conrad* into the search bar. And, of course, Taylor asked to see. So, he let her watch over his shoulder as he clicked on Erin Conrad after Erin Conrad. None of the ten or so clicks yielded results. He handed the iPad back. "She must not be on Facebook."

"Everyone is on Facebook," Taylor protested. "Well, everyone except you." She raised an eyebrow. "Who is she, anyway?"

"I thought you said you weren't going to ask." He rolled his eyes, smiling. "She was a childhood friend. We practically grew up together, kind of like brother and sister." He did his best to hide the wistfulness creeping into his heart and left out the part about almost killing her and ruining her life.

"Try her first and middle name."

"What do you mean?"

"Some people, women mostly, just use their first and middle name on their profile."

Landon took the iPad and entered *Erin Leigh*. Bam. There she was. He had never seen her with short hair; it suited her. He was a long hair guy himself, but didn't most guys prefer long hair on women? He studied the picture—her mature features (she didn't look old, but her face had a maturity about it, even when they were kids; she wasn't cutesy, like Taylor or Susan, for that matter), the intensity in her yellow-pepper eyes. He closed the lid and handed the iPad back.

"That's it? Don't you want to scroll through and see what she's been up to?" Taylor tried to hand the iPad back, but he held his hands in stop-sign style.

"This is a waste of time. I've seen enough. Erin used to wear her hair long, and now it's short. What more do I need to know?" He got up to get a beer out of the fridge and carried it out to the small balcony overlooking the ninth fairway on the base golf course.

Later, he feigned sleep when Taylor got friendly in bed, preferring to lie awake and ruminate.

Landon leaned against the piling and waited for Erin to get off the boat. God only knew what she was doing down below. If it had been anyone else, he would have figured she was standing in front of a mirror, applying a dab of lipstick or a swipe of mascara. Not Erin. The only time he had ever seen her wear makeup was during their junior prom. He had wanted to ask her to go with him but lost his nerve every damned time the topic of prom came up. He rehearsed several different ways to ask her, determined to keep the mood light and frame the request to not imply anything other than two best friends getting dressed up and hanging out together. Nothing more. Deep down inside, though, he wanted more. He just didn't know what to do with his feelings, didn't know how to begin unpacking them. He didn't even have the emotional language to understand that some things needed unpacking. He only knew it now because of the counseling sessions with Taylor. *That's a big emotion*, the therapist would say. *Let's unpack it.* Ad nauseam. In the end, Landon lost his nerve and asked Susan to the junior prom instead. And Erin was giddy happy when Nate Gibson asked her to go. Landon made a show of clutching Susan during every slow song, one eye open and glued to Erin, laughing in Nate's arms.

A slow stirring, the clanking of metal against wood, and the various other sounds of a person banging below deck. A black duffle bag flew out of the companionway hatch, hitting the deck with a thud and an even louder thud when a rolling suitcase followed. Two hands popped out, each one grabbing one side of the deck. Erin lifted herself, using only her upper body and swinging her legs through the opening like a gymnast on the parallel bars. He didn't remember her arms being so defined in the past. They weren't exactly bulky, suggesting a lifting routine with heavy weights. Her arms were simply firm, with tiny, bulging triceps. He supposed she used her arms frequently to compensate for having one leg.

"Daddy! Daddy! I got another Batman!" Willie came barreling down the pier, clutching a stuffed Batman doll to his chest. "Puppy took me to the toy store!" He held the doll out for Landon to see.

"Wow, Little Dude! That's awesome!" Grateful for the interruption from his inappropriate thoughts about Erin and her sinewy arms, Landon took the doll and pretended to study it intently. "That's the most awesome Batman I've ever seen." He handed the doll back. "Where is Puppy?" Landon had wanted Willie to call his grandfather Poppy like he had called his grandfather. Kids apparently mangle even the most seemingly simple words; Poppy somehow morphed into Puppy. Landon's dad embraced it. How could he not? Who, in their right mind, wouldn't want to be associated with a soft, playful puppy?

"Puppy fixing the big boat." Willie took his hand. "Come, Daddy. Let's go help Puppy fix the big boat."

Landon scanned the horizon, infuriated that his dad would let Willie run around unsupervised. Back in Coronado, he took Willie to the beach and the pool on base every chance he could. Landon even tried to teach him age-appropriate respect for the water. He was in no way worried about Willie deciding to jump in. But accidents happened. And if anything untoward happened to his son, Landon would kill himself.

"He's with me." Susan walked toward him, a kid-sized Batman backpack dangling from her hand. "Is that the boat you rescued?"

"Yeah. Sort of." He scanned the deck for Erin, but she had apparently flung herself back down below. He noticed the name on the hull: *Jolly Good Day*. The day was wrapping up to be anything but jolly good.

"I was waiting tables at my mom's and saw the boat get into trouble." She put an arm around his waist, then quickly removed it. "You came in like a knight in shining armor on a white horse."

"Except my boat is blue," he said, turning around to look for Willie. He exhaled when he saw his son sitting in the dirt next to the pier, constructing a tower out of small rocks and oyster shells. "Your mom doesn't need you at the restaurant anymore?" Earlier, he had looked forward to spending some time with Susan tonight. Not so much anymore. He was distracted and, at least internally, cranky.

"I saw you and wanted to come over." She shrugged. "The place is pretty slow tonight, and mom can get on without me." She put her hands on her hips. "Then your dad asked if I could watch Willie for a few minutes while he looks at that Catalina 22 that came in this morning."

Landon sensed Erin's presence, figuring she would reemerge from the cabin any second. And as if he was clairvoyant, she did, indeed, emerge, this time climbing through the companionway hatch normally, which was too bad because he would have liked to see her triceps again.

Ignoring him (and Susan), Erin lowered herself over the side, her upper body hugging the hull, the duffle dangling from her hands until it touched the finger pier. Her face, red from her head having been upside down, was tilted in his direction, but either she didn't see him or chose not to acknowledge him. And she was wearing an artificial leg donned with a running shoe.

"Ouch!" Landon glared at Susan, who had just punched his arm. Hard. "What are you doing? Why did you..." He softened, realizing that he hadn't been paying attention to anything she had just said. "I'm sorry. You were saying the restaurant is slow?"

"Never mind."

"Don't be like that." He took a deep breath and cocked his head toward the sailboat, and Erin, who was now on the pier fiddling with the rolling suitcase, her back toward him. "She looked like she was about to fall on her head."

"Sure," Susan said, turning away from him. "Hey, Willie, show me what you're building."

"I'm building a Batman house," Willie said as Susan shuffled toward the dirt.

LANDON FELT Susan's eyes burning holes through his tee shirt, into the flesh on his back, through his ribcage, and straight to his heart. Susan couldn't possibly know it was Erin who he was attempting to help with her bags. Couldn't possibly. More likely, Susan felt threatened by the beautiful intruder, the interloper, the outsider daring to wash up onto the shores of her hometown, her exclusive little cove. Like a bad romantic comedy, Susan probably already knew the ending. Happy for the beautiful intruder, pleased for the leading man. But decidedly unhappy for the hometown girl, the girl next door.

"Can't I help you with that?" Landon's frustration mounted. Erin never accepted his help. Never.

"I told you. I've got it. I'm good." She hoisted the duffle across her body like a messenger bag and took hold of the rolling suitcase's handle. Barely halfway up the pier, the suitcase burst open, eight or ten articles of clothing tumbling out. Landon crouched down and grabbed a flowery sundress right before it was about to flutter into the water. He held it up and regarded it. Daisies. "I don't remember you being a dress person."

"Give me that!" She grabbed it and crouched down to stuff it, along with the other items strewn about, back into her suitcase. She stood up and straightened to her full height, most of it in her legs. "There is a lot you don't know about me."

"I knew you pretty well back in the day." Landon let his eyes drift to her fake leg and wondered if anyone ever asked about it. The dweeb cardiologist no doubt had. He imagined them in the early bliss of new love, giggling as they showed each other their scars, comparing injuries, each contesting the other's claim that he or she had the most tragic story. Erin, he was sure, claimed victory every time. He sighed. "You're right. I don't know you. It's not like I didn't try."

"Try what? To take back what you did to me?"

"It was an accident."

"I don't want to talk about it, Landon." She pushed past him, dragging the suitcase behind her, its wheels catching on the finger pier boards. "Dammit, this thing!" She lifted the suitcase up and carried it the rest of the way.

"Daddy! Come see my Batman house!" Willie called from his play area in the dirt.

"Duty calls." Landon followed Erin the rest of the way down the pier. "I have a kid."

"I know." Erin stopped and looked him in the eye. "Susan makes sure I know about the key events in your life. I keep telling her I'm not interested in knowing." She shook her head as if flinging unwanted thoughts into the water. "Where is your son's moth—"

"Willie. His name is Willie." Landon shrugged. "Honestly, I don't know where Taylor is."

"They're no longer together." Susan sidled up next to Landon so that their arms were touching. Landon moved his arm a hair's width away, barely perceptive, yet he didn't know why he did it. "Erin," Susan said, nodding. "You're the one he 'rescued' today?"

"The one and only. Hi, Susan."

"What brings you to town?"

"My mother's family camp. This is the first one without Dad."

Landon looked at the ground and kicked a clump of sand, a tiny puff of sand-smoke settling on his sneakers. "I'm sorry about your dad," he mumbled. He didn't look up, couldn't bring himself to see the sadness he knew was in Erin's eyes. She and her dad had been close.

"Yeah, me too," Susan chimed in.

"Daddy!" They all turned to Willie, and Landon was grateful for the diversion from this awkward exchange. "Come see my Batman house!"

"On my way, little dude. On my way." He looked at Erin. "Give me a minute, and I'll take you to your mom's. I'll have my dad call you tomorrow about fixing the boat."

"Oh no. No. No. No." Erin dragged her suitcase across the dirt and into the parking lot. "I'll get myself home. And don't bother having your dad call me. I'll have BoatUS tow it to my mom's dock tomorrow and then back to Baltimore next week."

Landon stood and watched her, wondering how she would get home. There was no taxi service in town. And Uber or Lyft? Forget about it. He rolled his eyes. *Erin being Erin*, he thought. Not only that, but BoatUS would look at the damage and tell her to leave the boat right where it was. He shook his annoyance off as he plopped in the dirt next to Willie. They would build the best Batman house ever.

12

———

The nerve of him commenting on her clothing. The nerve! And standing, reminding her that blowing off her leg was an accident—on par with dropping a glass of red wine on a white couch. *It was an accident. It was an accident. It was an accident.* The nerve!

Erin traipsed through the parking lot; Wes's duffel bag was heavier than it felt this morning when she carried it onto the boat. Why couldn't Wes have just carried his own damned bag? That's easy to answer; he was on his phone, and Erin felt pressure to load their bags and orient herself to the boat before signing the rental agreement. He was always on his phone. Always put work before her. She took a deep breath, determined to quell the rising, misplaced resentment she felt toward Wes at this moment.

She stopped walking, letting the bag fall from her shoulder and hit the ground. *Deep breaths*, she told herself. *Deep breaths*. Wes did nothing wrong. She couldn't help that he was a doctor. A cardiologist! A surgeon! She laughed at the irony. She always thought she would marry a waterman—a sailor like her dad. Or someone who built beautiful things out of wood with his hands. Again, like her dad. There was never any question in her mind that she would get married and live in Canvasback Cove. Ever since she was old enough to understand that marriage was a partnership, living and working and laughing with your best friend, she always figured it would be Landon. Not until much later did she understand the rest of the story. The way two bodies rolled toward each other in the middle of the night and held onto each other for dear life. When she realized that, she knew it had to be Landon.

She picked up the duffle bag and draped it across her body, promising herself that she would direct her anger toward the person she was justifiably angry with: Landon. Wes had done absolutely nothing wrong. It wasn't as if he had hidden the fact that he was a surgeon who was frequently on call and needed to drop everything at a moment's notice. Their relationship had grown more serious over the past few months, and marriage was beginning to look like a distinct possibility, although they hadn't exactly talked about it. Did she even want to marry Wes? Was it significant that she hadn't yet brought Wes home to meet her mother? Why hadn't she done it last fall when it became apparent that their relationship had fallen into exclusivity? Or last Christmas? Or any of the many weekends between then and now? She would say yes if he asked. Even if it meant many nights sleeping alone while he was intimately entangled in other people's hearts. He fixed hearts. He was a hero. Who wouldn't want to be married to a hero who fixed hearts?

Sometimes Erin would open her laptop and try to start the novel she never seemed able to write. She tried on different bylines, seeing how her name looked on the screen and written in various forms: *Erin Conrad. Erin L. Conrad. E. Leigh Conrad. Erin Rubin. Erin Conrad Rubin. Erin Conrad-Rubin. Erin Leigh Rubin. Erin Shultz.* Many months ago, she had tried that last one on a whim, after a particularly fitful night dreaming about Landon. She quickly deleted the byline, wishing could delete the lingering something—she couldn't quite define what that something was—that persisted in her heart. If only she could delete Landon. *If only.*

Erin continued walking, clutching the handle of her suitcase, sweating profusely in the hot, humid, stagnant early evening, the damned thing growing heavier and harder to drag by the second. The B&B was a little over two miles away. In high school, she would run from her house to the wrought iron gate at the abandoned inn, then down Moss Street all the way here, look for Landon on the docks or in between jack stands in the boatyard. Sometimes she would find him, and he'd scam a cold bottle of Gatorade from the cooler in his dad's bait and tackle shop. She would guzzle half, then give the other half to Landon before turning around and running back to the B&B (touching the gate, as was her tradition), and then home. The whole thing equaled six miles; her best time, not counting stopping at Landon's, had been forty-five minutes.

She hoped to get at least one or two early morning jogs this week. Three miles was about all she could handle on Doris. And slower than shit. She looked forward to a few open water swims in the cove. She had taken up swimming last year with the someday-maybe goal of doing a triathlon. Someday. Maybe. Wes had expressed interest too, but he had yet to put a toe in the water. Or buy a bike. Erin had her friend's old Cannondale, which she sometimes rode around Baltimore on weekends. It took a while to get used to riding with her artificial leg. She hated navigating the other people on the roads, though, and hated yelling, "on your left." So, she didn't ride much. At all.

"LADY! MY SPIDERMAN! MY SPIDERMAN!" Erin stared at the blond, curly-haired little boy going through the contents of her suitcase. "My Spiderman! Daddy, look! The Lady got me a Spiderman!" How in God's name did her suitcase pop open—again? More importantly, how had she not noticed?

"That doesn't belong to you, buddy." Landon crouched down at eye-level with his son. "Let's put it back in my friend's suitcase."

"I have a Batman suitcase," the boy said to Erin. She stood, mouth agape, trying to imagine Landon with a child. She knew he had a child, so the fact of this little boy wasn't a shock. Her surprise was in how much he looked like Landon. Right down to the cowlick above his left ear and his steel gray eyes. "Puppy got me a new Batman toy, see?" He held out the stuffed doll for her to see. "It's soft. Feel it."

Erin took the toy and held it in front of her face. "Hello, Batman!" She handed it back. "And what's your name?"

"Willie."

"Hello, Willie!" She extended her hand, and much to her surprise, he took it and pumped three times. "You know, I think your Batman needs a friend."

"I'm his friend!"

"True. But I think Batman needs a superhero friend to help him save people." She winked. "Don't you?"

Willie nodded. She pulled the Spiderman action figure out of her suitcase and handed it to Willie. She had purchased it on a whim to give to her nephew this week. So be it. She could borrow her mother's car and drive to Target in Easton to get her nephew another. She peered at Landon and felt herself flush.

Are you sure? Landon mouthed, followed by *thank you* when Erin nodded.

"What do you say, Willie?" Landon mussed the top of his son's head. "What do you say when someone gives you something?"

"Thank you, Lady."

"This is my friend, Erin." He looked at her and smiled. "We've known each other since we were babies."

"Daddy is not a baby!"

"Not anymore, buddy, not anymore." He lifted Willie up and set him on his shoulders amid loud, raucous giggles.

Erin watched Landon struggle to remove the life-proof packaging. Landon, a father. How many Punnett squares had she dreamily drawn in her notebook during sophomore biology when she learned the archaic yet satisfyingly fun method for predicting the probability of her and Landon's future children having a particular hair or eye color? Reality would inevitably hit, causing her to tear out the pages and rip them into tiny pieces before tossing the whole wad in the trash on her way out the door.

Landon pulled a knife out of his pocket and cut Spiderman's

confines, almost like freeing a hostage. She wondered how many hostages he had freed as a SEAL.

"Are you sure I can't give you a lift to your mom's?" He said as he handed the toy to his son.

Erin considered this. What harm could possibly come of it? More importantly, what options did she have? She had tried calling her mom, but it went straight to voicemail. She supposed she could walk as far as Martin's Country Store and see if anyone there could drive her the rest of the way to the B&B. Her mom arranged with Billy Martin to drive guests from the B&B to the two drawbridge restaurants on Friday and Saturday nights. Maybe he'd give her a lift if he wasn't busy. Or she could simply walk to the B&B; much easier said than done, particularly with the bum wheel on her suit-case—and her bum leg. She pictured herself walking along Moss Street just fine, with its smooth, wide sidewalk. But at the bend right after the firehouse, Moss Street turned into Alfred Way, and the sidewalk disappeared, which was no big deal in and of itself. She feared she would look like a homeless woman, dragging a malfunctioning suitcase, a duffle bag dangling from her shoulder, and balancing the box of onion rings she still wanted to stop and get.

Of course, letting Landon drive her to the B&B was, by far, the most sensible option. Logically, Erin knew that, as an independent adult, she could accept a ride from an old friend. But she also knew she didn't want to subject her mother to the angst of seeing Landon and all the baggage that came with it. At least not the day before relatives started arriving for family camp. Her mother deserved better.

"I'LL DROP you off at your mother's place," Susan said, holding her hand out and touching the shiny, plastic Spiderman in Willie's clutched hand. "I don't remember seeing this toy before, and I didn't know you like Spiderman." Her raised eyebrow was incongruent with her sing-song voice.

"Spiderman is my favorite!" He giggled. "Wait! Batman is my favorite! Spiderman is my next favorite!"

"But where did you get him?"

"The lady gave me him."

"Buddy, the lady's name is Erin," Landon chimed in. "I told you she is my friend from a long, long, long, long time ago." He smiled and looked at Erin.

"She gave him a toy?" Susan crossed her arms. "Why would she give—"

"Excuse me, I'm standing right here," Erin said, tapping her foot. "Yes. I gave him a toy. What difference does it make?"

"I don't understand why you would buy a—"

"It fell out of my suitcase, and he picked it up. I guess he thought it was for him." Erin shrugged. "What was I supposed to do at that point? Take it away?" She shook her head, feeling utterly stupid for thinking she had to justify and explain. "I bought it for my nephew, Sandy's son. He's a little older than Willie, but not by much."

"Oh wow. Sandy! I haven't seen him in forever." Susan uncrossed her arms. "How is he doing? Is he still sober?"

Susan, Erin thought. She sighed. *Not quite forty years old, Susan is already acting like an old biddy.* Now she wondered why she bothered staying in touch with her—however sporadic it was; clearly, they didn't like each other all that much. And, except for their shared experience of growing up in Canvasback Cove, they had very little in common. She made a mental note to curate her Facebook friend list soon; Susan would be the first to go.

Erin glanced at Landon, who had lifted Willie off his shoulders and was now spinning him around, blond curls (and the cowlick) blowing around his little head. Erin supposed there was another thing she and Susan had in common—Landon. Susan's posturing around him, acting all concerned and motherly over a stranger giving Willie a toy. Susan didn't need to worry. As far as Erin was concerned, Landon was all Susan's. She smiled, thinking about Wes and looking forward to parading him around later in the week. She took a deep breath.

"I'll take you up on your offer," she said to Susan, ignoring the question about Sandy's sobriety. Yes, he was sober. She knew that Susan didn't care, one way or the other. All Susan wanted to do was dig at Erin's flawed family in front of Landon. And for what? To show some sort of superiority? Was Susan's family so perfect? Didn't her father have an affair with his twenty-five-year-old secretary last year? *Maybe I'll ask if her father came to his senses yet and ditched the secretary.* Erin hated herself for thinking like that, but she hated the prospect of spending even five minutes alone in the car with Susan even more. *It's only five minutes unless we get stuck behind Smokey Jones in his golf cart. It's only five minutes. It will only take five minutes to drive from here to the B&B. I can do anything for five minutes.* She kissed the prospect of onion rings goodbye, too; it just wasn't worth prolonging her time with Susan. She would walk if she wasn't so tired, hot, and cranky. Susan was clearly the best option. Better than Landon, anyway.

"Great! My car is just over there."

Landon, making airplane noises, dipped a horizontal Willie close to the ground, then lifted him back up again in an aborted landing.

"I want to land! I want to land!" Willie choked the words out between giggles.

"Mission Control, this is Wombat Willie coming in for a landing." Landon made the crackling sounds of static over a radio. "Wombat Willie is requesting permission to land." More crackling, more static. "Permission granted," came the response in a make-believe, official-sounding voice. "Wheels are coming down...and...landed!"

Twenty years ago, Erin had wanted to hold Landon's hand and had planned to do just that the night of the accident. She had the whole thing scripted out in her head. It was simple, really. Obviously, she and Landon would sit together during the fireworks. She "reserved" her dad's double-Adirondack chair near the water by draping two sweaters across the seats and placing a bag of potato chips on the built-in table in the middle.

Erin's plan had been to wait until the grand finale when her father lit the best fireworks. Amid the *oohs* and *aahs* at the colorful shooting stars, Erin would casually reach for Landon's hand as if doing so was the most natural thing in the world. The whole plan was brilliant in its simplicity. She had been so confident that he would welcome her hand in his that she didn't bother to devise a contingency plan. It had never entered her mind that Susan might insert herself into the evening or that Landon might try to blow her leg off. Yeah. That year, the grand finale had been her night in the emergency room, writhing in pain.

"Say bye to Miss Susan," Landon said.

"Bye, Miss Susan."

"Aren't you going to thank Miss Susan for playing with you today and for bringing you donuts for breakfast?"

Erin stood, mesmerized by how Landon talked to his son like a real father would speak to a real son. Landon was a real father, and Willie was a real son. It was just that the Landon in her mind, the one she buried the night of the accident, was still a seventeen-year-old boy with baby fat around his face and tummy. This man, with his chiseled jawline, granite torso, and arms that looked like he could singlehandedly lift a house off its foundation...well...this man was not the same Landon. The Landon she sometimes conjured was the boy Landon, the only Landon she had any context with. The Landon who once or twice a year showed up in her dreams, well, he too was always the boy Landon. This Landon standing before her, instructing his little son to be polite, might as well be a different person entirely. She felt like she was in a time warp where she had awoken from a deep sleep. Life had moved on, the world had changed, and the people in it had grown and aged. She, however, was stuck in the past, at least as far as Landon was concerned.

Willie stood in front of Susan, but his eyes were on Erin. "Thank you, Lady, for my new Spiderman." Ignoring whatever response came out of Susan's mouth, Willie ran to Erin and hugged her legs.

∽

ERIN CLIMBED into Susan's green Mini Cooper after struggling to stuff her suitcase and Wes's duffle bag into the joke of a trunk. There was no way she was getting both items in there. She slammed the trunk shut, not the least concerned that Wes's bag might feel like a hostage, alone in the dark. She maneuvered her suitcase into the backseat, nearly wrenching her lower back.

Settling herself in the front passenger seat, she glued her eyes to the side view mirror, careful not to be noticeable. She wasn't exactly sure why she felt like she needed to hide the fact that she was stunned to see Landon. Or shocked to see him with the kid that she only knew about through second-hand accounts. Landon and Willie walked toward the bait and tackle shop, their figures growing smaller by the second. She wasn't sure what Susan was doing outside the frame of her tiny TV, but she didn't care.

There's Ed, she thought, as an older man with thick white hair entered the scene. Seeing him up close would probably tell a different story, but from this distance, in the side view mirror, except for his once dark hair's pigmentation loss, he didn't look like he had changed much.

Landon's father crouched down and said something to Willy—a split-second glimpse at a tiny family on a tiny screen. Erin didn't know when the last time Landon had been home and wondered if this was Ed's first time getting to know his grandson.

The driver's side door slammed shut. Erin jumped, suddenly aware of Susan sitting in the seat next to her.

"Thanks for the ride," Erin said preemptively, just to say something, anything, to break any awkward silence before it even started. Not that Erin minded silence; she relished it at times. She just couldn't see making an already long drive (yes, five minutes alone with Susan was too long, as far as Erin was concerned) even longer. She figured a little bit of idle chit-chat would go a long way in speeding things up; at least, it would give the illusion of doing so.

"Oh! No worries!" Susan smiled her dimpled smile. "I'm happy to help. I know you would probably have rather gone with Landon, you know, to catch up and all, but he's been away from Willie all day." She shrugged. "I just figured I'd do this one little thing for him." She started the engine, the radio coming in softly, Elton John's *Tiny Dancer* already in progress.

So much for settling into or easing out of awkward silence, Erin thought. If she played her cards right, Erin could get away with a few head nods and strategically placed um-hums and not have to talk at all. Susan seemed to be doing a great job talking for them both.

Erin glanced in the side view mirror as Susan slowly pulled out of her parking space. Season Twenty, Episode One of *The Landon Show* had apparently ended. She wondered what Episode Two had in store, then quickly tossed the thought away. She didn't expect to see Landon again this week, and more importantly, she didn't want to see Landon again this week.

"I guess we missed each other the last time you were home," Susan said, her eyes fixed on the road. She pulled onto Main Street. "Oh, look, there's Charlie."

"Charlie?"

"Maverick's new wife," Susan said, pointing to the osprey circling overhead as they crossed the drawbridge.

"What do you mean, 'Maverick's new wife'? What happened to Goose? Ospreys mate for life."

"True, but Smokey said Maverick and Goose weren't successful last year, so they 'divorced.'"

Erin swallowed, surprised by the lump rising in her throat at this unexpected development. While she enjoyed seeing the ospreys, she certainly didn't care about them, at least not to the point where she would cry over them. Yet, she felt like the floodgates were about to be breached. She wrinkled her nose, which was her tried and true method for getting any tears that dared to emerge, to stay put. She wouldn't have taken Susan's word for it, but Smokey, well, he was an osprey expert. If anyone could distinguish one osprey from another, it was Smokey Jones. They all looked the same to Erin.

She remembered one summer, five or so years ago, when Smokey, slurping oysters at Lenny's, told her and her father that osprey parents often held back food to encourage the fledglings to leave the nest. *I didn't need to encourage this one to leave the nest,* Erin's dad had said, laughing, as they found their own table and settled in for an evening of picking crabs and drinking beer. If Smokey said Maverick "remarried," then Maverick did, indeed, remarry.

"So, Landon tells me you're here with your boyfriend?"

"Sort of." Erin was relieved by the abrupt topic change. "Wes had to go back to Baltimore." She adjusted her back, sore from lifting the suitcase. She made a mental note to sign up for Body Pump at the Y after vacation. "He's a cardiologist. A surgeon. He got called back to the hospital." She looked out the window, wishing she hadn't accepted the ride. She was tempted to ask Susan to pull over so she could get out. *It's only five minutes,* she told herself, and at least two of the five had already gone by. *Three minutes. I can do anything for three minutes.*

"He sounds important. Oh, fiddlesticks." Susan slowed the Mini to a stop, the red brake lights ahead an ominous sign. "I was afraid of this." She turned to Erin. "They're doing some road work up near Green's Pond." She looked at her watch. "It's after four. They should be done for the day by now." She sighed. "Oh well. At least that gives us more time to catch up."

Oh, great, Erin muttered, a little too audibly.

"What?"

"Oh, great!" Erin said, plastering a smile on her face. "I don't remember the last time we chatted in person!" She enthusiastically looked Susan up and down, searching for any compliment to toss in her direction. "I like what you're doing with your hair. Did you get highlights?"

"It's sun kissed." Susan turned her head to look at Erin. "And your hair. It's so...."

"Short?" Erin laughed. "It's okay. My parents had a conniption the first time they saw me like this. My mom thought I was hiding a cancer diagnosis, and it took me the entire weekend to convince her otherwise."

"It suits you." She kept her eyes on the road. "Landon had to grow his hair for a secret mission. I taught him some different ways he could wear it."

"Landon was never much into fashion hairstyles."

"You don't really know him, though, do you? Did you even know he had a kid?"

Erin straightened her back and glared at Susan. "You're right. I don't know him anymore. And yes, I knew about his kid. You told me. On Facebook. Remember?"

"Not really." Susan accelerated. "Yay! A gap!"

Not a very long gap, apparently. Erin closed her eyes, wishing she were anywhere but in this car. "We're not moving, Susan. How about you let me out, and I'll walk the rest of the way? It's not very far." She raised her eyebrows. "I really need to pee, and I think I'll make it home faster if I walk." She didn't need to pee; she simply wanted to be out of this car, away from Susan.

"Nonsense! I offered to give you a ride. End of story." She looked at Erin and smiled. "I like your hair short. I wish I had the courage." The Mini inched its way forward. "Willie is a cutie, isn't he?" She shook her head. "His mother just up and left him." She shook her head again, this time more violently. "Would you believe it? Who does that?" She sighed. "I've been helping Landon pick up the pieces."

Erin didn't respond, didn't quite know what to say. Then, finally: "So, that's why he's home?"

"Yep." Susan pursed her lips together. "I think he's better off without her. I don't think he loved her, based on the little things he's said here and there."

"They weren't married?"

"Nope. I think she might have liked to, but, in the end, it's a blessing he never married her." Susan perked up. "Hey, why don't the four of us—Landon, me, you, and your boyfriend hang out while you're here."

Erin thought about this for two seconds before deciding it was the last thing she wanted to do. "Honestly, Susan, I'm going to be busy helping my mom. I haven't seen Sandy and his family in a while, so I think Wes and I will just hang out at the B&B."

"Surely, you'll want to show your boyfriend your favorite haunts. Maybe Landon and I will bump into you two. Let's just see how it plays out."

Erin waved as Susan spun the Mini Cooper around and disappeared among the thick grove of trees on either side of the narrow driveway. Erin waved wildly to indicate a hearty *thanks for the ride* and an equally passionate *enjoy your evening;* in reality, she was waving in great relief. With the traffic, the five-minute drive had turned into almost twenty.

She left her suitcase and Wes's duffle bag in the gravel and climbed three steps to the side door leading to her mom's living quarters. She had always found it strange that her parents referred to their residence as if they were live-in butlers at a royal chateau. The section of the B&B that her dad renovated to live in was a bright, airy, one-story apartment sporting a kitchen worthy of an HGTV design contest, complete with an industrial-style Wolf stove, a massive island with seating for eight, and an unobstructed view of the Chesapeake Bay. A wall of French doors opened to a circular stone patio dotted with light blue Adirondack chairs—her father's favorite. A few years ago, he added an outdoor kitchen and fireplace.

Erin stood in front of the door—wide open except for the flimsy screen that her father somehow never found the time to replace and was a running joke between her parents—and peered inside. Her mother's gardening tools stood against the far wall, and Erin imagined her pulling weeds and pruning her herb garden. The sound of something sizzling in the kitchen danced to the door, still too far away to smell. She turned back for her bags and stepped inside, pushing the door open with her shoulder.

"Mom?" She dropped her bags next to the etagere and glanced at herself in the antique mirror on the wall. *Yikes! I look like crap!* Why hadn't Landon mentioned that she had several black streaks across her face, plus a gaggle of gnats that had apparently drowned in her sweat? Why didn't Susan, sitting two inches away in her tiny clown car, hand her a tissue or at least, in a whispered woman-to-woman way, told her that she might want to consider wiping her face? She imagined Susan was glad Landon's first impression after twenty years was that of a bedraggled orphan.

Horrified, Erin slipped into the hall bathroom and scrubbed her face, letting the cold water invigorate and soothe her. She splashed a palmful of water on the back of her neck and sighed in sweet relief. Satisfied that she no longer looked like a street urchin in *Les Misérables*, she stepped out of the bathroom, almost knocking her mother over.

"I thought I heard someone come in!" Lydia Conrad locked her daughter in a tight embrace, released her grip, and held her at arm's length. "You're getting too skinny, and you look tired."

"Nice to see you too, Mom." Erin laughed, letting her mother's comments roll off her back. "Oh, and for the record, I am tired. Dead tired." She sniffed, finally able to smell the source of the sizzling. "Omelets?"

"Come on," Lydia said, taking Erin's hand. "Let's get you fed."

ERIN PUSHED her stool away from the island; she felt stuffed. Her mother, intent on fattening her up, had given her a plate of food big enough to feed several burly men. "You should add this omelet to your menu," she said, carrying her plate to the sink.

"I'd never be able to replicate it, you know. It's one of my 'clean out the fridge creations." Lydia glanced at her daughter's plate and raised an eyebrow. "You didn't eat it all." She shook her head. "Honey, you're too skinny. Is there anything you want to tell—"

"Don't go there, Mom." She held up her hands. "Please, don't go there." Erin pulled a Pyrex container and lid out of the cupboard and scooped the remains of her omelet into it. "I'm exactly the same weight as I was the last time I came home, and that was only a month ago." Erin hated the thought that, forevermore, her mother would always see her as one bite-not-taken away from anorexia.

Lydia got up and joined Erin at the sink. "Your brother called me last night and..." She pressed her lips together, forming a straight line, a harbinger of an abrupt topic change.

Erin knew this harbinger all too well and braced herself for another round of concern about her weight. She had learned that the best strategy involved changing the topic herself, confusing her mother to the point where she would forget both the original and the new topic.

Erin rolled her eyes, exhausted just thinking about how she would get through the week, and wondered why she had looked forward to this, why she had orchestrated taking time off work to mesh her vacation days with Wes's crazy schedule. For what? To have her mother scrutinize everything she put (or didn't put) in her mouth?

Erin almost didn't come; she didn't know how to handle a week of family camp without her dad. He always made it fun, piling everyone in his boat for a day of sailing and lunch in Oxford, and a few days later, more of the same, the destination usually being Saint Michaels. One year, family camp coincided with the a Regatta in Cambridge. Her dad signed up, and the group raced (doing terrible, of course, but having a ton of fun in the process). They tied up at Snappers afterward for crabs and beer.

Carrying on the tradition of a few sails this week was partly why Erin had been so adamant about renting the sailboat; she wanted to metaphorically take the reins from her father. *Stupid me.*

Her anger and frustration over the events that had transpired today returned. She did a pretty good job of keeping her encounter with Landon tucked away during dinner, but now he was beginning to creep back into the forefront of her mind. She shoved him down and recalled Wes's friendly text an hour ago.

With sailing off the table, Erin wondered what her mother had up her sleeve on the entertainment front. Maybe just chilling in town would be enough for everyone. Perhaps just being together and remembering Dad was more than enough. The bottom line was that Erin didn't want her mother to be alone (not that she was better equipped to help her mother navigate this "first" than Sandy or anyone else).

She softened, suddenly willing to put up with her mother's watchful eye and not-so-subtle digs about her weight. "The property looks beautiful, Mom. When Susan dropped me off, she commented about the daisies and your petunias and the vivid colors. Oh, and you finally had the gate painted, didn't you? It's amazing what a coat of paint can do."

"Don't change the subject." Lydia reached into the cabinet above the microwave and pulled out a bottle of Baileys. "Fancy a glass?"

Erin nodded. Baileys had been her father's go-to special occasion after-dinner drink. *This is going to be a long week.* She took a deep breath. "You're the one who changed the subject. So, do you want to talk about how much I ate, or do you want to talk about Sandy? You said he called last night."

"Please don't sass me."

"I'm not 'sassing' you, Mom." She carried her drink into the family room and plopped on the couch. "I'm almost forty years old. You have got to stop it with my weight, my eating habits. Just stop." Erin's face grew hotter by the second. She leaned her head back and closed her eyes. "That was a long time ago." She opened them and glared at her mother. "A very long time ago. And I wasn't even technically anorexic. Remember, I was the one who noticed it. I was the one who came to you for help. Anorexics don't realize they look like skeletons. They generally don't ask for help. You know this. You didn't need to insist that I had a problem. I recognized the direction I was headed."

Erin had just finished her senior year of high school when she noticed she had put on a few pounds. More than a few. Still recovering from her injury and unable to run, she found solace in food. Ice cream. Chips and salsa with her dad. She did a lot of baking that summer, too, perched on a stool at the counter because standing for any length of time was against her doctor's orders. What else was there to do other than reading and writing? She found an old Betty Crocker cookbook and went through every cookie recipe in the dessert section—all twenty-two pages of it. That summer, she made chocolate chip cookies, oatmeal raisin cookies, spicy gingerbread cookies, zucchini cookies, lemon-cranberry squares, grasshopper bars, toffee bars, cashew triangles, and coconut macaroons. By the end of the summer, she had gained nearly fifteen pounds.

One day in late summer, she bit into one of her jumbo molasses cookies and spit it out, dumping the entire batch into the trash. She spent the first semester of college that fall losing the weight she had gained and then some. Her parents didn't notice it at first; she had enrolled in Chesapeake College, which was within a half-hour's drive, and they saw her every day. It wasn't until she was drying off after a shower one morning before Christmas that Erin noticed her rib cage; she had taken her dieting too far. She talked to her parents that night. They were supportive and rallied around her, for which Erin would always be grateful. But her mother took it upon herself somewhere along the line to ensure she didn't go down that slippery slope again.

"Then why are you so skinny?" Her mother whispered as if it were somehow shameful to be thin.

"I'm no skinnier than last month, last year, or the last decade." This, Erin knew, was true. She had weighed herself weekly for years, precisely because she didn't want to lose track of her weight, because sometimes, she often lost track of whether she had eaten. Mainly when she was hyper-focused at work, reading a client's story synopsis and puzzling together ideas for a catchy, compelling, creative synopsis. Her dad always forgot to eat when lost in an exciting project, and she loved how they were similar. *How could anyone forget to eat*, her mother would say, annoyed when her dad came in from his workshop and made a beeline for the pantry, scarfing down handful after handful of potato chips or peanuts right before dinner.

"You must stop it with the food police routine, Mom." Erin sighed. "It has gotten beyond old." Erin twirled her glass and watched the ice spin and settle. She took a sip, missing her dad.

"Sandy isn't coming." Lydia picked up the remote and turned on the TV. An HGTV show was already in progress, featuring a young couple looking at beach rentals in Panama City, Florida.

"What do you mean he isn't coming?"

"Covid concerns." Lydia selected the guide and scrolled until she found the soft rock station. She grabbed a lumbar support pillow from the other side of the huge sectional and carried it back to her favorite spot, stuffing it behind her back. She muted the volume and shrugged. "He called last night and said Pam isn't comfortable flying, and she doesn't feel safe traveling with Noah, either."

"But they're all vaccinated! Even Noah!" Erin thought about the Spiderman doll she had given to Landon's son. "So, they just canceled their flight?"

"Apparently, they never made reservations."

Erin shook her head, incredulous. Her brother's wife hated flying. Hated it. According to Sandy, he practically had to drag her kicking and screaming through the boarding tunnel for their annual visits home. Erin wasn't buying the Covid excuse. Two years ago, yes, it was a valid excuse. Now, not so much. She tried hard not to judge other people's choices—she still wore a mask in grocery stores and probably would continue to do so for the foreseeable future. But to use Covid to avoid flying when you hate flying anyway? Lame. She knew she was speculating, but she couldn't help herself.

"Of course, it would have been nice if your brother let me know weeks ago."

"Exactly! They should have let you know months ago!" Erin rolled her eyes. "It's all Pam. She just doesn't want to get on a plane. Covid or no Covid." She picked up the remote and turned up the volume when *Drops of Jupiter* came on. "He could have at least been upfront with you. God, we hadn't seen them in, what, since Dad's funeral?"

"Something like that."

Erin sat up. "Let me get my phone. I'll call Wes and put him in touch with Sandy. We will tell him how to fly safely in the age of Covid."

"My sister and brother canceled too, but not because of Covid.

Uncle Jack is still recovering from his prostate surgery, and Aunt Kate is in the middle of her kitchen renovation." Lydia was either in her own world and didn't hear Erin or chose to ignore her. "There isn't a practical way to do family camp this year." She sucked down the rest of her drink. "The vagaries of life, I suppose."

ERIN REGARDED her mother on the couch, the soft light of the family room making her skin look young and fresh. Even when the beams of a harsh summer sun highlighted the crevices around her eyes and the grid of lines on her forehead, she looked younger than most sixty-five-year-old women. In fact, a new client she had recently met in person for the first time was her mother's age and looked at least ten years older. Her mother had recently gotten her shoulder-length silver hair cut into an inverted bob, creating a playful yet sophisticated persona. The new look matched her mother's personality perfectly.

She got up and hobbled into the kitchen to get her phone. Her leg pain, which had abated during the distraction of dinner and post-meal judgment, had returned. "I'm calling Wes," she said as she plopped back down on the couch.

Lydia came out of her trance. "Please don't. Call him if you want to talk to him, but don't call him about Sandy. It's really none of our business."

"It is our business. Because of Pam, we're not getting to see him. Or Noah! I was looking forward to playing with Noah, and I even bought him a...never mind. I'm just frustrated with the situation."

"I know, sweetie, I know." She swayed gently to *Let's Get it On* and sucked down the last of her Bailey's. Erin turned away, unable to conflate her mother and that song. "I'd have another one of these, but I need to function tomorrow." She set her glass on the coffee table. "So, tell me about Wes."

"What's there to tell? I've already told you all the important stuff. You'll get to meet him in a day or so." Erin was still reeling from her perception that her brother's wife was keeping him from her, controlling Sandy's moves. "Why don't we forget family camp and book a flight to Portland." Her chest tightened with excitement. Okay, so it would mean spending the week without Wes and dragging him back in a few weeks to meet her mother. She imagined it would be better for him, with the critical surgery and all, if she pardoned him from spending the week with her. "If Sandy refuses to come to family camp, we will bring family camp to him!"

She picked up her phone and typed *cheap flights to Portland* into Google. Spending the week in Portland would be perfect. Perfect! It would get her away from here, away from the inevitability of bumping into Landon again. *Crap, the boat.* How could she have forgotten the boat? She would have to deal with Landon one last time to tell him she was sending a proper tow boat from BoatUS to drag it back to Baltimore. She waved her phone at her mother.

"We could fly out of BWI tomorrow at around eleven. It's not a direct flight, but we'd be there by two with the time difference."

"We can't just barge in on them."

"So, we'll stay in a hotel. I'll call Sandy now and tell him."

"Sweetie, stop." Her mother got up and ambled to the kitchen.

Erin picked up her mother's glass and followed her to the sink, where she was already loading the dinner plates into the dishwasher. "Why, Mom? Why should I stop? Why not fly out to see Sandy? Are you squeamish about flying right now? I understand if you are, but—"

"This isn't about Covid." She turned to Erin, a plate suspended in mid-air. "I'm not flying to Oregon tomorrow. Or the next day. Or the day after that." She put the plate in the dishwasher. "I want to stay here, is all. It's what your dad would have wanted. He never wanted me to go chasing after Sandy. When he wants to come, he'll come."

"This is all Pam's doing."

"Perhaps." She squeezed a thick glob of detergent into the dishwasher and slammed it shut. "We can't blame everything on the evil wife now, can we?" She laughed. "I love Pammy, you know that. Let's give her the benefit of the doubt. If she doesn't want to fly because of

Covid or another reason, so be it. Let's not twist her motivations into a tangled mess. She loves your brother, and she's a good mom."

Erin hung her head. "You're right, Mom." She was still angry and frustrated but felt humbled. She didn't want to be a person who judged everyone else's choices (mask or no mask, dine in or carry out, pro-vax or anti-vax). "I was just really, really looking forward to seeing them, and I thought, since we're all vaccinated, there would be no issues."

"There are no issues with us. It's the strangers on the plane she's worried about."

"Fair enough." Erin wiped down the island with a damp cloth. She held the edge of the counter for support and stretched her bad leg behind her, flexing her knee to help ease the pain that had progressed from her thigh down to her stump.

"What's going on with your leg, dear?" Her mother sat down at the island. "You've been hobbling around. Do you need a new prosthetic?" She raised an eyebrow. "You've been running again, haven't you." She tucked a strand of hair behind her ear. "Be honest."

The last thing Erin needed was to get into a debate about running. She never had to justify her passion to her dad, who had been the cross-country and track coach at the high school. Erin remembered a time when she was eleven or twelve years old, and her dad let her run on the track with the big kids during practice one afternoon. She tried to jump over a hurdle, and by some miracle, she cleared it but landed funny on the way down. Not wanting to embarrass herself in front of the older kids, she sprinted the rest of the way around the track, then retreated to the bleachers under the guise of doing homework. She sprained her ankle, but you would think she'd been paralyzed from the neck down based on her mother's reaction.

After the sprained ankle incident, Lydia tried to get Erin less interested in running and more interested in swimming, which was big on the Eastern Shore. Erin had been a pretty good swimmer in those days (and still was) but never liked it enough to compete. Running, on the other hand...God, how she loved running. Possibly even more than she loved sailing. And as great of a track coach as her father had been, he could teach sailing to a hummingbird.

"I miss Dad." Erin wrapped her arms around her mother.

"Me too." Lydia sighed. "I can't even begin to tell you...me too." Her phone buzzed and danced around on the counter by the sink. "Whoever it is can leave a voicemail."

Erin patted her mother's shoulders, a sudden urge to tell her about Landon overtaking her. She sat down next to her and tried to come up with an opening when Lydia's phone buzzed again.

"Oh, for heaven's sake." Lydia started to stand, but Erin gently returned her to a sitting position. She stepped across the kitchen to grab the phone.

"Here you go." Erin slid the phone toward her mother, not intending to look at the number (it wasn't any of her business), but couldn't help but see, in big, bold letters on the caller ID, *Shultz Boat Yard and Marina*. If Erin had been looking for an opening to tell her mom about seeing Landon, a ready-made one just fell into her lap.

"What in God's name is that man doing, calling me at this hour?" Her mother turned the phone over, covering the screen.

"It's only seven."

"Still. How in the world did he get my number? I've never given that family my new cell phone number." Lydia frowned. "Never. Ever."

Erin was amazed that her parents had been able to live in such a small town and avoid Ed Shultz all these years. And Joelle, when she had been alive. As hurt and angry as Erin had been at Landon after the accident, the years had softened the edges; she tumbled and rubbed the shards of glass long enough that the edges had smoothed. She suspected the fragments would never turn into sea glass, but at least they were no longer so painful to carry; she could pull one out from time to time and not bleed.

"He is probably calling about the boat."

"I thought you said you tied up on the floating pier near Rupert's."

"That was my original plan."

"Please don't tell me you tied up at that man's marina. The place is a dump. It's gone to hell in a handbasket since Joelle died. The man doesn't care about anyone. He's an old curmudgeon." Lydia rested her head in her hands, then looked at Erin. "Why did you go there?"

"I had no choice, Mom." Erin sighed. "I was planning to tell you, but then we ate, and you started on me about my weight, and I never got back to it. I was going to tell you tonight." She laughed. "Okay, so I might have waited until tomorrow." She glanced at her mother's phone, wondering if it had been Landon or his dad leaving a message. Probably his dad. "I ran aground in the channel then spun around and hit the pier pretty hard." She scratched her head. "I'm calling BoatUS first thing in the morning."

"You couldn't just drive here? You had to try and sail?" Lydia's tone was incongruent with the gravity of the situation; the situation simply wasn't grave. "Showing off for your boyfriend?"

"That's enough, Mom." There were a million words, phrases, or sentences she could spew at this moment, many of which she would regret, some harsher than necessary. She selected one of the milder possibilities and tried it on for size. "You never liked that sailing was such a thing between Dad and me." She took a deep breath and waited. When her mother didn't respond, she continued. "You never enjoyed sailing and only did it because—"

"What point are you making?" Lydia looked pained. "Yeah, I know. He couldn't even get Sandy to sail with him." She sighed and patted Erin's hand. "If you're implying I was a little jealous, you'd be right."

"I'm sorry, Mom." Erin immediately regretted dredging up old baggage. "I didn't mean to bring this—"

"It's okay, it's okay." Lydia shook her head, smiling. "I loved that you and your dad were so close. Loved that he took you everywhere he went. Truly, you were his shadow. I loved it. Sailing? I could take it or leave it. I was just happy he had someone to do it with."

"And then he just stopped."

"Well, of course, he did. Do you think he was going to continue sailing without you, after what that irresponsible, good for nothing, kid—"

"He's a Navy SEAL."

"I know."

"And he has a son." Erin suddenly craved another Baileys on ice. She got up to make herself one and carried it back to the island. "Want a refill?"

"I shouldn't. I really, really shouldn't." Lydia smiled. "Oh, what the hell."

ERIN and her mother sat at the large kitchen island, sipping their drinks, each lost in their thoughts, the music coming from the TV in the family room the only punctuation marks breaking up the silence. Thanks to her parents, she loved all kinds of music, from their go-to soft rock, cycling through song after song right now (currently, Tim McGraw serenading them with *Humble and Kind*). She still couldn't listen to Great Big Sea, her father's all-time favorite, without choking on her tears. A long time ago, when they played cards with Landon and his parents, they listened to a medley of Rat Pack classics.

"Mother-son dance," Lydia spoke into the air, gently swaying to the music. "It was a beautiful wedding."

Erin let the song end and the next one begin before responding. "I'm angry anew that Sandy isn't coming." She hung her head. "Maybe I'm being too harsh. No. I'm not being too harsh. I am angry."

"Sweetie, these are uncertain, difficult times."

"A year ago, maybe. But not now. Transmission rates are stupidly low. Sandy's entire family is vaccinated. They are young and athletic and have no underlying conditions, as far as I know."

"Pam is pregnant, so I guess that is an underlying condition."

"What?!" Erin's anger abated, making room for hurt feelings to emerge. "Why do I always feel like I'm the last to know about important things."

"I only just found out last night when he called."

"And you're only now telling me?"

"What did you want me to do? Call you the minute I got off the phone?" She sipped her drink. "Come on, Erin. Stop acting like the world revolves around you."

"But the world does revolve around me!" She lifted her glass and burst out laughing. Her mother's comment worked like a charm. Even at five years old, when Erin heard those words, she giggled. Every. Single. Time. Lydia raised her glass too and clinked it against Erin's. "To the new baby."

"Hear, hear." Lydia's eyes perked up. "Did I hear you correctly a little while ago? Did you say Landon Shultz has a kid?"

"How could you live in such a small town and not know this?"

"I have nothing to do with those people."

"It's a tiny town, Mom."

"He doesn't come home very often. I do know that much."

"He's home now."

"You saw him?" Lydia set her glass down and grabbed Erin's hands. "I'm sorry. You should have called me." She studied her daughter. "Are you okay? If this is going to trigger any—"

"Mom, I'm fine." Erin rolled her eyes. "It didn't trigger anything. He was accommodating. Wes took it upon himself when we lost the motor to Google tow boats." She sighed, then chuckled. "Of all the gin joints in all the towns in all the world, he walks into mine." Putting on her best Humphrey Bogart voice and employing the gift of peripheral vision, she peered at her mother, wondering what kind of reaction she would get. She braced herself for a tirade.

"Casablanca," Lydia said softly, defying Erin's expectations. "Let me guess. The first thing that popped up in the search results was Shultz."

"Something like that." Erin covered her eyes. "I had no idea. You could imagine my shock and horror."

"If this were a Hallmark movie, I would say that was one hell of a meet cute." Lydia raised her eyebrows.

Erin winced. "Not cute. Not cute at all."

13

L andon gave up. Mrs. Conrad obviously wasn't answering. He would have just tried calling Erin but didn't have her number. And the only reason he had Lydia's was that Erin had listed it as her emergency contact in the sailboat rental paperwork.

"I'll try again in the morning." He lifted Willie out of his dad's lap. Sound asleep, his little body dangled like a rag doll. Landon didn't usually put Willie to bed this early, but the little dude had a busy day with Susan and Puppy. Not to mention his excitement about meeting "The Lady," who he couldn't stop talking about. Erin did absolutely nothing other than give him a silly Spiderman doll.

Landon was intrigued that the little dude talked about her nonstop. He had initially wanted to spend some time with Susan tonight, but the day had worn him out. He told himself it had nothing to do with Erin dropping out of the sky and into his world. Absolutely nothing to do with any of that. He was just tired. Plain and simple. Anyone would be tired after a day like today. The heat and sun alone would do just about anyone in. Even a Navy SEAL, which he was beginning to feel less and like with each passing hour of his emergency leave. *It's been two weeks. Shouldn't that be enough?* Maybe he would call his commanding officer tomorrow and see if he could return early. He missed his guys, missed the routine. He touched the hair hanging down his neck and vowed to get it cut before heading back.

"Putting him to bed so soon?" Landon's father sat pointing the remote at the TV, flipping channels until he found something worth his time. He finally settled on a rerun of *Mecum Auto Auction*. "It's not even twilight yet."

"If I try to wake him now, he'll be grouchy for about an hour, then he'll turn into the Tasmanian Devil, and we'll be up all night with him."

"We?" His dad raised an eyebrow, then laughed. He muted the TV. "What will you do about the Conrad girl's boat?"

Landon hated when his father referred to Erin as *The Conrad Girl*. Not that they ever discussed her. They didn't. But since the accident, when her parents tried to sue his parents for the lost scholarship money, Lydia and Doug became *Those People*, and Erin became *The Conrad Girl*. In the before times, they had all been one big happy family.

"I'm not sure yet. I think I'll go back outside and poke around after I put Willie down. At the very least, I want to understand the insurance situation. I'll bring the paperwork inside. Maybe you could help me make heads or tails out of it?" Landon was good at many things. However, reading the fine print on forms, and under-standing all of the terms and conditions, usually spelled out in a vernacular that might as well have been a foreign language, gave him apoplexy.

"Sure. Will do." Ed Shultz unmuted the TV. "Two hundred and forty grand for that piece of shit. Would you believe it?" He pointed at a yellow Corvette, circa 1963. "Two hundred and forty grand! I could fix the pool and put in three new piers for that amount of money."

"Say 'night-night' to Puppy," Landon said when Willie stirred in his arms.

"No night-night."

"Woof-woof, buddy," Landon's dad said in response.

"No night-night." Willie lifted his head, then let it fall back onto Landon's shoulder.

Landon carried Willie to the bathroom and stood him in front of the toilet. "Come on, buddy. Time to pee."

"No night-night." Zombie-like, Willie did his business with surprisingly good aim. "No night-night."

Landon settled Willie onto the air mattress his dad had set up next to the bed in Landon's childhood room. "Good night, buddy," he said to the snoring kid as he gently closed the door.

LANDON HELD onto the piling and carefully lifted his leg over the lifeline onto Erin's rented sailboat. He didn't want to risk the boat moving around and causing more damage. Not that this thirty-five-foot hunk of fiberglass was going anywhere. Erin had managed to wedge it between the piling and the pier so tightly that he wasn't sure how he and his dad would dislodge it. There was no way he would let Erin call BoatUS or anyone else; with this much damage, the rental company would charge her a fortune, insurance or not. Even if the rental company did send her off on a boat with a bad motor. Unless she was somehow at fault for the engine crapping out. She was a great sailor (when he knew her) but wasn't very mechanically inclined. It was possible, if not probable that she did something terrible to the motor when she tried to turn it on. He was sure her boyfriend had been no help. The dweeb cardiologist may be good with a scalpel and stethoscope but likely useless with a greasy old boat engine.

He found two extra dock lines in the cockpit and used them to tie the boat to the pilings, just in case. The wind wasn't supposed to be too bad tonight. Bottom line: the boat wasn't going anywhere. Still, he wanted to be sure.

Jolly Good Day. What a silly name for a boat. He wasn't entirely sure why, but that name conjured up images of creepy clowns. If he ever had a sailboat, he would give it a one-syllable name that easily rolled off the tongue, like *Slice* or *Slash*. He remembered going to a sailboat race with Erin and her dad on his boat, *Flying Conrads*. Doug Conrad had told Landon to just be ballast, but Erin put him to work. It had been an enjoyable day. They didn't win. Didn't even come close.

Landon laughed at the memory. He didn't remember much of anything except sitting on the rail with Erin, legs dangling, laughing at all the silly boat names, their all-time favorite being *Flatulence*. Yep, anything to do with farting and pooping at eleven was hysterical. Maybe it shouldn't have been. But it was. He laughed out loud, thinking about it. Even now, at thirty-seven, a boat named *Flatulence* was funny.

Landon sat in the cockpit, watching the sun fade. He had been so lost in his head that he didn't see the sky changing. It was now bright orange as far as the eye could see. He pulled his phone out of his pocket and took a picture, tempted to text it to Susan. The feeling abated almost as quickly as it had manifested. It was a good thing—a damned good thing—that he didn't have Erin's number. Strangely enough, it wasn't anywhere on her rental agreement. He was taking a risk calling from his cell phone; obviously, Lydia didn't answer when he called earlier from his father's business line (damned caller ID). He should have just left a voicemail but didn't know what to say. He swallowed his nerves and pushed the buttons, reminding himself he wasn't some pimply teenager asking a girl out on a date. Of course, it rolled right to voicemail.

"Hi, Mrs. Conrad." He cleared his throat. "This is Landon. Landon Shultz." He cleared his throat again. "Landon Shultz of *Shultz Marina and Boatyard. Shultz Towing.*" He cringed at himself, tempted to hang up. He took a deep breath. "Could you please give Erin a message? It's about her rental sailboat, *Jolly Good Day.*" He chose his next words carefully. "Please tell her to call me at my dad's boat yard. Or she could stop by. I need to talk to her before she arranges to move the boat." There was more he wanted to say but couldn't find the words. "Thank you."

He set his phone down and watched the orange in the sky peak to its brightest and begin to fade.

"I'm getting married on a sailboat," Erin had announced when they were kids. They had been playing on the little beach behind his family's boatyard, making an elaborate highway system for his mountain of Matchbox cars. "On a sailboat just like that one." She pointed to a large vessel on the horizon, its massive white sails vivid against the cobalt sky.

They had been, what, eight or nine years old? The topic never came up again. He wondered if Erin and the dweeb cardiologist would someday get married on a sailboat. *The cardiologist is not a dweeb*, Landon told himself for the umpteenth time today.

He forced himself out of his reverie and went into the cabin to retrieve the rental paperwork. Sitting down at the navigation table, he thumbed through what seemed like a million pages of tiny print. The last hints of orange streaming through the portholes might be a pleasant backdrop to a romantic dinner, but it made lousy light for reading. He lifted the navigation table's lid to search for a flashlight. No luck. *Fine.* He folded up the rental agreement and stuck it in his pocket.

~

"I CAN'T SEEM to make heads or tails out of this rental agreement." Landon slid the packet across the kitchen table toward his dad, who had *The Washington Post* crossword puzzle in front of him, most of the squares filled in. "From what I can tell, Erin took out a one-week insurance policy, but the deductible is through the roof. Or am I missing something here?"

Landon's dad quickly flipped through the packet, pausing to lick the pad of his thumb between pages. He stopped about five pages in and held the packet to the light. "Holy shit!" Shaking his head, he handed the rental agreement back to Landon. "That girl never did have a head for numbers now, did she?"

She's not a girl anymore, Landon wanted to say but bit his tongue.

She may have been a girl the last time he had seen her, but that girl was gone, and the woman he met today gave him agita. And he hadn't even talked to her, not really. He dreaded the week ahead, dreading having to interact with her over the boat, and suddenly missed Coronado more than ever. He didn't care what his commanding officer thought was best for him; he was ending his leave. Tomorrow.

"Dad, I think I want to go back."

"Just be careful out there. I still need to get Tim Dillon to fix the dock lights. Since you've been here, two more lights have gone out."

"I'm not talking about going back outside. I'm talking about going back home to the base. Back to Coronado."

Ed Shultz took off his glasses and pushed them to the top of his head. "Home is here, Son."

"I know that, Dad. This will always be home. But Coronado is home too, and it's the only home Willie has ever known."

"I've been meaning to talk to you about retiring." He rubbed the bridge of his nose. "You're eligible soon, correct?"

"Retire?" He braced himself for the guilt trip he knew his dad was about to embark on. Ever since Landon's mother died, Ed Shultz dropped subtle and not-so-subtle hints about wanting him to retire from the Navy to help run the business. While Landon knew he could run the boatyard, marina, bait and tackle shop, and the towing aspect of the business easily and without fanfare, he wanted no part of it. As a matter of fact, Landon was shocked that the topic was only coming up now, for the first time since he'd been home. The jabs here and there should have started the moment he walked through the door. How could he be so stupid as to miss the signs? His father's silence was a harbinger of a nuclear war.

"I ultimately agreed to give you my blessing to join the Navy because your mother convinced me a change of scenery would do you good. We figured four years to get your head screwed back on straight." He looked at the crossword puzzle and pushed his glasses over his eyes. He picked up his pen and scribbled something in the margin, counting with the fingers on his other hand. "Ah. Toothy!" He shook his head and laughed. "That was my first choice, but I hesitated. Tough might have worked too. Your mother always said I should use a pencil, so I could erase my mistakes. Tried it once or twice and rubbed a hole right through the paper. Pissed me off."

"I didn't need your blessing." Landon's face grew hot. His first reaction was to get up and walk away, afraid of what might come out of his mouth. Instead, he bit his tongue and forced his butt to remain planted in the chair. He picked up Erin's rental paperwork and mindlessly flipped through it, pretending to read, giving himself a few precious seconds to cool off.

"It was always our expectation that after your enlistment, you would come home and help me run the yard." He pushed the crossword puzzle away, but he left his glasses on this time. "It was bad enough when you decided to reenlist." Using his feet, he pushed his chair away from the table, the legs screeching across the tile floor. "Bad enough. But when you announced that you had gotten into SEAL training, it almost killed your mother." Instead of getting up, he jammed his elbows into his knees and rested his head in his hands.

While Landon would never admit it to his dad, he had every intention of coming home after four years. He surprised himself by enjoying the structure and routine of basic training. Most of his bunkmates whined, cried, and complained, counting down the weeks —the counting getting more raucous the closer it got to graduation— until basic training ended. Landon took comfort in the repetition, having every minute of every day detailed and dictated by someone else—when to go to bed when to get up, when to shit. Twenty years later, he could still hear the blaring trumpet announcing reveille every morning at sunrise and the softer, somber trumpet announcing taps sixteen hours later. Four years came and went. And when an opportunity to go to SEAL training presented itself, he jumped on it.

"Mom got over it." Landon hated when his father did this. He knew his mom wrung her hands over his decision to become a SEAL, but it didn't almost kill her. When Osama Bin Laden was captured, she told anyone who would listen that her son was a SEAL. It didn't matter that his team was not involved in the attack's planning, plotting, or execution. Just that he was a SEAL was all that mattered to her, no matter how many degrees of separation existed between his team and SEAL Team Six.

"Don't disrespect me, Son."

"Dammit, Dad. I mean no disrespect." Landon took a deep breath and silently counted to ten. He exhaled. "Are you okay? You're acting weird."

Ed Shultz got up and carried his crossword puzzle and pen into the family room. He looked at Landon, standing in the arched opening between the two rooms. "I'm sorry, Son. I'm just tired. So tired. And short-handed. It's been nice having you here. Please don't go back early. Puppy wants to spoil the kid a little while longer." He plopped in his chair and turned on the reading lamp. "We need the Conrad girl's problem like a hole in the head." He rolled his eyes. "That family pissed me off to the bottom of my feet, you know that. But I can't, with a good conscience, let her pay that deductible and whatever other nonsense would come from her returning a rental boat in that condition. Let's pull that damned boat out of the water tomorrow and assess the damage."

14

E rin adjusted her fuel belt, making it tighter around her waist. The snugger it was, the less likely it would shift around and bounce during the ninety minutes it would take her to jog to the boatyard and back. She slid her phone and two energy gels into the zippered pouch and cringed at the thought that a flat, six-mile journey (round trip) would take her that long to complete.

The jog back would be even worse because the sun would be entirely out by then, and her legs will have stiffened up, even in the few minutes it would take her to retrieve her rental paperwork. She couldn't believe she had left the boat yesterday without it. In her previous life, before the accident, she could have run more than twice the distance in that amount of time. At least she was running. Okay... jogging. At least.

She pressed her hands against the kitchen island and stretched, flexing her artificial foot until she felt the burn on her left side, then repeating the motion with her real foot. She did those five times on each leg, making sure to be good and loose before she started out. Her father's philosophy had always been no stretching cold muscles, and he always had his students do a series of warmups (high knee kicks, walking lunges, marching in place, arm circles) before pausing for a minute or two to stretch. But since her injury, she needed to stretch and needed to stretch often—with or without running.

"What are you doing?"

Erin jumped three feet (or so it seemed) into the air. She hadn't heard her mother come into the kitchen. "You scared me half to death!"

Lydia stood several feet away, her blue crab emblazoned pajamas peeking out from under a silky, pink housecoat, her mouth a straight line of concern. She took a deep breath, then made a show of exhaling loudly.

"I know, I know. You're an adult, and I can't tell you what to do." She shook her head and padded to the sink, turning on the faucet with a flourish and filling the coffee pot. "I wish you would look into getting a blade for running. I hate the thought of you pounding on—"

"Please give it a rest, Mom." Erin continued stretching, this time grabbing her ankle and lifting it behind her until her artificial foot touched her butt, holding it for twenty seconds, then releasing it and switching to the other leg. Yes, she had thought about getting a blade for running—many times. But she had long ago made peace with the fact that her competitive days were over. With a blade there would be no excuses, no reason to not resurrect her long dormant competitive streak.

"Do you really need to run this early in the morning?" Lydia yawned and pointed to the window. "It's still dark outside."

Erin cocked her head and rolled her eyes, saying, without words, *you're kidding me, right?* According to the weather app on her phone, it was already seventy degrees with ninety percent humidity. Who, in their right mind, would wait much later to run? "It's plenty light enough."

"You won't be visible to cars."

"My fuel belt is reflective. So are my running shoes." Erin couldn't believe she was having this inane argument with her mother, yet she felt powerless to stop. She needed to have the last word. "Who's up at this hour, anyway? What cars? The only people out and about are the watermen, and they're already on their boats heading down the channel. Let's see. Maybe Andy and Bill are up opening the bakery. Oh, and Martin at the Country Store is scrambling eggs. I would say Smokey Jones might be on the road, too." She paused and looked at her watch. "But he's likely already in the bridge tender's hut with his thermos of piping hot coffee." She finished stretching and hugged her mother. "If I don't go now, I'll regret it later. It's just going to get hotter and hotter."

"Are you really running all the way to the boatyard? And back? Look, I'll throw on some clothes and drive you over. Or you can do your little jog around the property here, and then I'll drive you over. I'm uncomfortable with you interacting with those people at the boatyard."

Erin regretted mentioning her plan to combine a run with a trip to the boatyard to retrieve her rental paperwork. But that's what a glass of wine with dinner and two glasses of Bailey's for dessert will do. She had harshly admonished her mother about harping on her weight and told her to lay off the snarky comments about running. The one thing she didn't mention, thank God, was that she had been experiencing the same old pain in the knee, just above the stump, but in new ways. She kept telling herself that running would help; her leg always felt better after a run, at least for a day or two, but only if she was careful, didn't push too hard, and foam rolled her leg afterward.

"I'm not interacting with 'those people,' Mom." She wondered why nobody on either side had softened after so much time had passed except maybe her. Seeing Landon with his kid yesterday stirred something in her that she wasn't sure how to even begin to articulate. "Those people used to be like family."

"Please stop talking like that." Lydia poured coffee beans into the grinder and pressed the button. Within seconds the smell of freshly ground coffee—nutty and slightly burnt—filled the kitchen. "Look at you! Look what they did to you!"

"They didn't do anything to me." She lifted her leg and let Doris rest on the island. "Landon did this to me. Joelle and Ed had nothing to do with this." She blinked against the tears beginning to fill her eyes and lowered her artificial foot back to the floor. "I like my life, Mom. I don't know where I would be or who I would be if this hadn't happened. I like where I am and who I've become." She shook her head. "Just the other day, I thought about how I never would have met Wes if my life hadn't taken the exact trajectory it took."

"You're always looking for silver linings."

"It's better than wallowing." Erin focused on the rhythmic drip-drip-drip of the coffee maker, a soothing sound that always calmed her and gave her a warm and fuzzy feeling. She had her own personal coffee maker at her desk at work. Strangely enough, some of her best creativity came during the drip-drip-dripping of her coffee brewing. Her two office mates shared a Keurig and teased her about her archaic and lame Mr. Coffee. *It's the drip-drip-drip,* she always said in response. Listening to her mother's coffee dripping, she wondered if the sound was so soothing because it reminded her of a gentle morning rain hitting the water. Maybe she should buy a white noise machine with a rain setting.

"I've been doing a lot of soul-searching since your father died." Lydia looked at Erin, a slight wistfulness in her eyes. "He always maintained that I was being too harsh with them." The drip-drip-drip subsided. Lydia pulled two mugs out of the cupboard and poured coffee in one of them. She held up the other and shrugged.

Erin was tempted, oh so tempted to have a cup. If anything could sway her to alter her plans, it was her mother's coffee. She looked at her watch, frustrated that the dark morning was rapidly approaching sunrise. She shook her head. "I really need to hit the bricks."

"Okay, so the accident itself, I can forgive that. I think maybe I've even made peace with it." Lydia ignored the sense of urgency on her daughter's face. She poured coffee into the second mug, added a cream splash—just the way Erin liked it—and set it on the island. "Maybe. I don't know." She ran her hand through her hair. "Landon should have known better. Yep. He should have. Had he been ten years old, maybe I'd feel differently." Lydia put her hands on her hips.

"But Joelle and Ed, refusing to do anything about your lost scholarship? That was just inexcusable."

"You should have seen Landon with his little son yesterday. I'm telling you, Mom, he's different." Erin deliberately ignored her mother's comment about the real source of the two-decade feud between her parents and Landon's parents. If she had any good sense, she would walk away right now.

ERIN WISHED she knew why she was still standing in her mother's kitchen, having this conversation, the heat, and humidity outside rising by the second. More than anything, though, she surprised herself by jumping to Landon's defense. She had harbored her anger over the years and stubbornly refused to ever give him a chance to apologize or at least hear his side of the story. Not that there was much of a story to tell. He was a teenager wanting to impress her (and Susan) with his own fireworks display.

Defeated, Erin picked up the mug and held it under her nose, inhaling the aroma. Despite her best efforts at resisting, she took a sip. "Thanks, Mom." She set the mug down and threw her hands up. "For screwing up my plans."

"Why is Landon alone, then? Where is the child's mother?"

"I don't know anything about any of that. Maybe she couldn't deal with Landon's deployments? I have no idea." She took another sip of her coffee. "Susan Rupert seems to be cozying up to him." She grew wistful, then. "He looked comfortable with her, too. I won't be shocked if they end up together." She shrugged. "Susan always had a thing for him."

Bang. Bang. Bang.

"What in the world?" Lydia looked at Erin, who shrugged. The banging on the side door got louder, more urgent.

Bang! Bang! Bang!

"I wonder if Rosco is wandering around Bert Newton's property again," Lydia said.

"Rosco?"

"Oh, my new rooster. Just got him a few days ago. Twice, he's managed to get out of the yard. It's probably Bert telling me he put the dumb bird back over the fence."

BANG! BANG! BANG!

Lydia looked at her bare feet and tapped her housecoat. "You'd better answer the door for me. I'll be upstairs changing. If it is Bert, give him a couple of those muffins to take home." She pointed at a white cardboard box on the counter and scurried away.

FRUSTRATED BEYOND BELIEF, Erin hobbled to the door just as the person on the other side banged it as if trying to break it down. Over a rooster? She shook her head, readied herself to give Bert Newton a piece of her mind, and swung the door open. "For crying out loud, Bert! You could have at least waited until the sun was fully up before you—"

"Hello, Erin Leigh."

An older version of Landon—minus the Navy SEAL muscles (and man bun)—stood on the other side of the screen door. Three days of gray stubble decorated his chin, and the crinkles around his eyes were more profound and numerous than she remembered. "Is this about my mother's rooster?"

He pursed his lips, wrinkling his nose and making sniffing noises like a rabbit on the hunt for a garden of carrots. "I don't know about any rooster, but that coffee sure smells good."

Erin looked at him, incredulous as if he had just announced that the water in the Chesapeake Bay had turned into champagne. Or the ospreys and other waterfowl had grown exponentially and were swarming the skies, ready to eat everything that moved in a modern-day remake of *The Birds*.

More realistically, Ed Shultz might as well be Satan; he had been despised in Erin's family for so long. That he would hint at coming in for a cup of coffee made no sense.

Erin straightened her back, contorting her face into the most neutral, professional expression she could muster, and cleared her throat. "How can I help you?"

"You can start by opening the door and offering me a cup of coffee."

"Have you lost your mind?" *Love your enemies, right?* Erin sighed; she had long ago run out of reasons why Ed Shultz should still be an enemy. "My mother is going to be down any second. If she sees you standing here, she will—"

"Where did you find Rosco this time." If Lydia had been driving a car instead of walking toward the open door, she would have slammed on the breaks, the screeching so loud it would have been heard a mile away. "What the hell are you doing here?"

"I like what you and Doug did with the place." Ed waved his arm around the property, ignoring Lydia's shock. "You got quite the deal on this place. Intimidated a lot of people. The property, I mean. It would make a great boatyard if it wasn't so far off the beaten path."

"If Doug were here, he'd punch you between the eyes."

"Let's cut the bullshit, Lydia. Doug isn't here." He hung his head, then looked back at her, his eyes a tiny bit softer. "I'm sorry about Doug, by the way. Must have been rough not being able to see him or hold his hand at the end."

"Get out!" Lydia's voice cracked. She swallowed but didn't move, seemingly paralyzed with indecision.

"My mother asked you to leave," Erin said with equally unconvincing conviction.

"If she wanted me to leave, she would have slammed the door in my face by now." Ed cocked his head. "Now, are you going to let me in, or are we going to sand here like a bunch of school kids on the playground posturing for the best swing?" He sighed. "Look, I've been up half the night trying to figure out what to do about that damned boat of yours. The least you people could do is give me a cup of coffee."

Lydia stepped aside, letting her enemy squeeze through the opening in the screen door.

Erin unbuckled her fuel belt and set it on the far end of the counter, out of the way of the coffee maker and tray of muffins her mother was arranging. Any hope of running this morning before the heat and humidity kicked in had fizzled away.

She watched, in awe, as her mother took muffins, one by one, out of the bakery box and set them neatly on her favorite tray—the one painted with three red cardinals she had found at a yard sale years ago. Six muffins in all. As if the whole reason Ed Shultz was sitting in her mother's kitchen was to catch up over coffee and muffins.

Erin shook her head. It was one thing to let your enemy step over the threshold and maybe, just maybe, offer him a cup of coffee. Okay, maybe offer him a muffin too. Feeding one's enemy was undoubtedly a way to love one's enemy, right? Judging from the past twenty years of hate, discontent, feuding, unsuccessful lawsuits, and general everyday vitriol, she wondered why her mother didn't just shove the box of muffins at him. Or better yet, open the box and discretely spit on them, then shove the box at him. Or even better, simply conduct whatever business he had come here to conduct, standing outside on the stoop by the side door. Instead, Erin's mother set the tray in the middle of the island and handed Ed a mug of steaming coffee.

"These muffins come from that new bakery on Moss?" Ed grabbed one and took a bite, not bothering to peel away the liner. "Amazing. I didn't give that place six months to survive. And yet, it seems to be thriving." He regarded his muffin, holding it up and twirling it in the light. He took another bite and shook his head. "Absolutely amazing. Your coffee is amazing too." He set his mug down and wiped his mouth with the back of his hand.

Erin grabbed a handful of napkins and set them next to the muffins. "With all due respect, can we stop fawning over the muffins and get down to business?" She stood with her hands on her hips. "In fact, there's really nothing to talk about." She pulled her father's well-worn BoatUS card out of her pocket and waved it in front of him. "I'm about to call them to get the boat."

"And how do you suppose they'll get the boat out of the jam you got it into?"

"I beg your pardon?" Erin couldn't believe what she was hearing and seeing. First, the bold nerve of him to barge in here like this, knowing full well how her mother felt about him. And second, seeing him sitting in her mother's kitchen like he owned the place. Erin's stomach turned. "Why are you even here? You could have called first."

"It's not like I didn't try." He looked at Lydia and pointed to her phone, which was sitting on the counter next to Erin's fuel belt. "How many missed calls do you have?"

"Did you really expect me to answer?" Lydia leaned against the sink. She looked young and pretty in a pair of cutoff denim shorts and a pink scoop-neck tee shirt. Sometimes Erin found it hard to believe her mother was sixty-five years old. "I figured my daughter would get in touch to let you know to expect the BoatUS tow boat." She sighed. "Look, Ed, I'm not ready to let bygones be bygones or whatever it is you're trying to do here."

"Who said anything about bygones? You didn't answer your phone, and I wanted to talk to Erin Leigh about her boat." He rolled his eyes. "Plain and simple." Unable or unwilling to bite around the muffin liner, he finally peeled the thin, blue paper away and crumbled it into a tiny ball, which he flicked with his thumb and forefinger. Erin caught it before it pummeled to the floor. "Plus, you're the one pushing muffins at me." He plucked another one off the tray. "Do you mind?"

"Go ahead," Lydia said, as if with great effort. "So, how badly damaged is my daughter's rental?"

"Won't know that until I can pry it away from the piling." He looked at Erin. "I don't know how you managed to wedge it in there so tightly. Wish I could have witnessed the shenanigans."

"It's a long story," Erin said, sitting down at the island next to Landon's father—her second father, as she had affectionately referred to him during her childhood. She softened a bit, mostly because her mother seemed to be softening. "I basically ran aground in the channel, and I think I may have damaged the rudder. I couldn't steer and ended up scraping against the pier."

"According to my son, and let me tell you, he spent a long time trying to make heads or tails out of that thousand-page rental agreement." He shook his head. "A simple two-pager would have basically conveyed the same information." He sipped his coffee. "You don't want to file an insurance claim. According to my son, the deductible is through the roof."

"You don't even know how much damage there is. I know I broke the rudder; that's on me. And there is probably some superficial fiberglass damage on the hull. Again, on me. But the motor conked out, and that's on them."

"If you had let my son give you a tow like a normal person would have done, I wouldn't be here defiling your mother's beautiful kitchen." He chuckled.

"Don't imply that my daughter isn't a 'normal person.'" Lydia worked her way around the island and put her arm around Erin. "Any abnormality is because your son—"

"Whoa!" He held out his hands. "I didn't come over here to rehash any of that. Maybe my word choice is suspect. I didn't mean abnormal." He turned to Erin. "You always had an independent streak and wanted to do everything yourself. Drove my son crazy, sometimes."

"Like the time I wanted to reel in my own fish?" Erin glanced at her mother. Was it okay to laugh with the enemy as if everything had been forgiven and forgotten? Alas, Lydia had moved to the sink and was washing phantom dishes; Erin couldn't see her face.

"Yes, ma'am." Ed smiled. "You had to reel her in yourself after my son saw you struggling with the line. 'I can do it! I can do it!' Remember? And then whammo! Just like that, you're in the water."

"At least Landon was able to get the fish." Erin shook her head, remembering that day. The two families gathered at Ed and Joelle's house for grilled fish and a game of horseshoes.

"I should have sued you for reckless endangerment." Lydia suddenly appeared at the island, the phantom dishes she had been washing sitting in the drying rack. "You should have had your eye on her, Ed."

"Mom, it was a fun day. It wasn't like I was a baby. I was what, thirteen or fourteen?" Erin surprised herself by jumping to Ed's defense. "I swam back to the boat and climbed in. Trust me, I wanted to keep swimming. The water was glorious that day."

Lydia waved a muffin around, looking like she was going to throw it at her enemy. "The kids should have been in life jackets."

"They were hardly kids." Ed picked up his coffee mug and held it midair before putting it back down. "Plus, the waters were smooth." He picked up his mug again, raising it to his lips and taking a sip. "It was hotter than hell that day too. No way I would confine the kids to wearing heavy life jackets. They would have cooked from the inside. Anyway, they were both great swimmers."

"Your memory is flawed, just like your logic. I remember the day being windy." Lydia shook her head. "Never mind, I see you're still as stubborn as you were back then. And always right." She looked at Erin. "He always has to be right, even at the expense of..." She let her voice trail off and sighed. "The kids should have been in life jackets, that's all. Your son too, but especially my daughter."

Erin clapped her hands together three times. Her mother and Ed jumped. "Let's regroup here, please. I'm glad you two are finally talking, but we have bigger fish to fry, no pun intended." She turned to Ed. "You came here to discuss *Jolly Good Day*." She encircled the room with her arms. "You have the floor."

ERIN WALKED Ed Shultz to the door. Her mother had retreated to her bedroom, visibly tired of the discussion, getting more upset with each passing moment. What Erin had initially interpreted as one brick in her mother's defensive wall cracking and possibly falling out turned out to be something else entirely. Erin knew she would spend hours scratching her head over her mother's seemingly mild reaction to Ed, followed by the return of her vitriol.

It had taken two muffins and two cups of coffee for Ed to get through his soliloquy of technical mumbo-jumbo about how he and Landon planned to un-wedge *Jolly Good Day* and pull her out of the water to assess the damage. He was adamant that returning a damaged boat to the rental company was not in her best interest, no matter the insurance. Yes, she would need to disclose that it had been damaged and repaired, but they would cross that bridge later. Ed even said he would look at the engine for her and see if there was anything he could do about it.

"It will all work itself out." Ed stopped in front of the door with genuine compassion in his eyes. "It's a good plan, and it will save you a ton of money, for sure." He held out his hand. Erin hesitated for a moment and then shook it. "By tomorrow morning, I'll better understand what we need to do and how you can help. Trust me, I'm going to put you to work." He winked and stepped out the door.

Erin stood in the doorway and watched Landon's father walk gingerly down the three steps, holding the railing tighter than she would have expected. In her memory of Ed Shultz—the Ed Shultz of twenty years ago—he was fit and young for his age, just like her father had been. Ed looked like he had aged forty years instead of twenty. She waited until he climbed into his truck and was out of sight before letting her back slide down the wall and crouching on her heel in a deep squat. She took a few cleansing breaths and slowly rose until she stood, then repeated the process twice. It usually worked like a charm to stave off a panic attack. This morning, though, it was not working.

The rapidity at which Ed had shot off the play-by-play of what needed to be done to get *Jolly Good Day* out of the water left her shell-shocked and reeling.

In a nutshell, Ed and Landon would need to wait for high tide, which wouldn't be until around three this afternoon, then bring the towboat abreast and use the winch to slowly pull the sailboat off the pilings. He would need to use a ton of fenders and tie the sailboat securely to *Little Jo*. Oh, and let's not forget about the bridge tender! Landon and Ed would need to coordinate with Smokey Jones to raise

the drawbridge. The Department of Natural Resources also needed
to be notified so it could prevent smaller boats from coming through
the channel. The two Shultz men would carefully crab the tow across
and up the channel to the marina's entrance. If all went well, the next
step would be to move *Jolly Good Day* to the head of the pier where
the travel lift could pull it out of the water, enabling them to inspect
the keel and rudder.

Erin paced the length of the small entryway, trying to get her
heart to stop pounding. When she rented the sailboat, she had opted
for insurance with a huge deductible to keep the cost down. She had
no idea how she would be able to pay for the repairs, not to mention
getting the boat fixed by the end of her lease to avoid the five-
hundred-dollar per day late fee.

She wanted—needed—to talk to Wes. He would help her come
down off the edge. She hadn't mentioned running aground or
crashing the boat when they spoke last night. Stressing over her
stupidity was the last thing Wes needed the night before major
surgery. She looked at her watch—he was deep into it by now. And
Erin knew from experience that he wouldn't call her immediately
after; he would need time to destress before he would want to talk to
anyone. She braced herself for a long, miserable day.

15

It had taken almost four hours to extract the sailboat from between the pier and bulkhead. Finally, Landon and his dad had *Jolly Good Day* out of the water and safely resting on jack stands. Susan was at the house with Willie, supposedly teaching him how to make lasagna. The plan had sounded good this morning when Susan suggested it, but now it seemed utterly ridiculous. Teach a three-year-old to make lasagna? He shook his head, knowing that if an activity didn't involve Batman (and now, Spiderman) or Baby Shark, Willie had the attention span of a gnat.

Jolly Good Day was in worse shape than either Landon or his dad had anticipated. The keel needed new bottom paint, the bow pulpit would need to be removed and taken to the machine shop to be heated and straightened, and the road rash on the hull would have to be buffed out. The most serious issue, though, was the rudder. It was bent and would need to be removed so it could be taken to the machine shop and repaired. Landon didn't want to think about the time and effort it would take to get the rudder off this boat.

After chatting for a few minutes about their quick assessment of the damage, Landon's dad walked away to open the bait and tackle shop for an out-of-town customer who acted as though buying a bag of ice was a matter of life or death. Hell, maybe it was, for all Landon knew. He imagined all the ways one might put a five-pound bag of ice to good use: ice pack for a migraine or twisted ankle, filler for a cooler, cubes to make a Scotch or rum and Coke more palatable, used for stuffing down your shirt during the hottest day on record.

Landon remembered the only year his dad and Erin's dad raced in a local, long-course triathlon. That day was possibly, the hottest day on record. He and Erin, along with a bunch of Erin's cross-country teammates, worked a water station at the eight-mile mark on the run course. Of course, it was hot for the racers—many of them getting carried away on golf carts (the two dads made it through, yay) —but the volunteers were roasting in the sun too. Erin started handing out cups of ice to the runners, telling them to pour it down their shirts or fill their ball caps. When he wasn't looking, she poured a cup of ice down his shirt, which incited riotous laughter and an all-out food fight with ice. He remembered wanting to grab her at that moment—mush her sweaty, ice-cooled body into his—but he never did. Yep. One of his biggest regrets. Maybe if he had done that, he would never have concocted his ill-conceived fireworks plan a few weeks later.

He blinked the memory away and returned to judge the poor, innocent guy who just wanted a bag of ice. While today was hot, it wouldn't break any records like it did the day of that triathlon. The poor, innocent guy just wanted a bag of ice. Landon didn't like this side of himself, the cynical side that harshly judged people's inten-tions. This, too, had been pointed out by Taylor in counseling, and, like all good counselors, theirs sided with Taylor.

Crap. There he was, doing it again. He couldn't help it. A pinch or two of cynicism sprinkled on top never hurt anyone. He was being realistic, was all. True, it didn't matter to Landon personally what the guy wanted to do with a five-pound bag of ice. However, Susan trying to get cozy with his family by making dinner under the guise of teaching a three-year-old how to make lasagna was his business. He had been trying, for two weeks, to embrace the thought of Susan in his life, even celebrate it. If anything, he should be happy Willie was safe in the house with Susan, occupied and doing something educational and practical.

"What took you so long?" Landon eyed his dad, who returned carrying a small cooler and looking disheveled and sweatier than he had been when he left twenty minutes ago.

"Ice chest was empty, believe it or not."

"Didn't we get twenty bags delivered three days ago?"

"Nope. Only ten. And those went quickly." Ed knit his brow. "I thought Alan told me he would be back this morning with another ten bags." He shrugged. "I guess not. Anyway, I walked the guy around the house and gave him an old bag I had in the spare freezer. The bag was ripped and had a handful or so of cubes missing. I told him the ice was not good for making cocktails. He said he needed it for his cooler. They're anchored out just before the channel."

"That's just great, letting a stranger into the house while my son— your grandson—is inside." He shook his head. "I'm sorry. I keep forgetting, you don't know a stranger." Landon surprised himself with his blatant sarcasm and tone.

"Actually, you probably won't believe this, but, well, the guy isn't a stranger at all. He's Ned Truman's grandson from Annapolis, here with his girlfriend." He shrugged. "Nice fellow. You might remember him. He's not that much younger than you."

"Doesn't ring a bell." Landon glanced at the boat bottom he was standing under, imagining Erin and the dweeb cardiologist (who was probably cutting someone's heart open at this moment) spending a romantic week aboard. The whole thought of them cuddling on the foredeck under the stars made him want to punch a hole in the fiberglass. He took a deep breath and hung his head. "I'm sorry for my attitude, Dad. It's been a long day, and I'm hot, tired, and starving."

"You won't be disappointed, then." Ed patted his belly. "Susan has the whole house smelling like an Italian restaurant."

"Hot dogs on the grill sounds better, right about now. And a beer. An ice-cold beer." Landon's parched tongue longed for something cold and wet. He gulped from his water bottle, the contents now bordering on hot and unsatisfying. Still, the liquid quenched his thirst but did nothing to make his tastebuds happy.

"I knew you would say that." Ed smiled. "I can't do anything about a hot dog right now, but I can give you one of these." He opened the cooler and pulled out two Miller Lites, handing one to Landon. "Cheers to an interesting week ahead."

16

The air was cooler this morning than the last few days, but not by much. At least that's what Erin's weather app assured her. She had managed to slip out of the B&B undetected by her mother, unlike yesterday morning when Erin felt assaulted at every turn. She wiped the sweat out of her eyes as she jogged past Martin's Country Store—a mile before the boatyard.

Ed Shultz had called last night and left a voicemail. Erin had been about to step into the shower when her phone rang. But when she saw the caller ID, she let it roll right to voicemail. Whatever status he wanted to share about the sailboat could be conveyed just as easily in a message. In fact, a text message would have been better, but he was old, like her mother, and preferred chatter to emojis.

She reluctantly gave Landon's dad her cell phone number when he showed up at the B&B yesterday morning, and immediately regretted it. Hopefully, he would not share it with his son. Maybe she should just change her number; she was long overdue for a phone upgrade anyway. She smiled, thinking about the other call she received last night, the one that came a few minutes later when the sound of the shower masked her ringtone. When she got out and saw that Wes had called and left a message—she didn't even bother listening to it.

Still dripping wet, she called him back right away. *The surgery went well*, he had said. *Lasted longer than anyone expected. I'll spare you the gory details. I'm exhausted but looking forward to seeing you tomorrow afternoon.* He told her he wasn't exactly sure when he could break away, as he still needed to stop by the hospital to check on his patient. After that, he would hand the case over to his team. When they hung up, Erin felt a bit of post-call guilt, having left out the minor detail that her brother and the other family camp attendees were not coming. She didn't want to give Wes any reason to choose Baltimore over Canvasback Cove. The fact that she thought he would, was telling. She swatted the thought aside as she brushed her teeth and fell into bed, excited to see him. And now, she was excited that today was only Friday; she and Wes would be together until next Wednesday. Not counting today, they had five full days before they would have to rejoin the rat race.

THE WEATHER APP CLEARLY LIED. Clearly. When the drawbridge came into sight, Erin felt like she was enveloped in a thick wool blanket. Maybe the air temperature was five-degrees cooler, but the humidity was so thick it seemed hard to breathe.

Landon's dad left specific instructions in his voicemail: wear comfortable clothes, comfortable shoes, a comfortable hat, and plenty of sunscreen. She had shoved everything, including the sunscreen (even though her trusty weather app called for a cloudy day) into her Camelback. She would need to get out of her soaked running clothes at some point; hopefully, the showers behind the bait and tackle shop were in better condition than they had been twenty years ago. She could still smell those bathrooms in her mind: a combination of rust, bleach, and the sometimes salty, sometimes fresh scent of brackish water. Those showers may not have been pretty, but they were clean.

"You look like a Christmas tree!" Smokey Jones stepped out of the bridge tender's hut just as Erin approached the top of the drawbridge and pointed at Erin's blinking multi-colored illuminated vest. "Ms. Conrad! I thought that was you!"

Erin stopped jogging, unable to suppress her grin, despite how hot she was and how badly her knee hurt. "I'd hug you, but I'm drenched in sweat."

"How about an air hug, then." They both stretched their arms, embracing the pocket of air between them as if encircling a giant, invisible ghost—the pantomime that had become commonplace over the past two years, sweat or no sweat. "Where are you off to, at this hour? Or are you just trying to beat the heat?"

"I haven't beaten any heat!" She rested her hands on her thighs.

"Wait a minute. Don't go away." Smokey returned to the hut and came out three seconds later holding a plastic water bottle, and he handed it to her. "You look like you could use this."

Erin took the bottle. Not because she needed water (the bladder in her Camelback was filled and still cold) but because she didn't want to stand here for fifteen minutes debating the benefits of staying hydrated in the heat. She knew Smokey wouldn't let her proceed without watching her guzzle the water. She unscrewed the top and made a show of drinking—the icy water providing a jolt of joy that she didn't expect. She drank half and poured the other half over her head.

"Thanks, Smokey. I didn't realize how thirsty I was."

"How far are you running this morning?"

"Just over to the boatyard."

Smokey raised an eyebrow and smiled. "So, you and the Shultz boy getting reacquainted, are you?"

"Bite your tongue!" Erin shook her head. "No! Absolutely not! In fact, my boyfriend—a serious boyfriend, I might add—is coming in this afternoon. This was supposed to be the week of my mother's—"

"Family camp," Smokey interrupted. "So, why the boatyard, if not to see the Shultz boy." He raised his eyebrows. "Oh, yes. Your little mishap with the big sailboat the other day. I watched the whole thing unfold."

"He's hardly a boy anymore." Erin felt herself blush and hoped her already red, hot skin masked the embarrassment she was sure was written all over her face. She chose not to engage with him about *Jolly Good Day*.

"The two of you will always be kids to me." Smokey either down-played Erin's comment or was completely clueless; she didn't know which. No matter. She was grateful for him giving her the option to save face. "I saw your mother last week. Said this will be the first family camp since—"

"I know. I miss him more than I could say."

"He was a good man."

"The best." The first sliver of sun announced itself over the tree line on the horizon. "Look." Erin pointed at the second-by-second changing view. "I'll never get tired of that."

"And I have the best view in the house," Smokey nodded his head toward an approaching boat. "I'd better get back in there."

"Good to see you, Smokey." She smiled. "And thanks for the water."

"Screw it, I'm giving you a real hug." He leaned in for a brotherly embrace, then held her at arm's length. "You really do look like a Christmas tree!"

"Tell your wife I'll bring her some jalapeños."

"And I'll tell her to save you a jar of jelly."

Smokey disappeared into his hut. Erin stood on the sidewalk beside it and willed her legs to start moving again. She lost track of how much time had gone by; according to her legs, it was too much time. The sun, bright orange and well above the trees, confirmed that her legs were right; she had stood around way too long.

THE FIRST THING Erin did when she got to the boat yard—before she even looked around to see where Landon and his dad had put *Jolly*

Good Day—was test the bathroom. Sure enough, the combination on the cipher lock was the same as it had always been: 1224—Landon's birthday. As a kid, Landon never seemed to mind sharing his birthday with the eve of one of the most anticipated days on the planet. On the other hand, Erin always thought it would be dreadful. Landon's parents eventually assigned him a second birthday—January tenth—far enough away from Christmas yet close enough to his actual birthday to make it not feel peculiar.

The cipher lock combination was the only aspect of the bathroom that hadn't changed. Everything else looked as though it had been replaced. It was still a bare-bones bathroom, but at least the shower tiles were a modern blue, and none were chipped. The water pressure was better too. And it was hot. Very hot. Erin surprised herself by standing in the shower for so long, given how hot and humid it was outside, barely past sunrise.

She opened the door and stepped out, a puff of steam following closely behind, immediately regretting the hot shower. Within seconds of being back outside, she was drenched in sweat. She looked down at her clothes and immediately regretted her choice. What was she thinking, packing long pants and a long sleeve tee shirt? The pants and shirt were lightweight and touted SPF protection from the sun. Still, she would have been much more comfortable in shorts and a tank top. Well, she would only be here for a little while. Right? Just long enough to look at *Jolly Good Day*, do whatever little things Ed Shultz wanted her to do to help. Then call her mother to come to pick her up. At least that was the plan. She wasn't exactly sure when Wes would arrive, but she wanted to be sure she was back at the B&B when he did.

"I see you're making yourself at home." Ed Shultz strode toward her, two mugs in his hand. "Not sure why you're taking a shower before working, but whatever." He handed her one of the mugs. "No match for your mother's coffee, but I figure you'll need this."

Erin took a sip. Blech. She wanted to say, *this isn't coffee; it's coffee-flavored sludge*. Instead, she smiled and followed him behind the bait and tackle shop, where he typically stored boats that had been pulled out of the water for winter. In summer, the only boats on jack stands were broken boats or boats that, for one reason or another, were no longer loved, no longer used.

Beyond the boats sat the house Landon grew up in. The summer between fifth and sixth grade, Landon's parents added a second-story addition. She and Landon would sneak up there after the construction crew left for the day, pretending it was the upper deck of a pirate ship. After the construction was complete, they tried to resume playing pirate in the treehouse her father had built behind his workshop, but it was never the same. The treehouse was where they played cards and board games; it simply didn't have the right Feng Shui for pirates, even in pretend.

"Here she is," Ed said, breaking her reverie. Standing under *Jolly Good Day's* hull, he pointed to the rudder. "You really did a number on this thing." He stepped out from under the boat and moved toward the bow, shaking his head. "And the bow pulpit. Wow." He ran his hand along the side of the hull, outlining an extended, narrow area where the boat scraped against the pier. "This here is probably the easiest to deal with. Just some sanding, buffing, and repainting."

Erin perked up. Sanding, buffing, and painting were something she could do. She had loved helping her dad sand boat bottoms. She didn't love sanding—it was tedious and exhausting, but she relished the one-on-one time with her dad, their respective sanders humming a duet. Even though they couldn't hear themselves think, let alone talk over the humming and buzzing of their sanders, they were together. Last spring—only a few weeks before his age group was eligible for a Covid vaccine—was the last time they sanded together. It was the last time they did anything together. He got Covid a week later and died three weeks after that. She swallowed the memory. The last thing she wanted was to give Ed Shultz a glimpse into her vulnerability.

"I guess I'll need a ladder and a circular sander," she said. "And eighty-grit paper, too, if you have any laying around. If not, I'll walk to the hardware store and see if they have any."

"Whoa, now." Ed put his hands on his hips. "This road rash is the least of our worries. We'll get to that later. Much later." He scratched his head and took a sip of his coffee-flavored sludge. "Now that I think of it, just buffing it out might be enough. We'll try that before we sand, but like I said, that's the last thing we'll do." He shuffled to stern and tapped on the rudder. "Need to get this off the boat, so I can take it to the machine shop and see if I can straighten it myself. May need a new rudder if not." He looked at Erin as if seeing her for the first time. "How long did you say you'll be in town? Till Wednesday? Is that right?" Erin nodded. "Yep, okay. Yep. We need to get this rudder off the boat today. The long pole in the tent, if you catch my drift. Need time to get a new rudder if that's what it comes to." He pointed to two large wood blocks a few feet away from the boat. Erin followed, and they sat down. "You understand how hard it will be to get that rudder off the boat?"

Erin let her Camelback slide off her shoulder and hit the ground. She lifted the mug to her lips and pretended to take a sip. She knew a lot about sailboats—more than the average person—but didn't know anything about removing a rudder. If her dad ever had to remove a rudder, he didn't involve her. "I don't know. Unscrew it and lift it out?"

Ed laughed. "You don't lift a rudder out. You drop it. It has to be lowered to come out." He put his mug down and ran his hand along the dirt near his feet. "Small technical detail here, and the ground is kind of in the way."

"So, what are you saying? That you'll have to dig a hole?"

"No, I'm not saying that at all." He got up and walked to the other side of the boat, returning a few seconds later with four shovels of varying sizes and sharpness. "You, Missy, are going to dig a hole."

Erin stood up, paced the length of the boat, counting to twenty forward and backward, biting her tongue, clenching her fists—all to prevent herself from doing or saying something she might later regret. *Missy*. She will give him a pass this time, but if he ever calls her that again, she didn't care how old he was; she simply would not tolerate it. She returned to her wood block and stood over it, still flaming mad but confident she wouldn't rip his head off.

"Have a seat." He pointed at the block.

"No, thank you, I'd rather stand."

"Suit yourself." He downed the rest of his sludge and set the empty mug on her block. "It's simple. I'm going to save you a lot of money. And hassle. Sure, I could let you have the boat towed back to Baltimore like this. Yep. But I guarantee they would ding you for a lot more than what the repairs would cost if I wasn't being so reasonable by letting you work some of it off."

ERIN'S KNEE ACHED. Despite herself, she removed his mug from her block and sat. If she were smart, she would walk away right now. She didn't need his help and didn't need him to spare her any expense. Nor did she care if she were black listed from ever renting a sailboat again. She simply didn't care.

She bent down to reach for her Camelback. She unzipped the front pocket and pulled out her phone, stopping at the sight of a blur in the distance. Phone suspended mid-air, she momentarily forgot why she had pulled it out in the first place. Oh, right. She pulled out her phone to call her mother to pick her up; her knee simply wasn't up to the task of walking back to the B&B.

The blur came into focus, turning an abstract scene into something more realistic. Erin mindlessly dropped the phone back into her Camelback, her eyes fixed on the blur. She closed her eyes tightly and sat up straight, counting to ten, hoping the blur would be gone when she opened them. *One. Two. Three. Four. Five. Six. Seven. Eight. Nine. Ten.*

She opened her eyes quickly and sighed, the boat now at eye-level and blocking the scene unfolding in the front yard of the Shultz house. Like a magnet pulled to the ground, her body (seemingly without her consent) bent and hunched until her eyes were below the boat's bottom, and she could see the blur again.

Erin gasped. The blur was no longer a blur; it had somehow morphed into a man—Landon—on the front lawn, bending down to pick up the newspaper. He stretched, unaware of the two people sitting on wooden blocks under a broken sailboat. Shirtless and wearing those little brown shorts Navy SEALS wore in movies. Tanned chest and muscles she never knew existed.

"Okay." Erin turned to Landon's dad, still sitting beside her and texting on his phone. How much time had passed? A few seconds? "I'll stay."

He looked up from his phone. "Stay? You never said you were leaving."

"Oh. Right. Of course." She peeked under the hull, but Landon had already gone inside. "You were saying something about digging a hole?"

"Didn't you hear a word I said?"

"You were texting, so I gave you space." Erin was proud of herself for thinking so quickly.

"You were mesmerized by my son getting the paper." Ed Shultz turned back to his phone and resumed texting.

Erin would dig the stupid hole, but only if she could crawl into it herself. "I was distracted, I mean, not by Landon." She took a deep breath. "Look, I wasn't mesmerized. I wasn't even looking at him. Honestly, I was about to call my mother to come to get me. I think I will have BoatUS tow the sailboat back to Baltimore after all. I'll deal with any fall-out. I'd rather pay than sit in the heat and dig a hole."

"You really don't want to do that."

"With all due respect, Mr. Shultz, this is none of your business."

He put down the phone. "It's okay, dear. My son is a good-looking guy. But you don't have to worry. Whatever happened between the two of you..." He paused and looked down at her leg. "... he's over it."

"I never said anything about any of that." Erin hated how flustered she had become, hated that she didn't have the gumption to just get off the damned wooden block and walk away. "Look, Mr. Shultz..." She swallowed, trying to gather the right words and form a coherent sentence. "Landon and I were always just friends."

"Best friends," he added.

"Yes! Exactly! Like siblings." Erin emphasized *siblings*. "I'm happy for him. I'm happy that he has a beautiful son. Happy that he and

Susan reconnected." Erin tried to say all the right things but feared she wasn't coming across as very convincing.

Could she be happy for Landon and sad too? Sad at the possibility of what might have been? She flung the questions away. She loved her life. She loved Wes. God only knew what life with Landon might have been like. She let her mind drift to the blur—the shirtless Landon in his little Navy SEAL shorts. If she and Landon had ended up together, he never would have enlisted in the Navy and probably wouldn't look the way he looks now. Right! He would probably have a double chin and a beer belly. But would she have cared?

"I like how my life turned out, Mr. Shultz." She didn't know why she felt the need to justify her choice or assure him that she no longer had feelings for Landon—feelings that nobody knew about but her. Because she never told a soul. "Wait until you meet my boyfriend, Wes." She puffed out her chest a little. "He's a cardiologist." She paused, about to tell him about Wes's important surgery, but stopped herself. "He'll be here sometime today."

"Then you'd better get busy digging." He pointed at the shovels. "You might want to start with the small, pointy one until you get down to the softer dirt. The surface is pretty rocky, but then again, having grown up here, you already know that." He turned his head and looked over his shoulder. "Ah. Speaking of the devil."

Erin let her eyes follow the sound of tires on crushed gravel. Of course, Susan's green Mini Cooper. Ed waved as it rolled by. Susan, though, seemed fixated on looking straight ahead and didn't see him. The clown car disappeared into the jungle of boats. Erin bent her head to look under and beyond *Jolly Good Day* just in time to see Susan easing herself out of the car, a wicker basket dangling from the crook of her arm.

"You understand what needs to be done, then." Ed slapped his thighs and slowly stood, his knees creaking and popping. He put his hands on his lower back and stretched. "The hole needs to be deep enough so we can drop the rudder and get it off the boat. The rudder is about three feet long, so the hole needs to be at least four feet deep and about two feet wider than the dimensions of the rudder." He measured the width with his hands. "I'd say, make the hole three feet wide. Landon and I need to tow an old jalopy of a fishing boat from Oxford. Susan will be here watching the kid. If you need water or something to eat, just bang on the door and talk to Susan. I'll let her know you're out here." He walked away, waving goodbye behind his head.

God, she hated when people did that. Why not just turn around and wave properly? She clenched her jaw to help suppress the urge to scream. She dumped the coffee-flavored sludge into the dirt and kicked the mug out of the way. If she was going to dig a four-foot-deep hole, she might as well make it wide enough to lay down in. Because she would rather be dead than right here, right now. The only bright spot on what was proving to become a horrible day was that she would see Wes this afternoon. She took a deep breath and smiled, looking forward to falling into his arms.

17

Landon peeked out the window again. While he couldn't clearly see Erin, he could see that she was still on the ground, shovel in hand, digging away. His had planned to check on her after they returned from Oxford, but grabbed a handful of pretzels instead and hopped in the truck to head to an obscure boat salvage store in Annapolis. *Need to get there before they close*, he said as he ran out the door. His dad had called the salvage store the minute they got home, and against all odds, the shop had a rudder to replace Erin's broken one. And if, for some reason, the new rudder didn't fit, he and his dad would try to repair the broken one as best they could.

Landon wasn't entirely sure why his dad was so accommodating to Erin. Annapolis wasn't exactly next door. And on a Friday, to boot. Landon reminded him that he would likely sit in an hour's worth of beach traffic on the way home. *I need to do what I need to do*, is all his dad had said. *Oh, and make sure she eats something*, he added.

"I wanna dig dirt with the lady," Willie said, standing on tiptoes at the window. "Daddy, please. Dig dirt with the lady."

"Let's eat lunch first, buddy." He took Willie by the hand and led him into the kitchen. "Then we'll bring a sandwich and a drink to my friend." He studied his son, who was being so serious, as if the most essential thing in life, at that moment, hinged on digging in the dirt. Landon suspected there was more to Willie's request than that, and it troubled him. He had never seen his son warm up to someone so quickly. Not even Susan. And Willie loved Susan.

"Peanut Butter!" Willie ran to the cabinet where Puppy kept the bread.

"Yes! Peanut butter is Erin's favorite." Landon lifted Willie up and plopped him on a stool at the breakfast bar. "You know, her very favorite is peanut butter with marshmallow fluff."

"Jelly!"

"Yes! Jelly for you, little man!" Landon opened the pantry and pulled out his dad's jumbo jar of Skippy. "Strawberry jelly or grape?"

"Poisonberry!" Willie laughed.

"Boysenberry," Landon corrected, laughing too. "I think Puppy ate the last of the boysenberry jam yesterday, so your choices are boring old strawberry or boring old grape."

"Marshmallow fluffies."

Landon smiled, an idea formulating in his head. Erin always slathered a ton of marshmallow fluff onto her peanut butter sandwiches when they were kids. So much that it often seeped through the bread, sticky marshmallow oozing out like puss from a pimple. Most of the white stuff would end up all over her face. "Did you and Puppy use all the marshmallows when you made s'mores on the fire pit the other night?"

Willie shrugged. "Not hungry, Daddy. I want to dig dirt with the lady."

Landon poked around in his dad's snack cabinet and struck gold. An unopened bag of mini marshmallows practically leaped out. It wouldn't be quite the same as marshmallow fluff from a jar, but it was the thought that counted, wasn't it?

"I have a great idea." He put his forearms on the breakfast bar and leaned in until his nose almost touched Willie's nose. "Do you want to try peanut butter with baby marshmallows?"

"Yes!" Willie clapped. "Baby marshmallows!"

"Baby marshmallows it is!" Landon busied himself making four sandwiches—one for Willie, two for him, and one for Erin—each dotted with ten baby marshmallows. Smiling, he pressed ten more into Erin's sandwich, rendering any peanut butter invisible to the naked eye.

Susan had left suddenly after breakfast when she was called in to cover for the fifth-grade mid-morning summer school geography teacher, who had gone into early labor. He walked her to the door.

"They'll probably need me for a few days next week, too, until they find a permanent sub to take the rest of the session," she said. "If you weren't here, I'd do it." She kissed him then, and when he didn't kiss her back, she pulled away and looked into his eyes. "I'd much rather take care of Willie than deal with Leslie's fifth graders." She tilted her head back and laughed, exposing the side of her neck.

For reasons Landon couldn't figure out, he reacted to her neck, prompting him to grab her around the waist and pull her into him. He kissed her long and hard, then immediately regretted it when Willie ran in and asked them if they would get married. He shooed Willie away and shook his head. "Sorry about that."

"Kids say what's on their mind," Susan said with a dreamy look.

"I didn't mean sorry about Willie." He studied her, unclear about what this relationship was and what it wasn't. The clock was ticking; he would be back in Coronado soon, and the last thing he needed was a third wheel in his little family. He and Willie would be okay on their own. They would be. Period. "I'm sorry I got a little aggressive with that kiss." He looked at the floor, then back up at Susan. "That's what I was trying to say."

"You don't have to apologize." She looked up at him. "It was nice."

"Let's get you out of here," Landon said, ignoring her comment. He opened the door. "You don't want to be late."

Landon let the memory of kissing Susan evaporate and put the finishing touches on the sandwiches. He cut Willie's into four equally sized squares (a few days ago, Puppy had made the grave mistake of cutting Willie's toast into triangles before Landon could warn him) and put it on a plastic Batman plate. He poured the last of a bottle of apple juice into Willie's sippy cup and set the meal in front of him. "Chew it good, buddy."

"I like the baby marshmallows, daddy!"

Landon nodded as he wrapped his two sandwiches and Erin's marshmallow palooza sandwich in foil. He grabbed two cold cans of Pepsi and put everything into a soft cooler. "Finish up your lunch, buddy, and we'll take these sandwiches down to the dirt, where Erin is working. You can bring your pail and shovel and help her."

"BABY MARSHMALLOWS!" Willie ran toward Erin, his bucket dangling from his hand, swinging with every tiny, albeit fast, step. "Baby marshmallows!"

Landon took three giant steps and caught Willie's other hand. "Whoa. Buddy, slow down. We don't want to startle Erin."

"Erin doesn't startle easily." She looked up from her hole, a two-foot pile of dirt around her. She let the shovel drop as she stood, taking off the pair of gardening gloves Landon's dad had loaned her. She stretched, lifting her arms to the heavens, then bending down to touch her toes. She looked directly at Willie. "Did I hear you say something about baby marshmallows?"

Willie plopped down next to the dirt pile and started filling his bucket with a tiny, red shovel. "I use your big shovel?" Baby marshmallows, seemingly forgotten, he reached for the sharp, pointy shovel that Erin had been using to dig the hole for the rudder.

"I don't think so," Landon said, swopping in and gently pulling the shovel away from him. "Way too sharp. You have a perfectly good shovel." He picked up Willie's red shovel and handed it back to him.

"I want the real shovel!" His lower lip curled. And as much as it broke Landon's heart, he wouldn't fall for the curled lower lip routine. Not this time.

"Sorry, bud." Landon crouched down and looked his son in the eye. "Either you use your own equipment, or we go back in the house." He looked at his watch. "It's almost nap time."

"No nap!" Willie turned around and laid down on the dirt, his shoulders bobbing up and down with his muffled cries.

Erin picked up Willie's red shovel and started filling his bucket with dirt. Landon wondered what she was up to. She looked up at him, and his face flushed. *Damn, I hope I wasn't staring*, he thought. She raised her eyebrow and smiled. When the bucket was filled to the top, she patted the dirt down and smoothed it with Willie's little red shovel.

"Watch this," she said to Landon, obviously intending for Willie to hear. She smoothed a patch of ground several feet away from the dirt pile and inverted the bucket right in the middle. She pounded the bottom of the bucket with her fist. Looking at the back of Willie's head, which had stilled, although he was clearly still crying, Erin said: "Let me pound the bucket five more times, then I'll turn it over." She tightened her fist. "One. Two. Three. Four." She looked at Landon and smiled. "Five!" She lifted the bucket to reveal a perfectly formed...something. "Viola! The beginning of the greatest castle of all times!" She lowered her voice. "Now, I need to make four more." She handed the Batman bucket and little red shovel to Landon. "I could sure use some help."

Landon repeated what Erin had just done, mimicking her noises and gestures. He inverted the bucket and pounded on the bottom, counting to five, just like Erin had done. He lifted the bucket, his countenance falling with the sand. "Oh, no!" Willie lifted his head, tilting it just enough for Landon to see his tear-streaked face. He had, at last, appeared to have stopped crying.

Erin laughed. "I guess you're not a very good castle maker, Landon." She looked around. "Do you know anyone around here that could make a good castle? I have all this dirt and nobody to make a good castle."

"I make a good castle!" Willie sprung to his feet. "I do it!" He grabbed the Batman bucket and little red shovel and plopped down in front of the dirt. "Daddy, I knock down yours." He plowed into Landon's crumbling masterpiece with both hands, making a bull-dozer-like sound as he knocked it down. Without a word, he sat and carefully filled his bucket with the remains of Landon's sorry attempt at a sandcastle.

Thank you, he mouthed to Erin, who nodded. He popped open the cooler and produced the Pepsi, large pearls of condensation dotting the cans. "I thought you could use a cold drink."

Erin grabbed one and held it to her forehead, closing her eyes and smiling. She popped it open and guzzled. "Wow. I didn't realize how thirsty I was." She looked at the cooler. "And hungry. Did I hear something a few minutes ago about baby marshmallows?" She raised an eyebrow. "Or was that some sort of secret code word between you guys."

"We didn't have any marshmallow fluff in the house." He handed her a sandwich. "I was making lunch for Willie and figured you might be hungry."

Erin aggressively stripped the sandwich from the foil wrapper and shoved nearly the whole thing into her mouth. Several marshmallows fell out, one landing on her chest, just below her collarbone. He tried not to stare but couldn't help himself. He averted his eyes, hoping the marshmallow would dislodge and fall. He peeked. No luck. The tiny pillow was not going anywhere, her sweaty skin acting like glue. He couldn't stand it. He would need a cold shower soon if he didn't do something about the marshmallow. He gently plucked it off with his fingers, wishing he could have just used his mouth. He adjusted his position, crossing and uncrossing his legs, finally bringing his knees up to his chest. He held the marshmallow out to her.

"Thanks." She plopped it in her mouth and took another swig of her Pepsi. "So good. Better than marshmallow fluff." She wiped her mouth with the back of her hand.

"Remember when we argued whether a hot dog was a sandwich or a taco?" Landon needed a subterfuge and needed one fast. He didn't know what was wrong with him. He had Susan at his fingertips —all he had to do was say the word, and he would never be alone again. Plus, Susan loved Willie and would take great care of him when he was away on deployments. He was a fool to push her away.

And yet. And yet. And yet. He shook his head, amazed that the locked safe in his heart had burst open after rusting, decaying, and collecting dust for twenty years. He told himself that this was all just repressed guilt rising to the surface. Plus, Erin had a boyfriend. A cardiologist! He unwrapped the first of his two sandwiches and took a bite.

"Ha! I think I won that lame argument, didn't I?" She pointed at Willie, who was busily working on his third bucket of dirt. "Everyone knows a hot dog is a taco."

"We were never able to prove it, though." Landon was happy about the diversion, and he felt better, the craziness in his body subsiding. He finished the sandwich in three large bites and unwrapped his second one.

"But it is!" She shook her head. "Look, a sandwich is defined as filling between two slices of bread."

"And your point?"

"Two. Slices." She rolled her eyes. "A hot dog bun is the same as one slice of bread, folded. Calling a hot dog on a bun a sandwich is the same as folding a slice of pizza and calling it a sandwich. The two halves of a taco shell are attached. Just like a hot dog bun."

"Not exactly." He popped open his Pepsi and guzzled, disappointed at how quickly it had gone from being ice cold to lukewarm. "You're good with kids," he said, changing the subject. "You sure you don't have one hidden away somewhere?"

"Have what hidden away? A Batman bucket and a red shovel?"

Landon rolled his eyes. "A kid." He gestured toward Willie with his head. "You know, one of those." He paused. "How did you get to be so good with kids? Does Wes have one?"

"No to both questions." She shrugged. "You're good with him too." She blushed. "I'd better get back to work." She glanced at the hole and looked at her watch. "Wes is supposed to be here later this afternoon. And I still need to call my mom to come to get me."

"Nonsense. Willie and I will take you home." Landon tried not to let Erin see the disappointment on his face. He wasn't even sure why he was disappointed or what it was about. His stomach dropped in a familiar way—the way it had fallen so many times when he had been hopeful about one thing or another, only to have his hope dashed. The proverbial rug ripped out from under him, he supposed. He was so enjoying sitting under the shade of the boat, eating sandwiches and bantering like old times, he...well...he didn't know what. All he knew was he didn't need this new complication—Erin. He took a deep breath and looked at the hole Erin had spent the past few hours digging. "You haven't made much progress."

"The dirt is as hard as a rock." She looked up at him, her face bright red, tears streaming down her cheeks.

Landon glanced at Willie to make sure he hadn't grown bored with the task of filling his bucket with dirt and then dumping it out. Having a three-year-old was amazing in and of itself, but even more impressive was how easily a three-year-old was entertained. The simplest things—a bucket, shovel, and dirt—were fascinating in the eyes of a toddler. He turned his attention to Erin. "Hey. Did I say something or do something wrong?" Landon rolled his eyes at his own stupidity, his lame words. His very presence in the current story of Erin's life was wrong.

"It's not you, Landon." She lowered herself into the hole and stretched her arms wide. "You didn't do anything wrong. I'm just frustrated as hell. Half a day and look." She wiped her eyes. "Look!" She plopped down in complete and utter frustration.

Landon sighed. The hole was certainly wide enough. But at barely calf deep, she had a long, long way to go. He grabbed one of the other shovels and started digging around her.

"What are you doing?" She lifted herself out of the hole. "This is supposed to be my job, and I don't want your dad to come home and find you helping me." She wrinkled her nose, the harbinger of a full-on cry. Some things never changed.

LANDON PUT his shovel down and sat beside her on the hole's edge. *Everything happens for a reason,* his mother famously said—all the time. His mother said it after the accident when it was clear Erin wasn't going to die, even though she lost her leg. She said it a lot when Erin and her parents ghosted him and his family. Okay, calling it ghosting was extreme—the Conrads didn't ghost them, exactly. But to end a decades-long friendship over a childish move? Landon's childish move. The only problem, it didn't seem childish to him at the time. He had been in love with her and wanted to show and tell her. If only he could rewind time. He felt the old familiar anger welling inside him—anger at himself. Anger that he couldn't rewind time. Anger that he couldn't give Erin her leg back.

Everything happens for a reason. His mother's words. God, he missed her. He imagined sitting in the kitchen, a beer in his hand, his mother sipping a glass of Pinot Grigio, telling her about the broken boat heading here from Baltimore and that the skipper was none other than Erin Conrad. *Imagine that*, his mother would have said, a grin forming on her lips and a faraway look in her eyes, muttering *everything happens for a reason.*

Everything happens for a reason. What if he could rewind time, though? He looked at Erin, sitting in the dirt, hugging her knees, her head bent and resting on those bony bulges. He studied her artificial leg, a sick feeling in the pit of his stomach. If he hadn't blown her leg off twenty years ago, would they be together today, maybe married, with a child of their own? Or would they have drifted apart after high school? She was headed to Georgetown, and he was headed, well, at that time, nowhere. Maybe he would have stayed local and attended Chesapeake College. Maybe not. Georgetown was only a two-hour drive away. They could have made it work. Or not. Still, it would have been nice to have the opportunity to try.

Everything happens for a reason. He looked at Willie. If he could rewind time, he would have never joined the Navy. And if he hadn't joined the Navy, he wouldn't have met Taylor. And if he hadn't met Taylor, there would be no Willie. And right now, and forever, Willie was his entire life. *Everything happens for a reason.* He simply couldn't imagine life without his son. He swallowed the lump that had formed in his throat. *You're right, Mom*, he whispered. *Everything does happen for a reason.*

He picked up the shovel again and started digging. He needed to keep his hands busy, or he risked inching his butt in Erin's direction until their legs touched. Then, he would feel compelled to put his arm around her—to comfort her, nothing more. Maybe she would put her head on his shoulder and cry into his tee shirt. He thought about the cardiologist, probably in the car and on his way to Canvasback Cove. *Everything happens for a reason.* Maybe Erin and the cardiologist were destined to be together, get married, and give birth to a future United States president. Or the next Anthony Fauci. Or the first human to walk on Jupiter.

Landon picked up his shoveling pace, letting the tip of the blade cut the dirt, creating another pile opposite where Willie was happily playing. *Everything happens for a reason.* If Erin and the cardiologist get married and live happily ever after, then finally, finally, his guilt would be assuaged. Finally. Because if it wasn't for the accident, Erin and the cardiologist might never have met.

"Please stop," Erin said. "Seriously. There's no reason you need to be out here in the heat, doing my dirty work. I'm the one who got myself into this mess."

"You are absolutely correct on that." He laughed. "You should have waited for me at the channel like I asked you to." He leaned against his shovel and looked her dead in the eye. "In all seriousness, we need to get this rudder off the boat today. And by the looks of it, we have about two feet to go."

Erin looked at her watch and sighed. "I guess Wes will just have to wait. I suppose my mother could entertain him until I get back."

"Look, I'll take you home. Honestly, I'll finish this in half the time." He smiled. "No offense." Landon resumed shoveling, watching Willie out of the corner of his eye. He glanced at Erin and noticed her watching him, a puzzled grin on her face as if seeing him for the first time. He looked away from her and shoveled harder and faster.

Erin picked up her shovel and helped him, her pace much slower, one shovelful of dirt to his three. "I'm not letting you do my job.

Maybe I'm not as fast or as strong as you are, but I think we'll finish faster if we work together."

"What about the cardiologist?"

"The more I think about it, the more I like the idea of missing the awkward introductions."

"Are you saying your mom hasn't met him yet?" Landon raised an eyebrow. "And you've been dating for how long?"

"Six months." She shook her head. "It doesn't matter. He's busy, and so am I. Our time off from work doesn't often overlap."

"Interesting." Landon meant it. He found it very interesting that Erin hadn't introduced her serious cardiologist boyfriend to her mother. Very, very interesting.

"Stop talking to me," Erin said, laughing. "Or we'll never finish digging this damned hole."

18

Erin lost herself in the mindless task of shoveling—she on one side of the hole, Landon on the other. The sun had hidden itself behind a line of streaky clouds, making the task less onerous. It was still inhumanly humid. The job seemed less daunting without the sun pounding down her back.

Landon helping didn't hurt, either.

Admitting she needed help was hard—impossible when it came to Landon. Right now, she was grateful for his brute physical strength. Growing up, she dug holes with her mother around the house's perimeter, helping her plant colorful annuals to offset her other, less exciting plants. She struggled to dig the holes deep and wide enough to accommodate the root balls. Until her father swooped in, of course. *You ladies take a break,* he would say, and within a half-hour would have all the holes dug and annuals planted. On the other hand, this dirt had been compacted by the Shultz's thirty-ton travel lift, year after year, making it a million times more difficult to dig.

She stopped shoveling and regarded the progress on the hole. Landon seemed lost in the task, sweat glistening around his temples, his shaggy hair wet with perspiration plastered to his head. She liked him with long-ish hair; it unexpectedly suited him. The Landon who sometimes (okay, rarely...no, to be honest, a little more than rarely but not quite as often as sometimes...or maybe more often than occasionally...shit...she was losing her mind) appeared in her dreams at night, had close-cropped hair and boy next door innocence. This Landon, the one with the muscles and man bun (man bun!), was like a rugged Norseman Viking. And thanks to his help, the hole seemed almost deep enough to accommodate the rudder.

Willie was still happily playing in the dirt a few feet away, the shovel and Batman bucket tossed aside in favor of Matchbox cars and an elaborate dirt track. Where he had come up with the cars, she wasn't sure. When he had pranced out here with Landon and the "baby marshmallow" sandwiches, all he had were the pail and shovel. A medley of tunes rose from his lips as he pushed his cars around the track—Batman, Spiderman, Baby Shark, the alphabet song.

She was about to crouch beside him and challenge him to a car race when her watch buzzed on her wrist, indicating an incoming text. Her heart raced when she saw that it was from Wes. She lifted herself out of the hole and found her Camelback leaning against the jack stand closest to the keel. She didn't want to read Wes's text on her tiny watch face. Plus, she couldn't respond from her watch. Her heart raced, excited that he was finally here, probably holding a beer in his hand and walking the perimeter of the B&B property with her mother. She fished for the phone and opened the text, split-second confusion setting in.

She re-read his short yet poignant message: *Rare, post-surgery complications. Need to assess, consult with specialists, and monitor. Can't come until tomorrow, at the earliest. Realistically, maybe Sunday. Have fun, and I'll try and call you tonight.*

Have fun. Hahahahahahah. *Have fun, my ass,* Erin wanted to text back. Instead, she put on her supportive girlfriend persona: *I understand. Praying everything goes well. XOXO.* She hit send and waited—for what she wasn't sure. *I love you,* perhaps? A heart emoji? Three seconds later, it came: a simple thumbs up. So, that was it then.

She took a deep breath and reminded herself that Wes was a busy cardiologist in a prominent hospital, with life-or-death situations hanging in the balance. She imagined him rushing down the hospital hallway in response to a Code Blue announcement over the public address system, replying to her text quickly. Nope. Scratch that. He wouldn't text her on his way to an emergency. He sent her the thumbs-up emoji because that was all he had wanted to send her.

ERIN SHOVED the phone into her Camelback. For reasons she couldn't quite process, she didn't want Landon to know Wes was delayed. "Text from work. Sorry about that." She made her way back to the hole and picked up her shovel. "Looks like we're getting close." She sighed. "I hate to admit it, but I couldn't have done this alone."

Landon stopped shoveling and stared at her. "Another half-hour or so. Your leg okay?" He blushed. "Sorry, I didn't mean to bring that up. It's just that—"

"Stop. It's okay. I mean, I don't want to rehash all that. But my leg is okay. Doris doesn't like the dirt, but my leg is fine." She tapped the handle of her shovel, suddenly aware (and surprised as hell) that her knee didn't hurt. "Let's get back to work."

"Back to work? What do you mean, 'back to work?'" Landon laughed. "I never stopped working."

Erin shrugged. "You're right." She picked up her shovel and resumed digging.

"What did work want?"

"Huh?"

"Work? They texted you?"

"Oh yeah, that." Erin suddenly felt lightheaded. This is why she was a terrible liar—her body betrayed her whenever she tried to deceive. She took a deep breath and silently counted to ten. "I have this big client, an author—I'm not supposed to tell you her name right now—who contacted my boss and requested me by name."

"That's terrific!" Landon knit his brows. "Requested you by name to do what?"

"Write a blurb."

"Oh." He continued shoveling. "Blurb?"

Erin laughed. "You know, back cover blurb. When you pick up a book and turn it over to read the synopsis? That's a blurb."

"I know what a blurb is." He shrugged. "I just didn't know you wrote them."

"What did you think I do for a living?"

"Marketing? Book promotions? That sort of thing." Landon laughed. "Taylor, my ex, forced me to look you up on social media."

Erin frowned, giving too much away with her contorted facial expression. She quickly composed herself, unsure whether to be surprised, flattered, or furious that the only reason he had ever thought to look her up was that his ex-girlfriend goaded him into it. Erin had so many questions about that part of his life that she wanted to ask. With Willie playing so nearby, she tucked her questions away. Maybe she would ask him about Taylor another time. Or maybe never. Right. Probably never.

"I didn't realize you had any social media accounts. I thought SEALs were supposed to stay on the down low. You know, be anonymous and all that."

"It's discouraged, that's for sure." He stopped digging and wiped his brow. "Honestly, I don't understand the appeal of scrolling on Facebook. Seems like a huge waste of time." He shook his head. "Taylor would spend hours scrolling. The more she scrolled, the unhappier she became." He sighed. "It's much more complicated than that, but she was never satisfied. All the scrolling didn't help." He nudged his head toward Willie and lowered his voice. "You're probably wondering what happened between us."

Erin took a deep breath. Yes, she wondered. Ever since she learned Landon had become a father, she wondered. With his curly blond hair, Willie looked so much like the Landon she remembered from her childhood; it was like seeing a ghost. She swallowed the tinge of schadenfreude she felt bubbling to the surface, pushed it down into the depths of her heart, and tried as hard as she could to feel sorry that Landon's life with Taylor didn't end in a happily ever after Hallmark movie sort of way. No final scene with the two lovebirds flanking either side of the tow-headed kid, holding his hands and swinging him into the air on the count of three, giggles fading as they walked into the sunset. *Cut! It's a wrap!* Just as well, because Landon wasn't a Hallmark movie guy. At least not the Landon she remembered. Maybe all wasn't lost. Maybe Landon's happily ever after was with Susan. Yes, Erin had questions—a million of them. But now was not the time or place. She certainly wasn't going to go there, at least not today, not with Willie within earshot.

She chose her words carefully. "It must have been hard, losing her."

"I'm okay." He jammed his shovel into the ground, scooped up a tiny mountain of dirt, and flung it into the growing pile. "I didn't love her." He repeated the process three more times, then stopped and looked at Erin. "Seriously! I didn't love her." He hung his head. "I liked her well enough. I got her pregnant." He ran his fingers through his hair and looked at his feet. "You probably think I'm a bona fide jerk. I was prepared to build a life with her. I probably would have married her if she hadn't left." He closed his eyes and shook his head. "I feel horrible that Willie is missing out on having a loving mother in the picture. And I feel sorry for Taylor that she's missing out on all this."

"Missing out on what? Digging a freaking four-foot-deep hole? In the heat?" To lighten the mood, she smiled, unclear on how their conversation had taken such a dark turn. It wasn't like him to get so deep, so mushy-gushy. Maybe that's what digging a hole in the heat did to a person. Perhaps he needed to drink some water. She sighed. At least they weren't talking about their past, the accident, or the complicated jumbled mess of emotions that went along with it. She grabbed at the first neutral thought that popped into her head. "At least the mosquitos aren't too bad."

"Dad is at war with them." Landon laughed. "He even hired the Maryland Department of Agriculture to spray weekly." He leaned his shovel against the wall of the hole. "I think we might be done here."

With his palms pressed firmly on the ledge, he stood back and lifted himself out, as if he were in a pool, but without the help of the water.

"Well, that's just great," Erin said, a hint of sarcasm stuck in her throat. "There is no way in hell I'll be able to lift myself out of this hole."

"Bye!" Landon got up, walked a few steps, and then turned around, laughing hysterically. "Hang tight. I'll be right back with a stepladder." He stopped laughing and looked at her, puzzled. "Who is Doris, by the way?"

"Doris?"

"A little bit ago, you said 'Doris doesn't like dirt,' or something like that."

"Ah, Doris." Erin took it for granted that everyone who knew her knew Doris, and she supposed she had forgotten that she and Landon were strangers, though they shared a past. She tapped her artificial leg. "This is Doris."

"Daddy! I want to go in the hole!" Willie, covered in dirt and sand, sat down and let his little legs dangle over the edge. "I want to help the lady dig the hole."

"We're all done, buddy," Landon said. "You can help next time." He looked at his watch.

Willie's lower lip quivered and curled, breaking Erin's heart. She looked at Landon.

"Can he help me while you get the ladder? I have ten more shovels full to go before we're really done. If he helps me, we'll be all finished by the time you get back with the ladder."

Landon bowed. "Be my guest."

Erin held open her arms. Willie flew into them, almost knocking her off her feet. She regained her balance and lowered him into the hole.

"Here you go, hold the big shovel right here." Willie wrapped his hands around the handle where Erin pointed. She grabbed it a few inches higher, and together, they scooped up an impressive mound of dirt. "We'll make our own little pile right here. Ready?" Willie nodded.

"Let's count," Erin said. "One." They repeated the process several more times. "Two. Three. Four." She looked up, hoping Landon would return soon with the ladder but instead saw him crouched at the edge of the hole, watching. She felt herself blush. They locked eyes, and Landon mouthed, *thank you*. He stood up, brushed the sand off his shorts, and started back toward the house.

"Puppy!" Willie let go of the shovel and jumped up and down. "Puppy, I digged a big hole with the lady!"

Ed Shultz lowered the stepladder into the hole. "Good job, buddy." And to Erin: "Very impressive."

"This little guy here was a huge help," she said, mussing Willies hair and wondering where Landon was. "But I think he's exhausted and maybe even a little hungry."

"Nap time?" Ed raised his eyebrows.

"No nap!" Willie's face turned bright red. "No nap!"

"Okay, no nap right now," Erin whispered. She didn't see her nephew often, but she knew enough to understand that no good would come from arguing with an overtired toddler. Erin lifted him from the hole and deposited him next to his grandfather's feet.

Ed crouched down and looked at Erin. "I hate to ask this of you, but I need to borrow my son for a few minutes. Think you could keep your eye on the little guy? The house is open. Feel free to take him inside."

What about the great Susan? Erin wanted to say but stopped herself. Susan obviously wasn't available. "Sure." She climbed up the ladder and out of the hole. Kneeling in the dirt, she leaned over the hole, grabbed the ladder with both hands, and dragged it out.

"I got that," Ed said. "Obviously a little slow on my reflexes. Thanks a bunch." He took the ladder from her. "Let's touch base tomorrow and see where we are with the rudder." He crouched down and examined the hole, then stood and looked up at the sailboat's stern. "Should be plenty deep to drop the rudder. Plenty deep." He folded the ladder and lifted it, nestling it under his arm. He started to walk away but turned and came back. "Bad news. The salvage shop didn't have what I thought in terms of a rudder. So, we have no choice but to fix this one."

Erin nodded and watched Landon's father walk toward his pickup truck, parked next to the bait and tackle shop. He laid the ladder in the grass next to the shop, then climbed into the truck. She heard the tires crunching on the gravel as it backed away, and when it turned toward the street, she saw Landon sitting in the passenger seat, eyes straight ahead.

19

Erin felt like a prisoner inside the Shultz house. Willie hadn't wanted to come inside, so convinced he was that nap time was imminent. She risked her reputation by promising him a scoop of cherry-vanilla ice cream, a carton of which she was sure she would find in the freezer. Cherry-vanilla had always been Landon's favorite, and Erin had a hunch his dad made sure to have some on hand when Landon told him he was coming home. At least that's what she told herself. The fact that Willie registered recognition of the non-mainstream flavor gave her hope. With his interest piqued and his fear of nap time abated, Erin helped Willie load his Matchbox cars into his Batman bucket. She praised his elaborate road system, which surrounded his haphazardly constructed sandcastle, like the Beltway surrounding Baltimore.

Luckily, she hadn't lied about the ice cream. She and Willie sat at the kitchen table and enjoyed a scoop each, Willie talking nonstop about cars, sandcastles, Batman, Spiderman, Daddy, Puppy, Miss Susan (blech), and Bobo the big boat bird. As he jabbered on and on, she sat, mesmerized by the fact that Landon had a child, let alone one that looked exactly like him. From the bridge of his nose that was wider at the top than at the bottom, his gray eyes, cleft chin, double dimples, and crooked smile to the way his curls flopped around his ears. Plain and simple, Willie was a mini-Landon. Except that Landon's hair had darkened over the years and was now more of a muddy brown.

She looked at her phone to see if Wes had called or texted, even though she knew perfectly well that she would have felt any incoming communication vibrate on her watch. Maybe she missed the subtle buzzing when she lifted Willie onto the kitchen chair. Or when he explained that Captain Fred had a big bird named Bobo who liked to eat fish. *Bobo eats the wiggly fish*, Willie tried to explain. Erin pictured a one-eyed pirate with a macaw on his shoulder, tossing the hungry bird a squirming minnow. In Key West, maybe, but not here on the Eastern Shore. More likely, Captain Fred (who Erin had never heard of, and she knew pretty much all the watermen in Canvasback Cove) tossed bits and scraps to the seagulls, like many watermen did when they returned with the day's catch. A giant seagull named Bobo. Bobo. Like the silly waiter at the fictional restaurant, Grand Ticino, in *Moonstruck*.

Willie jumped off the chair and ran into the family room. She trailed behind, dropping the two empty ice cream bowels into the sink and filling them with soapy water. If she could, she would go back and wash them later. Later. Such an ambiguous concept. Would later even come? For all she knew, Ed Shultz was driving Landon to the airport, where Susan waited with a packed suitcase so they could elope and have a quick wedding and honeymoon combination in Vegas.

"Wait for Bobo! Wait for Bobo!" Willie's elated screams startled Erin out of her ridiculously annoying imagination. If anyone should be flying to Vegas for an impromptu wedding and honeymoon, it was her and Wes. Wasn't that the direction their relationship was headed? Erin wondered. And right now, standing in Landon's childhood home —which had barely changed in the past twenty years, except, maybe for the kitchen, which looked like it had been recently painted a modern, warm grey—she felt trapped and alone.

It was getting close to three o'clock; she thought she would be back at the B&B (showering for Wes) hours ago. And now, here she was, stuck taking care of Landon's kid. Not that she didn't think the kid was great—he was a hoot and probably the cutest little boy she could ever remember seeing. He was exhausting, though, but apparently not exhausted. After a full day in the hot sun, digging holes and building sandcastles, her nephew, Noah, would have passed out until dinnertime. She supposed Willie inherited Landon's tenacity. All she wanted was to be quiet and lost in her own thoughts. Impossible.

"Wait for Bobo!" Willie was sitting on the floor in front of the sliding glass door, which looked out at four boat slips inhabited by watermen's fishing boats. "Wait for Bobo!"

The three o'clock hour was usually when the boats came trickling in with the day's bounty. When they were kids, she and Landon sometimes "helped" the watermen by taking the scraps and tossing them into the creek for the seagulls to swarm over. There was never just one bird, and none of the watermen they knew back then ever named a seagull. Now, she wondered if Captain Fred was Freddy McKenzie, whose father, Chuck, had a fishing boat called *Reel Life* and would sell his crabs to Susan's parents for their restaurant.

Erin sat down on the floor next to Willie. "Tell me about Bobo. What kind of bird is he?"

"Big bird!" Willie stood up and raised his arm high up over his head. "Huge!"

"Like on *Sesame Street*? Is Bobo yellow like Big Bird?" Somehow, she suspected that Willie would know who Big Bird was. She hoped so, anyway. Not that it mattered. All she wanted to do was pass the time, the sands falling through the hourglass one by one as she waited for Landon and his dad to relieve her of her duties.

"No, silly!" Willie laughed, plopping back down on the floor. He set the top of his head on the carpet and raised his butt in the air. He peeked at Erin through his legs and did a somersault. "Bobo is blue!"

"Blue! Like *Blue's Clues*!"

Willie giggled and did another somersault. "Bobo, is a bird, not a dog!"

"Is he all blue, or does he have other colors, like the Fruit Loops bird?" Erin took a chance that a three-year-old would be familiar with Fruit Loops, particularly since it used to be Landon's favorite.

"Silly!" Willie assumed the somersault position again but apparently thought better of it and sat upright, his eyes glued to the sliding glass door. "Bobo not a toucan."

Erin's eyes grew big. Not only did this kid know Fruit Loops, but he also knew the type of bird. Perhaps she had been asking the wrong questions. Wait a minute. She did ask the right question, at least initially. Willie said Bobo was a big bird, which started her on the meandering path she couldn't get off, like an endless yellow brick road, neither leading her to Oz nor back to Kansas. She sighed, having a new respect for stay-at-home parents who had to find humorous ways to entertain little kids. Erin had only been at it for about an hour, and, except for eating ice cream (even though she didn't care for cherry vanilla), this was brutal.

She wondered how much of her waning patience had to do with not hearing from Wes after he texted that he wasn't coming down today. She shook her head, irritated with herself for being so needy. What did she expect from him, that he would text or call with hourly updates?

"So, tell me, what kind of bird is Bobo?"

"A great blue hero!" Willie looked at her as if to say, *Duh, Lady, don't you know anything?*

"Ah! A great blue heron!"

"No! A great blue hero!" He stood and pressed his nose against the glass. "Daddy said Bobo is a great blue hero! Like Daddy! My daddy is my hero!" He stretched his arms out and ran around the family room like an airplane, shouting, "My daddy is my hero! My daddy is my hero!" He paused at the couch, picked up the Spiderman doll she had given him yesterday, and resumed running in circles. "Spidey is my hero! Spidey is my hero!"

～

ERIN'S WATCH VIBRATED. A quick glance at her wrist told her it was her mother calling, probably wanting to know where she was. She left Willie circling the family room and stepped into the kitchen to grab her phone.

"Where are you?" Her mother's voice sounded clipped, irritated, and a bit concerned.

"I got roped into babysitting."

"Babysitting?"

"Yes, babysitting." She ran her fingers through her hair. "Look, it's a long story. I'll explain when I get home. I didn't think Landon and his dad would be gone this long, but then again—"

"You're watching Landon's kid?"

"What other kid would I be watching?"

"Oh, dear." Her mother grew quiet for a few seconds, then took a deep, audible breath. "Just be careful, would you?"

"Careful of what, exactly?"

"Never mind. Just get home as soon as possible, would you, please?"

"Of course." Erin's radar suddenly kicked in, the sound of silence in the family room deafening. "Mom, I need to go."

Erin shoved the phone in her pocket and stepped into an empty family room, the sliding glass door wide open, the sheer floor-to-ceiling curtains billowing with the afternoon sea breeze. She got tangled up in the fabric, trying to push the curtains out of the way. She stepped outside and saw Willie on the dock, "helping" a waterman tie his boat up.

"Bobo! Bobo!" Willie yelled. "Feed Bobo! Feed Bobo!"

Erin made her way toward the dock and stopped when a great blue heron landed just feet away from the boat. She could see now that Captain Fred was, indeed, Freddy McKenzie, which made her feel somewhat better about Willie interacting with him.

"Lady! Feed Bobo!"

"Erin Conrad?" Freddy put his hand on his heart, a massive grin on his face. "I'd give you a big hug, but I'm grimy. You watching the kid today?"

"Yep. I'm standing in for Susan, I suppose. Long story."

"What brings you to town?"

"My mother's annual family camp." She rolled her eyes. "Only with no family this year. Sandy's wife doesn't want to fly. Covid and all that."

"Yeah, I understand. I'm still wearing a mask when I go to Walmart."

Erin laughed. "I'll probably wear a mask in Walmart forever." She pointed at the great blue heron. "Bobo?"

Freddy shrugged. "That's what the kid started calling him. I had nothing to do with any of that. In fact, I call this bird Henry." He lifted a small fish from a Lowe's bucket filled with brackish water and handed it to Willie, who was waiting patiently next to the boat. "Here you go, little man. Go feed Bobo."

Willie stood, his arm outstretched, the fish trying to break free. The giant bird hunched his shoulders, his head jutting out suspiciously as if he didn't entirely trust this strange, little human. Erin could almost hear the bird's conflicting thoughts: *I see the fish. I've seen this little human before. This little human gave me a fish yesterday. I'm hungry. I want the fish. But I'm supposed to be afraid of humans. This human is little, but he is still bigger than me. And who the hell is that human talking to my friend Freddy? Dammit, I want the fish!*

Bobo, Henry, or whatever his name was, apparently decided the fish was worth the risk. He straightened himself up, head erect, and took several deliberate, regal steps forward. Keeping as much distance as possible while still allowing himself to grab the fish, Bobo extended his neck as far forward as it would go. Willie laughed as the bird took the fish, swallowing it whole.

"More fish! More fish!" Willie ran up and down the dock. The bird spooked and launched himself off the dock, flying low to the water and landing on the pier on the other side of Freddy's boat.

"Can I try?" Erin crouched down and caught Willie in a bear hug as he attempted to run by her on the dock. "I'd like to see if Bobo would eat a fish from me." Willie shrugged, and Erin stood, taking his hand. Together they walked up to the fishing boat. "Do you have two more fish, Freddy? Unless you think Bobo would get too full." She looked down and winked at Willie, who giggled. "We don't want Bobo to get a tummy ache, do we?"

"We certainly don't," Freddy said and handed one fish each to Erin and Willie.

"Where should we stand?" Erin asked Willie.

"Right where you are is good," Freddy said.

Erin and Willie stood still, their fish-bearing arms outstretched. She bent over and whispered in Willie's ear. "I'll bet Bobo takes my fish first."

"No, mine first," he said, his face turning red, a toddler meltdown imminent.

Erin was amazed that Willie had lasted this long without a nap. She braced herself for the kid to find fault with whatever answer she gave.

"Okay, okay. I'll put my arm down. You can give Bobo your fish first." Erin lowered her arm, the fish still squirming in her hand.

Willie smiled and waited for Bobo to approach. The bird seemed to be focused on something in the distance. Erin looked around but didn't see any other fishing boats coming. Suddenly she saw it: another heron swooped in, usurping Bobo's position as Captain Fred's bird. Willie ducked, then ran down the dock, chasing after his "big boat bird."

"Feed Bobo! Feed Bobo!" He cried, waving the fish in the air. Erin couldn't decide whether the fish's tail flapping meant it was still alive or was simply flapping with the motion of Willie's frantic arm gestures.

"Willie, stop! Stop!" Erin gasped, her breath catching in her throat. He stopped, thank God, at the edge of the dock. "Come this way. Bobo turned around. He's flying this way." She pointed in the opposite direction. She hated lying but wanted him to take a few steps in her direction, away from potential disaster.

"No! Bobo goes that way." He spun around, his feet dangerously close to the demarcation between the dock and one of the deepest creeks on the Eastern Shore. He squeezed the fish in his chubby little hand.

Erin's first instinct was to sprint as if her life depended on it. But she also knew that the sound of her feet on the planks (some of them loose; she would need to talk to Landon's dad about that) might startle Willie and cause him to lose his balance. She shouldn't have left him alone in the family room while she answered her damned phone. If she hadn't left the room, Willie would never have had the chance to run out the door. And if he hadn't run out the door, she might have had the good sense to rummage through the garage in search of a tiny life jacket, which she suspected Landon—being a safety-conscious Navy SEAL—had tucked away somewhere.

Erin walked lightly toward Willie. She glanced at Captain Fred, hunched at his cleaning table, a group of seagulls hovering above the bits of fish guts popping and floating in and out of the spray from his hose. Freddy was oblivious that a three-year-old with a dead fish in his hand stood dangerously close to the water.

She continued walking toward Willie while she scanned the horizon for Bobo. *Ah, there he is.* The bird sat perched on a piling two piers to the left of where Willie stood. Bobo was happily preening himself, seemingly not interested in Willie's offering. Smart bird. Smart, smart bird. *Please, Bobo, stay put.* He might take Willie down with him if he tries to take the fish. *Please, Bobo, stay put. Stay put. Stay put.* She repeated the mantra to herself as she continued to make her way toward Willie.

"Fuck!" Erin slammed her hand against her mouth, horrified that she cursed loudly. The bird was now flying in the opposite direction. Willie turned and looked at her, then started running toward Bobo, his little eyes fixed on the bird and not paying attention to where he was on the narrow dock. Erin sprinted, but she couldn't reach Willie before he ran right off the end of the pier, hitting the water with a thud, the fish launching in an arc and landing with a much smaller plop several feet away.

"Holy shit!" Captain Fred's voice was the last sound she heard before jumping off the dock.

THE FIRST THING Erin noticed when she hit the water was how heavy Doris felt. Innately, she knew she wouldn't be able to slice her way through the water in her running shoes or wearing Doris. Keeping her eyes on Willie, she used the heel of Doris to pry her running shoe off of her real foot. She repeated the process on the other side until both feet were free. Within seconds, she was gliding toward Willie, Doris surprisingly weightless in the water.

She had never swum with her faithful companion before and wondered if Doris might slip off. Erin spotted Willie and quickly forgot about her fake leg. He appeared to be standing upright—impossible, given the depth of the water—the top of his head visible and tilted back, his little mouth agape. That he wasn't yelling, wasn't crying, wasn't still trying to go after that damned bird was a bad sign.

"Are you okay?" Freddy teetered on the edge of the dock, life ring in hand. He tossed the ring into the water, the rope too short to reach her.

Erin ignored him and kept swimming toward Willie, confident that once she had an arm around him, she would be able to make her way back to the dock. She tried to remember which side the ladder was on to keep her mind from panicking as she approached her target.

"Willie! I'm right here. I'm going to help you." Despite her best effort to keep her voice calm, it cracked. She was close enough now to see him thrashing. She swallowed her rising panic, and swam breast stroke the rest of the way until she was within arm's reach. She grabbed him around the waist just as his face began to sink under the water.

20

L andon helped his dad unload the truck. They had stopped at Martin's on the way home to pick up steaks to grill tonight. Landon texted Susan and told her to come by for dinner if she wanted. He felt terribly guilty for leading her on with that kiss and planned to make it up to her with a friendly, G-rated family dinner. Okay, PG-rated, but only because beer and wine would be involved. But no kisses, no playing footsie under the table, no wistful longing glances. Not that there had ever been footsie under the table with Susan, but she tended to shoot him those damned glances. And even though he wasn't in love with her and never would be, those glances had a habit of stirring up longings that he didn't need in his life. He had enough on his plate, raising Willie alone as an active-duty Navy SEAL.

Landon caught of glimpse of Willie standing by the boat. "Dad, do you mind if I—"

"What are you waiting for? Go relieve Erin of her babysitting duties. I've got this."

He smiled as he trotted toward the docks toward his son, hoping Freddy had saved a few fish for him too. One of his and Willie's favorite routines over the past two weeks was waiting for Captain

Fred to show up with minnows to feed Bobo. His phone buzzed, and he paused to answer it.

"What time?" Susan's voice was perky, full of hopeful anticipation.

"What time, what?" Landon suddenly wished he hadn't texted her about coming over and hoped she was calling to say she couldn't come.

"You invited me over for dinner, silly."

"Oh, that." Landon forced a laugh. Any hope he'd had of her canceling was gone.

"Come by at six."

"I'm free now." She paused as if waiting for Landon to tell her to come over early. "Anyway, maybe I'll see you before six, and I'll bring dessert."

"Sure." Landon's eye caught something subtle on the dock, something not entirely wrong but not quite right. He hung up.

LANDON DIDN'T KNOW why he was in the water, fully clothed, or how he had gotten there. He swam as fast as he could toward an orange life ring that bobbed in subtle waves that hadn't been there a few minutes ago. Freddy was visible in his peripheral vision, yelling and waving and pointing. His loud voice billowed and carried over the water, yet Landon couldn't make out his words.

He kept swimming, unsure of what he was after. Whatever it was, he had a feeling it wasn't good. He instinctively grabbed the ring and kept swimming, ignoring the burning in his lungs. He was in excellent swimming shape; he had been swimming to the lighthouse and back—a little over two miles roundtrip—at least every other day since he's been home. So, the burning lungs made no sense other than a manifestation of the sheer panic rising in his body, turning his limbs into lead. He saw two heads—an adult and a child.

Grabbing onto the life ring for support, he frog-kicked with his leaden legs the rest of the way. Landon imagined telling Erin about this—his crazy, unexpected rescue—and hoped that she could give him answers about what had happened. Surely, standing on the docks with Captain Fred, she would have seen what had happened. He figured Willie was on the fishing boat, talking nonstop and oblivious that his daddy was swimming in the creek.

As he worked his way toward the two heads, his fantasy of dragging two random people back to the dock amid cheers and hugs and maybe even a case of beer brought in by the husband or wife of the bigger of the two heads shattered. He recognized both, yet his brain continued to play tricks on him. It wasn't until two pairs of terrified eyes locked on his that he began to fall apart.

"What happened? What happened!" Landon immediately felt like an idiot for asking the only question that popped into his head. It was like demanding someone high on drugs tell you what they had taken. As if they could string together two words, let alone a pharmaceutical list. Stupid, stupid, stupid of him to ask a person struggling in the open water what happened. What happened didn't matter. Treading water with his feet, he pushed the ring toward Erin. "Hold on! Hold on! Hold on!"

"I have him." Erin's voice was a barely audible, mere squeak. She was treading water herself, holding Willie up, trying to keep his head above water. "I can't let go of him."

Landon's brain kicked into sharp focus. His instinct was to grab Willie around the waist, freeing Erin's hands so she could hold onto the life ring. The only chink in this seemingly rock-solid plan was someone would need to take the rope and swim, towing the life ring with Willie and Erin holding on. He knew Erin was a strong swimmer. And while track and cross country prevented her from competing on the high school swim team, she could have beat any of their classmates in the pool or in the river. Damn. Maybe if she had focused on swimming instead of running, him blowing her leg off would have had no bearing on any scholarship she may have won. And she would have won a swimming scholarship; she was that good. But Landon knew from his Navy experience that fatigue sets in quickly for someone trying not to drown. Not to mention her arms were probably numb from holding Willie up.

"Daddy!"

"You're doing great, buddy. Keep holding onto Erin." Landon reached for the life ring, but it had drifted with the current and was several yards away. "I'll be right back."

Landon put his head down and swam as fast as he could. In the pool, he could swim twenty-five yards in twenty seconds. He counted his strokes until he reached the life ring to keep his breathing steady. Fifteen. He fished under the water for the rope, wrapped it around his wrist, and counted fifteen strokes back to Erin and Willie. Only they weren't where he had left them. Treading water, he scanned the area, swiveling his head right and left. His heart pounded against his chest so hard that he thought he might die. He took a deep breath and struggled to get air into his lungs.

"Daddy!"

Daddy. A single word, the sound of music, billowing from behind. *Daddy.* The most beautiful sounds Landon had ever experienced. When Willie had said *Da-Da-Da-Da* for the first time while pointing at Landon, well, if his heart could have exploded from too much love, it would have. Over the next few months, *Da-Da-Da-Da* morphed into *Da-Da* and eventually *Daddy.* Most of the time, when Landon looked at Willie, he was awestruck that he was a father. Overwhelmed that such a beautiful little creature shared his DNA. Today, treading water in a rescue attempt, *Daddy* took on a whole new meaning.

Landon turned around at the sound of his son's voice. His body—on high alert since he dove into the creek—relaxed. Holding onto the life ring for support, he wrapped the rope around his waist, securing it with a bowline knot. That he had the mental acuity to remember how to tie a bowline under duress was nothing short of a miracle. That Willie hadn't drowned was also a miracle. He needed to get to the bottom of what had happened, how Willie and Erin ended up in the water in the first place. There was time for that later. For now, his sole focus was getting them to solid ground.

"I'm going to slide the ring over your head," he said to Erin, who nodded, her face contorted in pain, effort, and exhaustion. "Just hang onto him, please." She nodded again, her teeth chattering, bending her neck into the hole. A second later, she was safely inside the ring, helping Willie guide his arms into position, sighing audibly to be free from the load she had been carrying.

"Daddy." Willie's lips quivered, and massive tears escaped his eyes. "Daddy."

"Daddy is going to swim like a dolphin," Landon said, his voice light and full of adventure. He knew it was a long shot, knew Willie was scared. Willie loved the water but had never had an accident. While he didn't see it happen, Landon was sure this had been an accident. Erin would tell him everything. Hopefully. "You hold onto the ring and listen to Erin. If she tells you to do something, you do it." He winked at Erin, who stared at him blankly. *She's just tired*, he told himself. *Probably a bit shell-shocked too.*

"WHAT IS IT?" Landon's heart raced, looking at Erin. Her face was bright red, and she seemed out of it, like she was in a trance. When she didn't respond, he tried reassuring her. "It's okay. We're safe," he said as gently as possible. He knew basic first aid—he was a Navy SEAL, after all—and should be able to clearly assess the issue. He ran through a litany of potential problems: heart attack, stroke, shock, hypothermia, hypoxia, a panic attack. None of the options he listed in his mind seemed to make sense. Erin was young and healthy, and while a heart attack or stroke was certainly possible at her age, it was doubtful. Probably not hypothermia, either, as the water felt like a comfortable seventy-eight degrees. Nothing like the icy ocean water in Coronado.

Of all the painful training drills his team regularly performed, the ones he hated the most involved running across the beach and diving into the frigid waves. He shuddered, thinking about it. If Erin was hypothermic, the skin around her lips would likely be blue by now. So, scratch that. Hypoxia? Scratch that too. She had been upright in the water, holding Willie above the surface. Things would have gotten bad quickly if she had been unable to breathe. The most likely scenario had to be either shock or a panic attack. Shock, he could understand. A panic attack was not likely, because the danger was clearly over. The three of them huddled in the shallow water, a hundred yards from the dock where Freddy's boat was tied. Willie was in the middle, seemingly stuck in some weird, suspended animation.

"Is the lady sick?" Willie's voice was a small, apprehensive. "The lady is a superhero." His voice grew louder. "Spiderman Lady!"

Landon lifted Willie up and hugged him, then pointed toward the small beach where he and Erin used to play when they were kids. "Go sit over there and wait for me. I want to make sure Erin is okay."

"Is Spiderman Lady sick?" Willie asked again, his voice quivering.

"I don't think so, buddy." Landon hoped with all his heart that he wasn't lying. "I think she's just very tired from rescuing you." He smiled and mussed up Willie's hair. "Now, please do as you're told and sit over on the beach." He conjured his not-so-convincing serious dad face. "Please do not move or go anywhere. I will come get you in a minute, and we will go to Puppy's house and have a bath."

"But I already had a bath." He giggled. "A big river bath." A serious look fell over his face. "I dropped Bobo's fish."

"That's okay, buddy. Bobo has plenty of fish to eat. We'll try again tomorrow, okay?" Willie nodded. "Now, go sit on the beach, please."

"Aye-aye," Willie said, laughing. He turned around and ran for the beach.

With Willie safely on the beach, Landon turned back toward Erin, who looked no better but no worse. He took her hand and pressed two fingers into her wrist. Her heart rate seemed high. He moved closer to her, the water lapping around their ankles. A sea nettle brushed against his toe. *Strange*, he thought. *This is the first nettle I've seen since I've been home.* He remembered his dad telling him that it had been a stormy spring, changing the salinity of the water, making it less hospitable to the jellyfish. Only three times during his life had that happened. Here it was, the middle of August, and the little pests were just beginning to arrive.

He leaned in and pressed his fingers into Erin's neck as if somehow her heart rate would register differently there. Still rapid. Too rapid. He put both arms around her and rested his ear on her chest, unsure what he was looking for. The little hairs on his neck stood at attention; her heart was beating so fast and hard. This couldn't be good.

"Erin." He shook her gently, then with a little more urgency. He held her close, not sure what else to do. He stepped on something bulbous and slimy—another sea nettle. *Wait a minute. Sea nettles. Jellyfish.* "Holy shit." How had he not figured this out sooner? The damned jellyfish. His mind raced backward when he and Erin were kids playing in the shallow water behind her house. She got stung and turned red, then blue. Her mother pumped her full of Benadryl. "Erin! Say something!" He studied her face, which, thankfully, hadn't blown up like it had that day when they were kids.

"I'm okay." She choked the words out, then took a huge breath. "I think I might have gotten stung. I'm a little shaky, though."

The relief Landon felt brought unexpected tears to his eyes. Aside from his relief a few minutes ago when Willie called out for him, he had never been so relieved. He held her close—to alleviate her shakiness, he told himself—and felt her heart rate slow. He stood like that until he could no longer feel her heart beating through her chest.

"Deep breaths," he said, unsure if he meant it for Erin or himself. "Just keep breathing." He pulled her in tighter. "You're doing great. Deep breaths. There you go. Deep, deep breaths."

21

"What the hell is going on here?" Susan ran through the water, her feet splashing, sending angry geysers spewing dirt and water with each step.

Landon jumped, cringing at Susan's frantic, high-pitched voice. She could have auditioned for *Alvin and the Chipmunks* and gotten a part. He could understand the urgency if he had still been out in the deep part of the creek. But now, here on solid, albeit silty, ground, there was no need for such commotion. He was about to tell her to calm the fuck down but stopped himself when he realized what this might look like—two young lovers embracing in the water. *If only*. He let go of Erin and held out his hands, stop-sign style.

"She's allergic to jellyfish!"

"And that's why you're hugging her like you just finished making—"

"Susan! Go find my dad. Ask him if he has any Benadryl."

Susan snapped to attention as if she was just now beginning to realize that Landon wasn't messing around—with Erin or the information he was providing. She ran toward the house, tripping once and catching herself before she did a face plant in the dirt. Landon shook his head and glanced at Willie, who was, thankfully, still sitting on the beach just like he told him to. He turned his attention back to Erin.

"What was that all about," Erin said, her voice gravelly, her body more unstable. Landon took her hands and squeezed them, lingering longer than he should have. She shook herself loose and took a few steps toward the shore where Willie was sitting, wavering and losing her balance. Landon's arm jutted out like a giant strap and wrapped itself around her waist, steadying her, helping her take one step, then another toward the beach.

"I think she thinks we—"

"Oh my God! Why would she think that?"

Landon shrugged, forcing a laugh, hoping his heart plopping out of his chest and into the water didn't make too big of a splash. She might as well have punched him in the face or poured a bucket of ice over his head. *What the hell was I thinking?* He wasn't thinking; that was the problem. He got caught up in being so close to Erin, rescuing her from rescuing Willie. The fact that she had jumped into the water after Willie was a whole other bag of puzzle pieces he would need to pull out and try to put together. Not that she had jumped in after him —anyone would have done that. He wanted to know why Willie was in the water, to begin with. Freddy could tell him what had happened or why Willie hadn't been wearing his life jacket. Why did Erin let Willie run around the docks without a life jacket? Wouldn't it be obvious that a three-year-old needed to be in a life jacket around the water?

Who am I trying to fool? Landon knew precisely what the puzzle pieces in the bag were about, and they were not about life jackets or even about Willie. They were about the way Erin's body felt next to his. Not just the physical sensation of having found his heart's missing puzzle piece, but all the feelings he had buried for the past twenty years. How did he bust open an iron safe with multiple locks? He didn't think it was possible.

"You two okay over there?" Captain Fred stood on the beach next to Willie. "Miss Conrad is quite the hero."

"What was he doing on the docks without a life jacket?" Landon addressed Erin with possibly a bit more tone than he had intended. He needed to steer himself back to reality, and reality, sadly, didn't include Erin. She had a boyfriend—a cardiologist! And he had a team of Navy SEALS waiting for him back in Coronado.

Erin plopped onto the sand and brought her knees to her chest and hugged them. "I'm sorry." Her voice was barely audible. "We were in the family room watching TV. My phone rang in the kitchen, and I stepped out to take it. When I returned a minute later, the sliding glass door was wide open, and Willie was on the dock getting fish from Freddy." She held out her hands, which were shaking wildly.

Landon felt like a complete ass. He took her hands. "I'm sorry, I didn't mean to sound harsh." He turned his attention to Willie. "You know you're not supposed to be near the water without your life jacket."

"If I had known where it was—"

"Stop. It's okay," Landon said to Erin as he shook his finger at Willie. "He knows where his life jacket is. Don't you, buddy?" Willie nodded. "Tell Erin where it is."

"On the hook."

"It's on the hook in the mudroom." Landon shook his head. "He knows this."

"He's three." Erin exhaled. "He was trying to tell me about Bobo, and I had no idea what he was talking about, then I got distracted with my phone." She hung her head. "I'm really sorry."

"I'm sorry, Daddy." Willie padded over to Landon and threw his arms around him.

"It's all over now. It's okay. You're safe, and that's all that matters." Landon made a fist and held it out to Willie, who made his own little fist and bumped it against his daddy's.

"I DON'T EVEN WANT to know how you got into this mess, but here you go." Ed Shultz towered over Erin, who was still sitting in the sand. He was carrying a reusable grocery store bag covered with cartoon-like images of avocados and limes, with the store's logo zigzagging around the pictures. Susan trailed behind, stopping to sit in the sand next to Willie.

"What in God's name possessed you to go for a swim in the creek, knowing how allergic you are to sea nettles?" He addressed Erin and set the bag down. He pulled out a bottle of vinegar, shaving cream, baking soda, and a plastic tumbler. He looked at her artificial leg. "You might as well take that thing off. You don't want it smelling like vinegar, now, do you?"

"I, well, I'm okay, Mr. Shultz." She held out her hands. "They're not shaking as badly as they were earlier." She touched Doris (Landon still couldn't believe she named her fake leg). "It's already smelly from the river. A little vinegar might be good for it."

Ed touched her forehead. "Clammy." He opened the bottle of vinegar and held it to the sun. "Nice color, huh? My wife used to have me taking a teaspoon of this crap every day. Said it would improve my cholesterol levels." He rolled his eyes. "I've been looking for an excuse to pour this shit down the drain." He took her hands, helped her stand, and then looked over his shoulder at Landon. "Hold onto her, would you."

Landon stood behind her and placed his hands on her shoulders, but she wiggled out of his grip.

"I don't need help," she said, her voice clipped.

"Suit yourself," Ed said. "Any idea where you got stung?" Erin shook her head. He moved closer to Landon and lowered his voice. "What the hell were you thinking, leaving your son sitting on the beach while you go for a romantic swim?"

"I can hear you." Erin whipped around and glared at Landon. "It wasn't a romantic swim."

"Dad, she jumped in after Willie. You were in your own world when we got home. You didn't even notice all the commotion over by Freddy's boat."

"It's true," Captain Fred chimed in. Landon didn't realize Freddy was still there. "The kid ran after the heron and, well, plop! Miss Conrad was in the water after him in a split second."

"Spiderman Lady!" Willie ran around in circles with his arms outstretched. "Daddy, I'm hungry."

"Puppy is going to grill your favorite broccoli," Ed Shultz said, laughing.

"No broccoli! I want hot dogs!"

"Hot dogs? How about I grill some big, juicy mushrooms?"

"No mushrooms, Puppy! Hotdogs!"

"I think I would rather make cottage cheese with pickle juice!" Ed bent down and mussed Willie's hair. "Never mind. Hot dogs it is!

Landon enjoyed watching his dad interact with Willie. Eye-opening, in fact. Landon doesn't remember his dad ever teasing him like that. His earliest memories involved following his dad around the boat yard, handing him tools, and helping him fix small things in the machine shop. But his favorite activity was helping his dad open packages in the bait and tackle shop. Wiggly worms, lures, boat supplies of all ilk—from stainless steel screws to nautical-themed can Koozies—every package was like a present. His dad let him run around the store and find where things went, stacking them in front of the shelf until his dad wandered by and told him to go ahead and put them up.

When Landon got older, he went on towing runs with his dad. They always had a close relationship, yet he never remembered his dad being silly with him, the way people—his dad especially—were silly with little kids. Yet, Landon's awe and wonder at how his dad talked to and played with Willie paled compared to his frustration that Erin was sitting in the sand suffering while his dad screwed around. Timing was everything, and his dad's timing now was abysmal.

"Dad, don't you think we should be helping Erin instead of playing silly games about food?" He glanced at Susan, drawing pictures in the sand, while Willie seemed much more interested in watching what was happening with Spiderman Lady.

"I'm fine, really," Erin said. She tried to stand but sunk back down in the sand. "A little lightheaded. I probably just need to eat something."

"Let me look at you." He turned to Landon. "Help her up, please, and for God's sake, hold onto her. Don't let her fall."

Landon stood behind Erin and gently placed his hands under her arms. He lifted her to a standing position, astounded at how wobbly her legs were. *Like soggy strands of angel hair pasta*, he thought, remembering how she used to describe her legs after a cross-country meet. He held her up while Ed looked her over.

"Soggy strands of angel hair pasta," Landon said, barely audible, his face so close to Erin's that he could see the crusted salt in her hair. "Remember that?" She nodded, a tiny hint of a smile forming on her lips.

Susan cleared her throat loudly. "I have Benadryl here."

Landon was startled, then remembered he had told her to get some. "Great. Thanks."

"Dad, did you bring anything for her to take the meds with?"

"Quiet, I'm concentrating." Ed looked up at Erin. "Are you sure you don't remember where you got stung?"

"Dad! She was busy saving my son's life. I'm sure she doesn't recall how—"

"My ankle," Erin said weakly. "My calf." She coughed, then sunk back to the ground, with Landon guiding her. She hung her head between her knees. After a few seconds, she looked up. "I'm sorry. I'm just a little woozy."

"Give me the Benadryl," Landon said to Susan, holding out his arms and cupping his hands. "Just toss it to me." The box of pills flew like a missile aiming straight for his head. He ducked just before impact and plucked it out of the air. "Thanks." He smiled, not wanting to give Susan the satisfaction of acknowledging her apparent anger at the fact that he was helping Erin. He knew Susan would soften after Erin left, and they were alone on the back deck. The problem was that he didn't want Susan to soften. He wanted her to be angry enough to leave. Any desire on his part to spend the evening with her had long since evaporated.

He popped two pills out of the blister pack and turned to Erin. "Open your mouth." He placed the pills on her tongue. "Go ahead and swallow. I don't have any water to give you." She nodded and swallowed, wincing.

"Let's see what we have here," Ed said, lifting her leg. "Humph, this one looks red and splotchy." He poured vinegar on her leg, the smell strong in Landon's nostrils. "Hopefully, that doesn't burn too badly." He pulled a can of Barbasol from the bag and let it shoot out onto several spots on her leg. "Rub this in, would you? I'll be right back with some water from the creek." Tumbler in hand, he left Landon and Erin alone, Susan watching them like a hawk. Erin did as she was told and rubbed the shaving cream into her leg until it was all absorbed.

Ed returned with the water. He pulled a box of baking soda out of the bag and dumped some into the cup. He picked up a small piece of driftwood and stirred like a wizard mixing up a special elixir. He handed the cup to Erin and instructed her to slather it on her leg. "Really thick, please."

"Dad, shaving cream? Baking soda? Really? Are you just making this up as you go along?"

"We don't have any meat tenderizer in the house."

"So, you just randomly selected items from the pantry? What about the shaving cream? That's kind of incongruent with the rest of the stuff."

"Like I said, I don't keep meat tenderizer in the house." He shrugged. "I looked up alternatives on Google." Ed turned to Erin. "We're going to wait until it dries and gets crusty."

"Then what?" Landon's voice was clipped, his tone harsh. "I'm sorry, Dad, but this makes no sense."

"The first hit Google gave me was a medical site, and this is what it said to do." Ed wrapped both hands around Erin's foot and lifted her leg. He studied it, pressing the baking soda paste with his finger. "Well, I'll be damned. It's dry and crusty already."

"It makes no sense, Dad." Landon's frustration was palpable.

"Just hold on, would you?" Ed reached into his back pocket,

pulled out his wallet, opened it, and produced a credit card. He handed the card to Landon. "Scrape the mixture off her leg."

"Me?"

"Yes, you." Ed nudged his head toward Erin's leg. "Go ahead and scrape it off. Time is of the essence."

"Honestly, Dad, this is ridiculous, but whatever." Landon began at Erin's knee and dragged the credit card to the bottom of her ankle as gently as he could, leaving a smooth path on her leg like a freshly snow-shoveled sidewalk. He shook his head, mumbling the only words he seemed able to say. "This makes no sense."

"No, it doesn't. It doesn't make any sense at all." The unfamiliar voice cut through the scene like a streaker at a baseball game. Landon slowly turned, the unknown voice morphing into a sound he had heard before, one he wished would go away. The hand attached to the body attached to the voice snatched the credit card out of Landon's hand. "Would somebody please tell me what's going on here?"

Erin tried to get up but wobbled again and sat back down. "You're here." The smile plastered across her face made Landon's heart sink. So, she was happy to see the dweeb cardiologist. Why shouldn't she be? She loved him, didn't she? He looked at Susan, who was doing a great job keeping Willie entertained. Maybe she wouldn't be such a bad companion, after all. Susan looked up and caught Landon looking at her. She smiled and shrugged. Landon shrugged back.

"How about I take him inside," Susan said.

"Looks like she's in good hands with my dad and the doctor." Landon got up and walked toward Susan. "I'll go with you."

"Start the grill," Ed said, calling out to him.

Landon nodded and ran toward Willie, pretending to be a football player, stopping just shy of tackling him to the ground. Amid screams and giggles, Landon swooped him up in his arms, forever grateful to Erin for rescuing him. He had been teaching Willie about water safety in Coronado—he could doggie paddle halfway across a twenty-five-yard pool. But this was different. Very different. Landon doubted he would have been able to doggie paddle to safety, especially with the current. He looked over his shoulder and immediately regretted it. He put an arm around Susan and tried to unsee Erin kissing the cardiologist.

22

"You're here." Erin's voice was barely a whisper as she fell into Wes's arms. If she was ever happy to see him, it was right now, at this beautiful, horrible moment.

"Yes, you said that already." Wes laughed, holding her tightly. "It wasn't easy, but I found a way to take a few days off."

She pulled away slightly and looked at him, her peripheral vision catching a glimpse of Landon swatting Susan's butt as they walked into the house. Her heart sank a little, which she attributed to Wes's confusing words, not the intimacy between Landon and Susan. "I thought you already took the week off. I mean, I know you had to go in, but...I'm sorry. It was a rough day, and I'm not firing on all eight cylinders."

"Hey, calm down." He brushed Erin's cheek with the back of his hand, then ran his fingers through her hair. He lowered his voice. "I love you and want to be here with you the whole week, but, you know, I have this patient. And look, I wasn't even supposed to come today, remember? I found a way to get here."

"I know. I know." She scooted back a little and examined him. He looked freshly showered and was dressed in a pair of olive-green shorts and the white golf shirt that accentuated his sexy forearms.

"I wish I could help you understand how serious this surgery was."

"Of course, I understand." She shook her head. "You know I do. When have I ever given you a hard time about your work?" She took his hands. "Never."

"You're giving me a hard time now."

"How can you say that?" Her face grew hot, and she felt like she could throw up at any moment. She hung her head. "I'm sorry. I'm not at my best, and it's been a very long and frustrating day."

"That's the part I don't understand." He lifted her chin with his finger. When her face was level with his, he raised his eyebrows. "This was an odd and surprising scene to walk in on."

"I told you they were making me help them fix the boat."

"And I told you not to worry about the money, to just enjoy the time with your mother, not spend time fixing a boat—that's not even yours, I might add—with your ex-boyfriend."

"That's the point, Wes. It's not my boat. I can't send it back damaged. I wanted to, but the more I think about it, the more I realize it just isn't right." Unexpected and very unwelcome tears sprang from her eyes. She wrinkled her nose and swallowed, coughing on her next words, which she had great difficulty forming. "Landon and I never dated. We grew up together. Our families were best friends. We were like siblings." She bit her tongue, fearful of what she might say next. She chose her words carefully. "We haven't seen or talked to each other in twenty years, Wes. Please, whatever you're doing, stop." She gave in and let the tears flow freely. "Just stop."

THEY SAT FOR A LONG TIME, each lost in their thoughts. Erin noticed Ed's credit card lying in the dirt next to Wes's foot. She looked at her leg and ran her finger down the smooth surface where Landon had scraped away his dad's strange mixture. She almost burst out laughing from the absurdity of the whole thing and what it may have looked like in Wes's eyes.

She touched the rest of the cracked and crusty coating, which felt like the crackled top of perfectly baked brownies. She picked up the credit card and shoveled away at the rest, feeling more and more like herself with every passing second. She knew she needed to unpack the horror of seeing Willie fly over the dock's edge. Yet, now, she needed to normalize things with Wes, who was staring off into the distance, lost in whatever thoughts a cardiologist coming out of a touchy surgery would think about. Or whatever thoughts a boyfriend catching another man gently scraping her leg with a credit card might think. She cast off the baking soda mixture, letting the pieces fall to the ground, mixing them into the dirt with her fingers.

"I'm sorry," Erin said, breaking the impasse. She smiled.

"Me too." Wes continued staring into the distance. "I wanted to surprise you. My patient is stabilized now, in good hands in the ICU. I need to go back Monday, at the latest." He finally broke out of his blank distance-staring and looked at her. "Can we start over, please?" He wrapped his arms around her. "I missed you." He held her for a few seconds and pulled away. "I met your mother. She told me where to find you." He laughed. "Very nice lady. She tried to shove food in my face, but I told her I wanted to take you out to dinner tonight."

"Nonsense!" Ed Shultz popped out from behind the boat next to *Jolly Good Day*. "I got some beautiful steaks from Martin's and several nice bottles of Cabernet. "I'd be remiss if I didn't ask you love-birds to join us."

Erin stood, surprised at how wobbly she felt. She bent down and brushed her leg where the shaving cream and baking soda paste had been. The red blotches were still there—tiny little mounds already beginning to itch. Every time she had been stung, she had gotten dangerously close to anaphylaxis. True, she had felt abysmal, dizzy, clammy, nauseous, and flush. And yes, her heart rate had been through the roof. But this reaction was unlike previous jellyfish reactions, and she wondered if she really had been stung. More likely, her reaction was the stress of almost losing Willie.

Her mind flashed back to Landon and Susan walking back to the house with Willie, like a happy little family. What if her weakness and symptoms resulted from Landon's arms around her in the water? His face was so close that she could see the variation of colors in his eyes—the flecks of silver reflected from the sun on the water—and the unique colors of the tiny hairs poking out on his upper lip and chin. Nope! Nope! Nope! It wasn't a jellyfish, and it wasn't Landon. It was the adrenaline of jumping into the water after Willie. Swimming to reach him, holding him, and ensuring his face stayed above the surface. Fighting the current with only her legs—one of which was fake and weighed about three pounds.

"Thank you, Mr. Shultz, but it's been a long day. A crazy long day." Erin made circles with her arms, wincing in pain, figuring her shoulders would be sore for days. "I'd like to go home and shower, then have a nice quiet evening with my mother and boyfriend." She took Wes's hand and smiled.

"Oh, now, we haven't been properly introduced." Ed shoved his hand at Wes. "Ed Shultz here. This is my boatyard. Wes took his hand and pumped it three times. "Nice firm handshake, smooth hands, though."

Erin blushed. She didn't remember the Ed Shultz of her childhood lacking in filters to this degree. Commenting on the texture of another man's skin? She touched her cheek. Yep. Hot, just as she figured. "He's a cardiologist." She observed Ed for his reaction but was disappointed by his poker face. "At Johns Hopkins," she threw in for good measure.

"Nice to make your acquaintance, Doctor, um, I didn't get your name."

"Wes. Wes Rubin."

"Ha! Like the sandwich!" He turned away from Wes and addressed Erin. "Won't you reconsider staying for dinner? It's been such a long time. And you're a celebrity now." He took a step closer to Wes and leaned in. "This one here was like a daughter to us. I'm still irritated she stayed away for so long." He clapped his hands together once, quite loudly, and Erin jumped. "Now that she's here, we don't want to let her go so easily. Oh, and did you know she saved my grandkid's life?"

Wes shrugged, then looked at Erin. "It's a long story, Wes." She squeezed his hand. "I'll tell you everything after I shower and have a glass of wine."

"You can shower right here," Ed chimed in. "She jumped right off the dock after Willie and saved him from drowning." He turned to Erin. "I talked to Freddy. He watched the whole thing unfold." He took a deep breath. "I'm forever grateful."

Erin blushed again. She didn't have the strength to unpack Ed's comment about being forever grateful. She had to remind herself that this was a man her parents had refused to talk to after the fireworks accident many years ago, essentially poisoning her perception of the entire family. And here he was, acting like none of that had ever happened. After twenty years, it might as well have never happened. She looked down at her dirt-encrusted pants, her shirt splotched with the brown remnants of brackish water.

"My clothes are so grody." Her resolve was waning, mainly because, in her imagination, she could smell the lighter fluid that Landon was pouring over the charcoal briquettes and, later, the intoxicating smell of steaks on the grill. She wondered what Susan would think of her and Wes staying for dinner. Probably not much. Not much at all. She looked at Wes, making circles in the dirt with his shoe and being surprisingly quiet and noncommittal.

"You're feeling better, though, right?" Ed nodded for her. "Look, I kept some of Jo's things. She was about your size."

Wes cleared his throat, finally finding his voice. "Honey, I was hoping we could have a quiet evening."

Erin slowly, gradually, came back to reality. The only good thing about having dinner with Ed and Landon (and Susan) would be to show Landon how happy she and Wes were. She wasn't even sure why she felt like she needed to do that. Any vibes coming off Landon were all in her head, and he seemed perfectly content with Susan. She again reminded herself of the scene just a little while ago. Landon holding Willie, Susan beside him, walking into the house as if they had just spent a lovely, tiring day at the beach. But, most importantly, Erin wanted no part of wearing anything that had once belonged to Landon's mother. She needed to get this awkward moment over with, and she needed to do it soon.

"I'm sorry about your wife, Mr. Shultz." The embarrassment she felt over the fact that she hadn't come home for the funeral would likely be forever implanted in how her brain perceived Ed's opinion of her. Of her whole family, really. It was bad enough that her family judged and harshly punished the Shultz's over the fireworks incident. The least they could have done—all of them—was to acknowledge Joelle's death. She hung her head. "I really and truly am sorry."

23

"What was that back there?" Wes opened the trunk of his Acura and pulled a towel out of the gym bag he kept in there, ready to go, in case he needed to sleep at the hospital. He handed Erin the towel.

"What was what back where?" Erin opened the passenger door and set her camelback and pile of crumpled running clothes on the floor behind the seat. It was only then that she remembered her sneakers were at the bottom of the creek. If she wanted to do any running during this debacle of a vacation, she would need to have Wes (or her mother) drive her into St. Michaels or Easton for a new pair.

"You know what." He pointed toward the row of boats on jack stands, *Jolly Good Day*, and the four-foot hole among them. "What are you not telling me?"

"Actually, I don't know what you're talking about. And I'm not, 'not telling' you anything." As happy as she was to see him, Wes's demeanor bordered on jealousy and control. He had nothing to worry about, but she was not about to give in and admit any wrong-doing or apologize for a crime she had clearly not committed. She looked at the towel draped over her arm. "What am I supposed to do with this?"

"Never mind." He yanked the towel away and spread it across the passenger seat. "There. Now you can get in."

"What? I'm not clean enough for your precious leather upholstery?" Erin didn't like that she was taking his bait. She was being argumentative for no reason other than she was tired, hungry, still a bit woozy from the sea nettles, and very much still shaken up from Willie almost drowning when she was supposed to be watching him. She felt like a failure.

She replayed the look on Landon's face when he first reached her and Willie in the water; she couldn't quite place the emotion she had read in his eyes or on his grimace. Confusion? Anger? But then...then...after Willie was safe and she was falling apart, his face said something else entirely. His face was close enough that she tasted (without licking him) the salt from the water mingling with the salt from his sweat—the taste of her childhood. She closed her eyes tightly and willed the image away.

"I'm sorry, Wes. I'm a bit out of sorts right now." She smoothed the towel with her hands and climbed into the Acura.

"I have the perfect remedy." He smiled and closed the door, apparently deciding to, as he sometimes said, press the reset button on their reunion. Poof. Just like that. He climbed in and fastened his seatbelt. "Fries."

"Fries?" Erin's eyes lit up, and she smiled. She supposed pressing the reset button wasn't such a bad idea. Proud of herself for not giving in to his inquisition a few minutes ago, she embraced the reality that he had surprised her by arranging his schedule to come down earlier than she had thought. "Rupert's has the best." She pointed. "Just up the road, right there. Turn left."

Erin tried not to think about Susan playing family with Landon as she and Wes sat on the patio at Rupert's, scarfing down a double order of fries and sipping beer. A cool breeze off the water replaced the day's heat and humidity.

She poked through the plate of fries, searching for the crispiest ones—a habit that had fascinated Wes at first but now simply annoys him. He has learned, though, not to hound her about it. *I don't do it in polite company, only with you* was her most common refrain. And he would volley back with some version of, *so, I'm not polite company?* And then she would hug him, plant a passionate kiss on his lips, and say, *I don't kiss polite company.* Usually, they ended up laughing.

This afternoon, however, Wes seemed off somewhere, not present, not even raising an eyebrow at the French fry excavation, the promise of good cheer evaporating with every crispy fry she plucked out of the pile. She set her treasures aside, wondering what Wes was thinking about. She pulled a big, fat fry off the top of the pile, dipped it in ketchup, and waved it in front of him. He took it from her and stuck it in his mouth.

"Where are you?" Elbows on the table, she rested her chin in her hands and searched his eyes.

He came into focus as if waking from a deep sleep. "Just thinking about work."

She raised an eyebrow. "Usually, when you think about work, you have your nose in your phone." She rubbed his arm. "Seriously, what's wrong."

"Nothing." A pair of seagulls swooped in, eyes on the fries, then thought better of it and aborted their approach. Wes picked up a fry and held it out. The bolder of the two birds came rushing back, furtively grabbing the fry with his beak before flying away. Other seagulls came from out of nowhere. Wes grabbed another fry and held it out.

"Stop!" Erin slapped his hand, sending the fry tumbling onto the patio, where it sat for approximately two seconds before five seagulls jockeyed and squawked for the prized possession. "Do you want to get us thrown out of here?"

"Since when is it a crime to feed birds?"

"Seagulls learn quickly. They've been known to land on the tables and steal packets of crackers."

Wes shrugged. "So, what's next on the agenda?"

"What agenda?"

He looked at his watch. "Did you have anything in mind for tonight?"

"What are you talking about? I didn't even know you were here until an hour ago." She took a deep breath and exhaled slowly. "Are you okay?"

"I'm sorry." He took her hands. "I'm worried about my patient." He looked away. "And you seem distracted."

"Me?"

"Yes, you."

Erin considered his statement; she could interpret it in several ways. She decided to go for the low-hanging fruit and be truthful.

"A little boy almost drowned today. A little boy who was in my care." Her breath caught in her throat. She tried to distract herself with a sip of beer but ended up swallowing it funny and coughing into her elbow. She cleared her throat. "You can't let anyone see you cough these days." She looked at Wes, the indifference on his face palpable, her attempt at humor falling flat. She didn't understand his lack of empathy for what she had been through today. This was so unlike him. She blinked back tears, but the gates of her eyelids could only hold the flood back for so long. She felt his arm around her shoulders, pulling her close. Instead of his comforting gesture helping, it made her cry even more as she struggled to reconcile his odd countenance with his loving embrace.

After a long time, Erin lifted her head from Wes's shoulder. Thank God no one approached the table while she was crying.

"Doing better?" Wes stretched, rolling his neck from side to side and lifting his arms above his head. "What happened out there, anyway."

"You didn't see it?" It suddenly occurred to Erin that she had no idea how long Wes had been at the boatyard this afternoon or what, exactly, he saw. "You didn't see me jump in the water after Willie?"

"Willie?"

"Landon's son." Erin rolled her eyes, frustrated by this conversation.

"Landon? Oh. Landon. Landon Shultz of Shultz Towing." He smiled and shook his head. "I didn't make the connection. You knew him from before." She nodded. "And you were helping fix the boat, but the kid fell in the water, and you rescued him." She nodded again. "So, why didn't Landon Shultz of Shultz towing save his son?"

"Because he wasn't there."

"He was there. I saw him." Wes knit his brow as if he didn't believe her. "You were already out of the water. But he was wet too like he had jumped in."

"Landon jumped into the creek, Wes." Erin felt her face grow hot, and her already swollen eyes fill. Damned tears. She willed her eyes to reabsorb them, and much to her surprise, her eyes complied. "He saved both me and Willie. I was struggling to keep Willie's face out of the water."

"I'm so sorry, babe. I didn't realize." He reached under the table and touched her leg. "And then you got stung."

"Yep. I truly wasn't thinking about jellyfish when I jumped in. I had one and only one thing on my mind." She shook her head. "Willie was watching TV, and I left the room for less than a minute to take a call from my mother. The next thing I knew, he was outside, running to meet the fishing boat so he could give scrap fish to a great blue heron. He lost his balance and went in."

"The water is deep there, then?"

"Very deep."

"Why didn't the fisherman help?" Wes raised an eyebrow. "Surely he had a flotation device or something."

"Stop." She pulled away from him. "Please, please, stop." She glared at him. "Why are you doing this?"

"Doing what?"

She threw a fry at him. "The Spanish Inquisition."

"Oh, come on." He laughed and threw the fry right back at her. He took a swig of his beer, then set it down and ran his fingers through his hair. He picked up the fry, dipped it in ketchup, and shoved it in his mouth. He took a deep breath. "I'm sorry. I am distracted by my patient, but there's something else."

Erin's heart popped out of her chest and fell to the ground. She began to hyperventilate as she braced herself for a breakup speech. She didn't see this coming. How could she have missed the signs? She could usually tell when something was bothering him, and, until today, nothing in his demeanor raised any red flags. As a matter of fact, they had been quite passionate with each other a few nights before the *Jolly Good Day* sailboat debacle.

"I never want to be one of those guys," Wes continued, "but I didn't like how your old friend was looking at you." He shook his head and chuckled. "It made me a little jealous." He covered his face with his hands and peeked at her between two fingers. "I guess that means I really do love you." He burst out laughing. "Seriously. I. Love. You."

Erin took a massive gulp of air, relieved that it filled her lungs. Her happy heart flung itself off the ground and back into her chest, where it started to resume beating. She threw her head back and joined in Wes's laughter. She knew there had to be a logical explanation for his odd behavior. Why in the world did she suspect the worst? Why did she think—based on nothing more than her cardiologist boyfriend being distracted after having performed a complicated open-heart surgery—that his distraction and aloofness meant he was breaking up with her? She promised herself that she would dig deep and figure it out later. For now, there were fries to eat and beer to drink.

24

Erin texted her mother and told her not to worry about dinner; she and Wes would fend for themselves. Holding hands in the car, they pulled out of Rupert's parking lot and onto Moss Street. There were a few things she wanted to show him, but first, she wanted to see her old house. Not because she had any great desire for him to see it, but because her mother had mentioned that it was listed for sale. Her mother had driven by a few weeks ago and reported that the house was vacant. Unlike many people she knew, Erin was not sentimental about the places she had lived. Yes, there were many happy memories in that old house by the water. But some sad ones too. Like the year after high school when she lugged herself to and from Chesapeake College instead of enjoying her freshman year in Washington, DC. And then Landon joined the Navy. Not that she had wanted to see Landon during that lonely year —she didn't. Or at least that's what she had told herself.

There was one part of the house she was curious about—the treehouse. Her father had built it for her during a weekend, and the following weekend she helped him paint the walls purple and lime green, her favorites at the time. Erin was already living on her own in

Baltimore when her parents sold the house and bought the B&B. They had packed everything in the treehouse except the ratty old couch, which had been a hand-me-down from her grandmother. She also had a few floor pillows, a lantern, books, and a selection of her cross-country medals, which hung from a deer antler that Landon had found and brought over one Saturday.

She remembered her father asking over a FaceTime call if she wanted to keep the antler. *Just throw the damned thing away*, she had said. And in response to her father's raised eyebrow: *What? That silly antler means nothing to me.* She remembered finding it strange that her father would ask about the antler or even care that it was something Landon had given her. Because, as far as her parents were concerned —even after all those years—Landon was, and always would be, persona non grata.

Erin wondered now if her father had been trying to tell her something. If so, she would never know what his message had been. Her father's death was another area of her life that she needed to sit down and unpack. Sometimes she had to remind herself that he was gone. It just didn't seem possible; he had been so alive. Immortal. Larger than life.

She knew, in her heart of hearts, that she hadn't even begun the grieving process. She feared she was due for a complete and utter breakdown. And now, with what had happened this afternoon with Willie—what could have happened, what almost happened—it might be time, finally, to swallow her pride and talk to someone. She kept a list of therapists on her laptop and promised herself she would call at least one when she got home.

"THE TURN IS COMING UP." She let go of Wes's hand and sat up in her seat. "Here it is! Right here!" She pointed. "Make this next left." Her eyes darted around, taking in the treelined gravel road leading to the old house. Wait a minute. The gravel road was no longer gravel. "I'll be damned," she muttered under her breath. She turned to Wes. "Everything is different. The verge of the woods looks neatly manicured."

"It's pretty back here," Wes said. "Peaceful. I could see why you loved growing up here." A sliver of water on the horizon grew bigger and bigger as the Acura crept farther down the road.

"I wouldn't give up my childhood for anything." Erin grew wistful as she said the words, the unhappy times of her last few years here fading as the happy times from the past vied for position at the forefront of her memory.

She saw the *For Sale* sign first. Then the mailbox came into view, the house number etched into the wooden post—another of her father's artistic creations. She could barely contain her excitement. "Here it is! Right here!" She squeezed Wes's hand as he pulled into the long driveway. She instructed him to park in front of the barn. She unhooked her seatbelt and climbed out.

"Are you sure this is okay?" Wes said as he gently closed his door. "There are probably cameras everywhere."

"The house is clearly for sale." She made her way beyond the barn, up to the house, and onto the front porch. She cupped her hands on the living room window and looked inside. "And it's clearly vacant," she yelled to Wes, who was several yards behind her, scanning the property, taking it all in, and, if she knew Wes, he was silently searching for booby traps.

"I don't know about this." Wes opened the car door and slid back in. He rolled down the window. "This seems creepy."

Erin grew more frustrated by the minute. How could someone who sticks his fingers inside raw, open, and bleeding hearts, possibly feel squeamish about looking in the windows of a vacant house? One that was for sale. The most normal thing in the world would be for a couple to check out a place before even contacting the realtor to see it.

"If anyone asks, we could just say we're interested in the house." She thought about her statement, shook her head, and took a deep breath. "Come on, Wes. We're out in the middle of nowhere. Nobody is going to know, and nobody is going to care." She opened his door, but he yanked it away and slammed it shut from the inside, waving at her as he rolled up the window. "Wimp!" She laughed and headed toward the barn.

"Just be careful," he yelled from inside the car.

Erin brushed Wes's concerns aside as she stood in front of the barn, remembering the last time she and her father worked on a project, about a year before her parents moved to the B&B. So trivial were the projects that she couldn't recall what they were. Could it have been the kid-sized wooden pirate ship—complete with wheels and a seat that opened for stowing important toys—he built for Sandy and Pam when she was pregnant the first time? How could he have known that Pam would miscarry?

Later, when Noah was born, her dad put it away for when his first grandchild got older. But then her dad had the nerve to die. Of Covid-19, of all things—two months before he was eligible to get vaccinated.

Erin had come home and visited her parents for three days during Christmas that first year of the pandemic, despite well-meaning friends (and her brother) urging her not to. She had gotten tested the Tuesday before and drove down from Baltimore Thursday morning after receiving word that her test was negative. She had even offered to wear a mask in the house when she wasn't eating or drinking, but her parents had poo-pooed the idea. Instead, they set up air purifiers around the house and, thanks to global warming, had the windows open most of the time.

During breakfast two days later, her dad complained about the coffee. Nobody ever complained about Lydia Conrad's coffee; Lydia's coffee was its own food group. The reviews B&B customers left on Google or Yelp always mentioned how good Lydia's coffee was. *The muffins were excellent, but, OMG, the coffee!* Even if the review was less than stellar—*narrow staircases, hard to navigate after a glass of wine* or *bed squeaked* or *ran out of hot water toward the end of a thirty-minute shower*—there was always a mention of the coffee and how it *turned an otherwise unpleasant stay* (the nerve!) *into something tolerable.*

"What do you mean the coffee is 'thin'?" Lydia had said. She was at the stove flipping pancakes when Erin walked into the kitchen wearing the flannel pink flamingo pajamas her mother had given her for Christmas just a few days before.

"Watery," Erin's father said. "Like the ratios are wrong. Something like that." He stared into his cup, taking his spoon and swirling the coffee as if the cream hadn't entirely incorporated the first time around. He held the mug to his lips, blew on it, then took a sip. He set the mug down and shook his head. "Thin."

"Oh, come on, Douglass. Stop messing around." Lydia took a deep breath. "Sweetheart, watch the griddle, please," she said to Erin, who was pouring her own coffee, determined to either agree or disagree with her dad.

Erin alternated watching bubbles form on the surface of the pancakes and watching her mother take a sip out of her dad's mug. "Tastes fine to me," she heard her mother say. Erin eased the spatula under a fully pocked pancake and flipped it, holding her breath, then exhaling in relief when she saw that it had turned the perfect golden-brown color. Most of her attempts to make pancakes ended in disaster, usually because she attempted to flip them too soon, resulting in volcanic lava oozing out of the top and the rest of the pancake stubbornly sticking to the griddle. She flipped the others—all equally lovely—counted to thirty, like her mother had taught her to do, then divided them onto three plates, still warm from the oven.

Standing in front of the barn, reliving the scene in the kitchen when her dad complained about the coffee, she hung on her mother's words: *Oh, come on, Douglass. Stop messing around.* Her mother never called her dad Douglass. Only when she was irritated. Or when he was playfully teasing her, and she wanted him to stop. Her mother's voice always had a lyrical tone when she called him Douglass. But not this time. Had it been foresight? Or a foreboding? The memory came back to her in bits and pieces.

"I didn't change anything. The beans are the same beans I've been using for the past ten years, and I ground them the same way I always do—very fine—and I used the same filtered water from the fridge door that I've been using to make coffee since we moved into this place."

Erin distributed the plates of pancakes around the table, then went back to the counter and poured herself a cup of coffee, determined to either stick up for her dad or have a coffee intervention with her mom. She laughed at the thought of an intervention, looking forward to siding with her dad, her eyes crinkling with imminent laughter until she took a sip, and well...it certainly wasn't "thin" and may have even tasted a little bit stronger than usual. Making her way to the table, she thought back to the spicy tuna they had eaten the night before.

"Maybe your tastebuds are still reeling from dinner last night." Erin studied her dad, who looked a little pale and a little worn around the edges. She knew it was a long shot that the spicy tuna impaired her dad's tastebuds. Seriously, she and her mom had eaten the same dinner, and neither of them complained about the coffee being thin. In fact, Erin had even gone to the fridge to get the bottle of sriracha sauce—much to her mother's chagrin—because the tuna wasn't spicy enough for her.

Erin slathered syrup on her pancakes and took a bite, savoring the taste of maple mingling with the smell of the cinnamon her mom always sprinkled into the batter. "The cinnamon smells great," she said, more as a test than a compliment or a complaint.

"That's probably it," her mother announced, ignoring the comment about the cinnamon and fixating on the spicy tuna explanation. Satisfied that the issue had come to a logical conclusion, she took a bite of her pancake. And then, as if Erin's comment about the cinnamon just registered in her brain, she mumbled about having added too much this time.

They ate in silence as Erin stole glances at her dad. She

watched him dunk a hunk of pancake into the glob of syrup on his plate. He held it up to his nose, sniffed, then shoved it in his mouth. The look of confusion and...panic(?)...in his eyes scared Erin. Pretending to be engrossed in her breakfast, she continued watching her dad.

You take ordinary smells and tastes for granted until you lose them, Wes had said during the getting-to-know-you phase of dating. Despite having been vaccinated, he had gotten Covid a month or so before they met. His symptoms had been mild—a headache and two days of fatigue—but the loss of his ability to taste the foods he loved or to smell the ordinary things of his life was almost as bad as not being able to breathe. Erin had been skeptical—how could not being able to smell or taste anything be akin to not breathing? *Try not talking to yourself,* Wes had said. Erin argued that she never spoke to herself. She sometimes did, when she was alone in her apartment; for example, she frequently talked back to the TV, or sometimes, to her houseplants. Wes explained that wasn't what he meant. He was refer- ring to the internal chatter, the endless loops running through her brain. *Just try to shut it off, even for a minute or two.* Erin did. And she tried again by herself the next day. Wes had been right: not hearing the constant chatter felt like not being able to breathe. And if losing your sense of taste and smell felt anything like it did to silence the chatter, Wes had been correct.

If her dad did, indeed, have Covid, was she the one who had brought it into the house? Erin pushed the thought away. She and her dad went for a jog earlier that morning, and he seemed fine. In fact, he kept ratcheting up the pace until Erin told him to go on ahead. When she finished the five miles (fifteen minutes slower than her dad), she found him panting on the porch.

Picking at a slice of bacon, she retraced her steps—reminding herself that she had tested negative just two days before.

"Are we out of cinnamon?" Doug stopped eating and looked at Lydia. He raised an eyebrow and smiled. "Or did you get distracted and forget to put it in?"

"Mom never forgets the cinnamon," Erin said, trying to keep her tone light. She turned to her mother and shrugged. "Maybe you didn't put in as much this time?"

"I most certainly did," Lydia shot back.

"Hmm." A look of puzzlement washed over Erin's dad's face. "Last night's tuna must have been spicier than I thought." He shook his head. "My taste buds are pretty much dead." He stood and carried his plate to the sink. "Come to think of it, I'm not feeling all that great." He returned to the table and kissed his wife on the top of her head. "I'm going to lay down."

Erin's mother stood and pressed her hand on his forehead. "Call Dr. Lamb," she said to Erin. "Tell him we think Doug has Covid." Two weeks later, Douglas Conrad was dead. Her strong, invincible dad. None of it made sense.

Damn you, Covid. Damn you. Her eyes filled with tears, blurring the barn, making it look like it was suspended underwater. Underwater. Willie. A little boy on her watch almost drowned. He almost drowned! But he didn't drown. What if Landon hadn't come home at the exact moment that he had? Would she have been able to swim while still trying to keep a frightened three-year-old's head above the water? She pressed the heel of each hand into her eye sockets and held them there until she stopped hyperventilating.

"You okay?" A voice cut through Erin's thoughts. She turned around to find Wes standing in front of her, creating a barrier between her and the barn and her memories. She rubbed her eyes.

"Just remembering my dad." She sniffed. "We spent a lot of time together in this barn."

Wes put his arms around her and squeezed. "I envy the relationship you had with him." He turned her around to face him and hugged her. "The only things my father and I did together were, well, never mind." He stroked her hair and took a couple of steps back. "Let's get back in the car and head to your mom's. You look like you could use a glass of wine and a nice hot bath."

Erin didn't want a hot bath or a glass of wine. She suddenly realized all she wanted was to be alone with her thoughts. If it wasn't getting so late, and if she wasn't so exhausted, oh, and if her running shoes weren't at the bottom of the creek—probably sinking deeper and deeper into the mud with each passing minute—she would insist he drive to the B&B without her. It was only a mile and a half away—an easy jog. She swatted at a mosquito on her arm. She had been so engrossed in her sadness and remembering that she hadn't noticed the mosquitos until now. She braced herself for a long night of itching and scratching.

"Come on. Let's head to your mom's. I don't know about you, but I'm hungry, even after all those fries." He took her hand and pulled her toward the Acura, but she resisted. "Come on, babe. The bugs are going to eat us alive."

"The damage is already done." She examined the exposed parts of her body, relieved to finally be finished crying. She felt around for any remaining lumps in her throat and squeezed her eyes shut to expel any straggler tears. Empty eyes, empty throat. Thank God. She exhaled, relieved. "Plus, there's one more thing I want to see since we're here." She nudged her head toward a massive oak tree with thick, sinewy branches creating a canopy that could shade the world. It was overgrown, and she couldn't exactly see the tree house through the leaves. She let go of Wes's hands and shuffled toward the tree's base, where the steps her dad had nailed to it begged to be climbed.

"Dammit, Erin. I need to pee."

"There is a multitude of trees to choose from." She laughed, feeling playful, and took the first step up the tree. "I spent a lot of time up here as a kid." She climbed two more rungs, remembering her dad widening them after the accident, so she could more easily climb the tree with her artificial leg. She glanced back at Wes, his arms crossed tightly over his chest, his face red and contorted.

"Let me guess. You and your dad built the tree house together."

"I'll only be a minute." She chose to ignore his snarky comment. It probably wasn't fair of her to do this to him, to make him wait while she took a long meandering stroll down memory lane. But they were here now, on the property, in the almost dusk. There was no better time. And while stopping to see her old house wasn't something she had planned to do during her trip here this week, it was all she wanted to do now.

Wes looked hopelessly frustrated. He uncrossed his arms, clasped his hands behind his head, then released them and lifted his arms up as far as he could stretch them. "Come on up with me. It's a cool place. Or at least it once was."

"No thanks." He shook his head and waved her away. "I'll be in the car."

THE TREE HOUSE was just as Erin remembered. She climbed the old ladder, wincing as the wooden rungs—rough, weather-worn, and splintered—dug into the skin on her bare foot. She wished she hadn't impulsively kicked off her sneakers when she was in the water trying to rescue Willie, but she had no other choice. It had been hard to keep his head above the surface, and adding wet shoes into the mix would have increased her exhaustion exponentially. She tried not to think about this afternoon's events as she took one rung at a time, planting her feet as gently as possible to avoid tearing her foot up. As usual, Doris was a trooper and didn't complain one bit.

By the time she reached the platform, she had snapped what felt like a million little branches, watching them flutter. It felt like a lifetime since her parents sold the house and moved to the B&B. She hadn't lingered the last time she was here, her purpose solely to clean out the inside of the tree house and remove everything she wanted to keep. In and out. No time for memories. No desire for memories.

Today felt different; the smell of the tree bark and fresh cut grass made her dizzy with longing—exactly for what, she wasn't sure. She sat down on the platform and gazed through the trees, the creek a sliver where it once was the prominent landscape. Her father had kept the overgrowth to a minimum, so she could have "waterfront views" from her special house. Her *special house*. That's what she called it when she was a kid—her special house.

The sun sighed and took on the orange hue of exhaustion—a final yawn before turning in for the night. Erin slowly stood, gripping the railing for support. She was still a bit shaky from her ordeal this afternoon and needed to be careful. Luckily, the platform, railing, and structure seemed in good condition, as if the people who moved in after them had cared for her special house and maintained it.

She pushed the door open and went inside. The previous family had cleaned out everything she had left behind, including her pillows and the old couch. She sat on the floor, her back against the wall, and gazed up at the wall in front of her, her eyes fixated on Landon's deer antler, hanging in the same place for over two decades. She stood up and walked over to it, running her fingers over the smooth bones, remembering being up here with Landon, a freshly won cross country medal around her neck.

They sat down to play scrabble, and at some point during that game (as always, she was pulverizing him with her command of the English language), he removed the medal from around her neck and hung it on the antler.

Scrabble. Scrabble. Scrabble! It had been one of their favorite activities. Why hadn't she bothered to take her Scrabble set when she cleaned the tree house all those years ago? Could she have been that distracted? Or still so angry at Landon that she didn't want to possess any tangible object that had been an essential part of their friendship?

Erin knew the hiding place by heart, and, like steel to a magnet, a force took her straight to the loose floorboard. She lowered herself to the floor and tapped it with her knuckles, happy to hear the hollow sound of the crevice her dad had deliberately left when he built the tree house. For the *map to your buried treasure*, he had told her. She stood up and whacked it with her bare heel.

"Holy Shit!" She sat back down, frustrated. "All that, and the floorboard didn't budge," she mumbled as she pounded it Doris's hard heel. Over and over again. Pound. Pound. Pound. She was about to give up when, just for good measure, she pounded it again, this time with every ounce of strength she could muster. No luck. "It's only a stupid *Scrabble* set," she said to the empty tree house. Someone obviously tightened things up. They probably even took her *Scrabble* game before hammering the nails into the coffin. "Not meant to be."

"WHAT'S NOT MEANT TO BE?" Wes stepped into the tree house, the beginnings of a grin on his face. "I heard a lot of pounding up here and wondered if you needed help." Erin looked up at him and wiped her eyes. "Are you okay? What's wrong?" He sat down next to her. "Are you crying again?"

She shook her head, then nodded. "No, I mean yes. I'm not crying now, but I was." She decided to be honest with him. "I had a secret hiding place under this floorboard. My dad left the board loose so I could store all my secret treasures." She shook her head. "The only thing I ever kept in here was a *Scrabble* set. I don't know why I didn't take it before, but I figured why not now?" She banged on the floorboard with her fist. "Someone obviously nailed the floorboard down."

"Are you sure about that?" Wes stood and jammed his heavy foot onto Erin's spot, banging. The floorboard moved like a loose tooth. Crouching down, he wedged his fingertips between it and the plank abutting it, and gently pried it free. "Hmmm. Is this what you're after?" He lifted the small box out of the crevice and examined it. "The way you were crying, I thought it was a vintage, limited edition, black walnut set with a rotating board." He laughed and handed it to her.

Erin grabbed the game, suddenly wishing she were alone to relish the feel of the tattered cardboard. She held the box to her nose and sniffed, the musty, earthy scent expanding her heart like a balloon. She glanced at Wes, who, thank God, was not watching her. Instead, he was standing at the tree house's only window, looking out at the water.

Taking advantage of Wes's distraction, she lifted the lid and stuck her hand inside, feeling for the velvet bag, not wanting to see it with her eyes because that would just be too much to bear. She tried to recall the last time she and Landon had been up here, the last time they had played *Scrabble*. Too much time had gone by, too many hours, days, weeks, years—she simply could not recall. With her eyes closed, she moved her fingers around inside the box. Instead of velvet, she felt paper, stiff and folded, the corners thick and sharp, with a soft, ruffled edge as if torn from a spiral notebook. Her heart pounded so hard she feared Wes could hear it. She willed her cheeks to not turn fifteen shades of red.

Without looking, she knew. Of course, she knew. To ensure she wasn't crazy or plagued with hallucinations from her harrowing afternoon, she opened her eyes, only to confirm what she already knew. Multiple sheets of paper, carefully torn from a spiral notebook, folded once, twice, three times, and placed inside the box. Her name was scrawled across the top in unmistakable handwriting—the E and N flourished with angular edges and finished with a small circle containing a frowning face. Sometimes, especially in art class, when his pieces looked more like kindergarten than high school, he would draw a frowning face in the palm of his hand and flash it at her, making her laugh. Her art wasn't much better. The frowning face had become a private symbol between them. She wondered if they had stayed in touch over the years if the ubiquitous frowning face emojis would have become part of their private vernacular.

"Great view," Wes said, his back still toward her, his forehead pressed against the window. "Is this yours too?" He slowly turned around, unwittingly allowing Erin to either open the note in front of him or tuck it back into the box.

"Let me see," she said, furtively tucking the note into the box under the playing board and velvet bag of tiles. She stood, her knee aching anew, and walked toward him. "It's pretty." She took the object in question out of his hand and examined it. "A petrified starfish." She set it on the window ledge. "Nope. Not mine." She looked him in the eye. "What do you see in me?"

"Huh?" Wes stared at her, his brows knit, a flash of confusion on his face.

"You heard me." She stepped back and regarded him. His dark hair and turquoise eyes. His sleek, always-put-together-even-when-he-dressed-down good looks. She ran her hand through her cropped hair, then looked down at her body—knock-kneed, lanky, and child-like. Her bare foot was dirty and, without question, quite smelly. Oh, and a missing limb. "What did you, a sophisticated doctor, ever see in me, a sloppy eccentric?

"Sloppy?" He took a step toward her and put his hands on her shoulders. "Yeah. Right now, you're sloppy. Smelly. Dirty." He laughed. "The woman I fell in love with is quirky. Unique. Colorful." He pulled her in and pressed her against his chest. "I love you, Erin."

She melted into him, new tears streaming down her face. After a few seconds that seemed more like minutes, she eased out of his grip and sat down against the wall, under the window, the flood of earlier memories forgotten, the note tucked into the *Scrabble* box suddenly holding less import.

Wes sat down next to her, their shoulders touching. Finally, he pointed to the *Scrabble* box. "Fancy a game?"

Erin shook her head. "I had something else in mind." She didn't really, but she didn't want to play *Scrabble* either. She didn't want to open the box, and she didn't want to share whatever Landon had written to her twenty years ago with Wes. All she wanted was to return to her mother's house with the box in her tight grip, take a hot shower, eat a good dinner, and forget this day.

"Oh yeah?" Wes's eyes gleamed. "Such as?"

She put the events of the day behind her and kissed him, then raised her arms and let him pull her shirt over her head, still damp from the brackish creek. She closed her eyes tightly and allowed herself to enjoy the moment.

~

WES STARTED DOWN THE LADDER, a bit gingerly at first, then taking two rungs at a time. He stopped to pick at a wedgie, then continued. Already at the bottom, safely on solid ground and clutching the *Scrabble* box, Erin watched him, shaking her head and wondering, suddenly, what she saw in him. Sure, she had asked him that question a little while ago, feeling unkempt, ugly, and somehow broken. Undeserving of his attention or affection. And now, watching him gingerly take one rung at a time, she wondered what she was doing with this dainty doctor. She recalled Landon—true, twenty years younger than Wes was now—climbing down to the halfway point and jumping the rest of the way. Most of the time, he landed on his feet, though sometimes he ended up in a ball on the ground, head tucked in like one of those rollie-pollie bugs.

Tapping her foot in a fit of impatience and defiance, Erin crossed her arms and uncrossed them about a hundred times. Or so it seemed.

"Are you sure this was okay?" Wes made his way to the second-to-last rung. He lowered his left leg and felt for solid ground with his foot but came up with only air. He looked down, then slowly bent his knee until he could set a toe in the dirt. He lowered himself to the ground and smoothed his shorts with his hands. "There are probably cameras everywhere. Crap. There might even be cameras in the tree house."

"I'm sure your reputation will be ruined." Erin rolled her eyes. "I could imagine the headline: *Cardiologist Caught Screwing His Girlfriend in Tree House.*" She shook her head.

"Correction. *Cardiologist Arrested for Trespassing on Private Property and Screwing His Fiancée in Tree House.*" Wes smiled his crooked smile, and dammit, Erin fell for it and smiled too. Wait a minute. Had Erin heard him correctly? *Fiancée?*

"Um. Uh. Okay." She laughed, unsure what to do with his sleight of hand or, should she say, a slip of the tongue. A week ago, she would have grabbed ahold of his word choice with both hands and not let go. Now she wasn't so sure what to say, what to do. She wasn't even sure if she wanted to marry him. Again, given the opportunity a week ago, she would have said yes without hesitation. She grabbed his hand and led him to the car. "Let's go home and get cleaned up. I'm hungry, and, honestly, I want to put this day behind me." She opened the passenger door and carefully placed the *Scrabble* box on the floor.

"Even the last half-hour?" He squeezed her.

She squeezed him back. "That was the one bright spot on an otherwise lousy day." She slid into the car and set foot on the box, silently and desperately wanting to go hide in a corner and read Landon's note.

25

The late evening, late summer sky looked purple, turning everything—as far as Landon's eyes could see—purple. Purple just happened to be Erin's favorite color. Landon, full to the gills from his steak dinner (and the massive baked potato slathered with butter, fresh green beans from the small, raised bed behind the house, and corn on the cob that Susan brought from the roadside stand on the winding road off Moss Street, and four bottles of Miller Lite) wondered if he had lost his mind. Or his sense of color. Hey, maybe he had Covid. If Covid could make you lose your sense of taste and smell, surely it could mess with your sense of color. Had to be it. He made a mental note to buy a rapid test kit.

As he walked along holding Susan's hand, he marveled at the fact that he didn't feel the least bit tipsy, thank God. Instead, he felt completely and utterly purple. From the top of his head to the bottom of his toes. Purple. Everything was purple. He abruptly stopped walking, Susan's arm stretching like that toy he'd had a long time ago. What the hell was that toy's name?

"Stretch Armstrong!" he yelled, lifting Susan up and twirling her around. He stopped, holding her above him in weird, suspended animation. "That's a nice purple shirt," he said. "Your hair too. I love that shade of purple on you." He smiled. "Your purple makeup is very complimentary. Brings out the blue in your eyes."

"What are you talking about?" Susan was airborne and looking down at him, like Baby looking down at Johnny in *Dirty Dancing*. "And what does any of that have to do with Stretch Armstrong?"

Landon lowered Susan to the ground. They still had several blocks of walking before he could deposit her at her house. He wasn't even sure why he had agreed to walk her home. It's not like she'd had too much wine with dinner—she easily could have driven home, couldn't she have? The walk was her idea, wasn't it?

"I'm a little tipsy," she had said. "Your dad never let my glass get empty." Maybe so, but she certainly didn't seem the least bit drunk. She might even be less tipsy than him, and he wasn't terribly intoxicated. Hell, he wasn't tipsy at all. "Anyway, I don't think I should drive," she had said. She batted her eyes at him at that point, and he fell for it. "Walk with me?" Had she said that, or had he? Dammit, he couldn't remember. And now, here he was, under a purple sky— Erin's favorite color—with a million miles yet to walk.

Suddenly tired and overwhelmed, he plopped in the middle of the sidewalk. He looked up at Susan, who was looking down at him, this time without Baby's and Johnny's wistfulness. It was more like, well, he wasn't exactly sure what he saw in her eyes. Confusion? Frustration? Whatever it was, it certainly wasn't wistfulness. Or love. Or even lust. He cocked his head to one side and studied her.

"Come. Sit down." He scooted over a few inches and patted the sidewalk next to him.

Susan knit her brows and carefully lowered herself to the ground. She brought her knees up to her chest and hugged them. "What's with you?"

"I was about to ask you the same question." He gazed at her purple face and into her purple eyes. "You're acting mightily strange."

"Mightily strange?" She stared at him. "Purple this and purple that?" She shook her head. "Are you okay? You're drunk, aren't you."

"I had a jolly good time tonight," he said, thoughtfully, thinking about Erin's broken rental. "Or is it jolly good day? No, I didn't have a jolly good day. But I had a jolly good time tonight." He laughed. "I'm not drunk, though. Not in the least." He pressed his lips together and stood, moaning and pressing his hands into his back. "I think I'm more out of shape after these past two weeks than I've been in the past twenty years."

He dropped back down to the sidewalk and did a push-up. Then another. Then five. He stopped counting at a hundred and looked up at Susan, only to find her halfway up the street instead of being impressed by his athletic prowess like he figured she would be. He sprinted after her, taking long graceful strides like a deer or a gazelle. By the time he caught up to her, he was panting like a sick dog, yet he felt exhilarated in a way he hadn't felt in a long time.

Susan stopped long enough to turn around, seemingly reassured that it was Landon standing behind her and not the boogeyman. She raised her eyebrows, shook her head (in awe or disgust?), and continued walking.

"Come on, Susan." He took two giant steps toward her and draped an arm around her. "We had a good time tonight, didn't we?" He let his eyes tip upward toward the sky—filled with stars but no longer purple—and felt the last bit of his exhilaration slip away.

"You were distracted."

Landon thought about that for a second. Distracted. Of course, he was distracted. His son almost died. Oh, and his face had been so close to Erin's in the murky water that he could feel her shallow breath on his forehead and smell the almost imperceptible scent that was uniquely hers. That scent brought him back a thousand years. Okay, twenty years, but it felt like a thousand. Everything he thought he had buried bubbled up to the surface at that moment; he spent the entire evening shoving it back down. And if anything was reason enough for him to re-bury Erin, it was watching her with the dweeb cardiologist riding away into the sunset. Blech.

"My son almost drowned." It was all he could muster. He knew he owed Susan the truth—he just wasn't that into her. Sure, he liked her well enough. And sure, during the past two weeks, he had seriously thought about sleeping with her; it wouldn't be fair to her, and he knew it. And so, he didn't.

Susan wrenched her shoulder out from under his arm. "I know. Willie almost drowned. And you still have feelings for Erin, don't you."

Landon felt himself blush as he silently thanked God for the dark, moonless night. "She's in a serious relationship. Whatever I felt a long time ago—if I even ever felt anything—is long gone." He hated lying but wasn't ready to lay his heart out there like that. Nope. Vaguely alluding to the fact that he may have had some sort of feelings for Erin a long time ago was as far as he was willing to go. And even at that, the topic was no longer up for discussion. And, to ensure that it stayed that way, he wrapped his arms around Susan's waist and pulled her toward him. Not sure how she would react, given her mind-reading capabilities, he was surprised and pleased when she melted into him.

They ran the rest of the way to her house, and Landon swallowed the regret he knew he would feel in the morning.

IN THE END, morning never came. Standing on Susan's front stoop, kissing her, nearly did him in. But, in a split-second cosmic shift, she struggled to dig her key out of her purse and struggled even more trying to fit it into the ancient keyhole. Well, that tiny pause was enough to make Landon's hormones come to a screeching halt. He hugged her, kissed her lightly, and said goodbye. He ignored her pleas to go inside.

"I'll behave myself," she had said, laughing. "Unless you don't want me to." She stood on her toes and wrapped her arms around his neck, nuzzling him and trying, without success, to lead him through the door.

He mumbled something about needing to get home and relieve his dad in case Willie got up during the night. This time, a bold-faced lie, Willie has been sleeping through the night since he was about six months old.

"I'll see you tomorrow, then?" Her voice was timid and hopeful.

"Maybe. I'm going to be busy working on—"

"Her boat?" Susan let her arms drop as she stepped away from Landon.

"Technically, not her boat."

"Hilarious, Landon." Susan shook her head and stepped inside. She pulled the storm door shut, then popped her head back out. "Why don't you just let your dad work on it? Or better yet, let her get her ass back down here and help him."

If Landon had been tipsy before, he was stone cold sober now. He narrowed his eyes and tried to speak, but speaking through clenched teeth was next to impossible. He loosened his jaw and tried to find the right words. Dammit, he couldn't find any words, let alone the right ones. Suddenly, all the wrong words came rushing from his brain into his mouth, ready to tumble out at a moment's notice. But he had learned in counseling that spewing vitriol all over someone was a decidedly ineffective way to get one's point across. He swallowed the wrong words, feeling them putting up a fight as they clung to the slippery walls of his esophagus, desperate to be heard and not end up splashing around in all that stomach acid.

"Susan, I really don't want to argue with you." It was all he could muster, yet he felt yucky for the tone he knew he had. He softened with the last of the wrong words, safely trapped in his digestive tract. "Look, it was a brutally long day." He forced a smile. "I had a good time tonight. And now I'm going home."

He turned on his heel and leaped off her stoop, flying over the two steps, and ran down the driveway, not looking back, feeling Susan's eyes casting aspersions and making him the bad guy. Yep. He was the bad guy. Indeed, he was.

He ran the mile back to his dad's house and vowed to stop leading her on. In fact, that wasn't the only vow he made. He also vowed to call his Commanding Officer and tell him he wanted to come home. Home to Coronado. Or wherever else the Navy might send him.

Because this wasn't his home anymore. Not by a long shot. He didn't need the remaining two weeks of his emergency leave; the first two weeks had served their purpose. And that purpose had been to assure him that he and Willie would be okay. And they would.

THE FIRST THING Landon did when he got home—out of breath and out of shape—was to guzzle a shitload of water. His dad was asleep in the recliner, *The History Channel* droning in the background. It wasn't all that late—just past nine—but when Ed Shultz fell asleep in his recliner, it was for the night.

Landon didn't bother waking him; he simply scrawled some cryptic words on the back of an envelope, which he picked up from an ever-growing pile of junk mail on the kitchen counter. *Junk, it's all junk.* Landon flipped through the stack. Holy crap, his dad received a lot of catalogs—some even touting early Christmas shopping. *It's only the middle of August,* he thought as he tore up the small pieces (his dad didn't own a shredder), gathered all the catalogs, and tossed all of it into the recycle bin.

All except the envelope on which he scribbled his note: *I'm working on Erin's boat. Come get me when Willie gets up.* Meaning he had every intention of working all night. The last thing he wanted to do was crawl into bed and try to force sleep. He might as well be productive. Because if he could keep his hands moving and focus on the tangible act of boat repair, there would be no room in his brain for anything else. And right now, that was where he needed to be.

But first, there was one call he needed to make. The evening was just beginning in Coronado—no risk of waking him or disrupting his dinner (Commander Diaz's idea of dinner was inhaling a foot-long sub while pacing the command center). Better yet, Landon would text. That way, he could get his point across without going through the obligatory inquiries and niceties.

Done all the healing I'm going to do. Need to come back. It's true what they say: you can't go home again. His finger poised over the send button, he thought better of his words and backtracked, deleting the part about never being able to go home again. Too mushy. Too revealing. Too red-flaggy. The whole thing sounded somewhat desperate.

He deleted it all and retyped: *Head's up, I'm coming back early. Looking at flights. Will text you with details tomorrow.*

Landon grabbed the headlamp off the hook by the back door and strapped it around his forehead. He desperately needed a haircut but would wait until he returned to the base. Unless Commander Diaz wanted him to keep it long. He was barely out the door when his phone buzzed with an incoming text.

"Well, that was quick," Landon said to himself as he pulled his phone out of his pocket.

Sorry about my attitude earlier. Crap. It was Susan. *I'll make it up to you* (with a winky emoji), came two seconds later. He decided not to answer and shoved his phone back into his pocket when it buzzed again.

"Dammit, Susan, enough," he mumbled. But it wasn't Susan this time.

Shultz, you read my mind. We need you back here, pronto. Arranging a flight out of Pax River the day after tomorrow. Details to follow via email. Oh, and don't cut your hair.

LANDON QUELLED the rising excitement at Commander Diaz's response. *Oh, and don't cut your hair.* Not cutting his hair could only mean one thing—he was going covert again. This excited him more than he cared to admit. The logistics of the whole thing threatened to overwhelm him—the last time he went on a covert mission, he and Taylor were still together. Worrying about Willie wasn't an issue then, but it certainly was now. He wished he had the nerve to continue stringing Susan along. He was sorry he had strung her along for the past two weeks. He was sorry he allowed himself to kiss her. Sorry. Sorry. Sorry. He knew Susan would jump at the opportunity to fly to Coronado and play happy house with him. Or perhaps that was just his arrogance talking. Standing in a four-foot hole looking up at a broken rudder, he thought about a night in Coronado, a few days before flying home.

"Would you like me to read your palm?" A woman sitting next to him at the bar broke into his thoughts. Landon shook his head wildly. He'd never been one to fall victim to superstition, but now that he was a parent, he couldn't bear the thought of someone looking at the lines on his palm and telling him that some sort of calamity would befall his son.

"Come on, Shultz, it's just for fun." Landon's buddy grabbed his wrist and shoved it at the woman.

The woman turned toward Landon and grabbed his hand, turning it over, so it was palm-up (a little too aggressively, as far as Landon was concerned). She had long black hair, a broad nose, and looked like a young Cher. He was about to tell his buddy to find the song *Dark Lady* on Touch Tunes, but the woman cut him off before he could get the words out of his mouth.

"I'm not really a fortune teller, you know." She dropped his hand.

"I know," Landon said, suddenly embarrassed.

She shrugged. "I've been told I look like a fortune teller."

Landon laughed. "Well, you kind of do."

"I'm a psychologist back home—Minneapolis, just to save you the trouble of asking—and can predict much about a person without any woo-woo-hocus-pocus." She took Landon's hand and studied his palm, then let it drop. She stared at him, looking so hard into his eyes that it made him uncomfortable. "Something you lost will turn up soon," she said. "And..." She paused and leaned into him; her face was close enough for him to smell buttery Chardonnay on her breath. He moved back a few inches. "And...the one you love is closer than you think."

"That's it, I'm out of here." Landon jumped up and grabbed his buddy by the arm, dragging him away from the bar. "If I had a dollar for every time I heard that line." Landon shook his head. "Desperation," he said. "That's what that was. Pure desperation."

Something you lost will turn up soon. The one you love is closer than you think. What had he lost recently? Or, perhaps more importantly, who had he lost? Taylor? Sure, he'd lost Taylor, but that was because of Taylor. In other words, Landon didn't view that as a loss because she was the one who walked away from him and their son. And the fact that he wasn't even all that upset was telling.

So then, what? Was the fortune teller's non-fortune telling him something about Taylor? That he will find her again when he goes back to Coronado? That she'd had a change of heart? That she loves him after all? None of that would matter one iota. Because he didn't love her. Sure, Willie would be better for having her in his life, but in some ways, Willie was better off this way, gradually forgetting the mother who walked away from him without a glance backward.

Something you lost will turn up soon. The one you love is closer than you think. Standing in the hole he and Erin had dug just that day, he ran his hands over the broken rudder. The section where the rudder was bent didn't seem as bad as it did two days ago. He placed both palms on the ground outside the hole and launched himself up and out, wincing in pain as his triceps spewed vitriol for making them work like that. Surprisingly, his shoulders and triceps were no worse for the wear—probably from the multiple times each day he lifted Willie up over his head and carried him on his shoulders.

Landon climbed the stepladder that was still standing at the stern of the boat and tried to take the rudder off with his bare hands; the two pins that held it in place had loosened from the trauma of the accident. He let the rudder drop into the hole (hopefully not incurring even more damage), then climbed back down to examine it closer. *No big deal,* he thought, as he lifted the rudder out of the hole and laid it on the ground. An hour in the machine shop to straighten it, maybe less. But first, he needed to examine the keel.

He turned on his headlamp and crouched next to the most critical part of the boat. *Needs new ablative bottom paint,* he thought, wondering if his dad had any in the workshop. If not, a trip to West Marine was in order. With no real plan of attack, he climbed the stepladder again and onto the boat, fumbling toward the bow. *Great job, Erin,* he thought. *We need to remove the whole damned bow pulpit and take it to the shop to be heated and straightened. That will be your job tomorrow. Unless I can get it done tonight.* He imagined her standing next to him on the boat, discussing these issues like two old buddies might do. If only.

He returned to the stern, climbed down the ladder, and walked around under the boat until he found where the hull had scraped against the floating dock. *You can buff out the road rash, my friend.* He smiled and shook his head, then berated himself for allowing his imagination to go there. Erin was with Wes. Wes, the cardiologist. Wes, the dweeb cardiologist.

He took a deep breath and contemplated Susan again, softening to the idea of perhaps trying, in earnest, to have a relationship with her. Willie adored her, and, honestly, Susan was easy to be with. Maybe a spark would ignite over time. Perhaps in time, he would feel excited about spending the rest of his life with her.

26

L andon was in the machine shop, holding onto the bow pulpit, which he had been straightening before he suppos- edly fell asleep. The rudder was on the floor by his feet— not perfectly fixed but darned close. Close enough that the boat rental company wouldn't notice. Close enough even that a boat surveyor wouldn't see—on the off chance that the rental company would ever try to sell *Jolly Good Day*.

"I made breakfast." Ed's voice gently stirred Landon from a stand- ing-upright sleep. "Erin will be here soon to buff the road rash on the hull. Willie has been asking after her all morning." He looked at Landon but didn't make eye contact. "I invited her for breakfast."

"You did what?" Fully awake, Landon looked at the ceiling, grab- bing fistfuls of hair with both hands. He felt heat rising—the angry kind, not the good kind—from his toes all the way up to his head. He let go of his hair and paced from one end of the shop to the other— past the floor-to-ceiling pegboards—every inch with all tools known to mankind—past the cabinets with drawer after drawer of stainless steel screws, nuts, and bolts. If you needed a tool, Ed Shultz likely had it in his shop.

Landon stopped pacing long enough to stop in front of one such cabinet, open a random drawer, pull out a cotter pin and twirl it between his thumb and forefinger. He held it to the light and then let it drop back into the drawer, which he slammed shut. He gathered the hair at the base of his neck and twirled it into a man bun, just like Susan had instructed. Alas, he didn't have a rubber band to secure his work of art in place.

"You suffer from emotional dysregulation," he remembered Taylor spewing at him one night shortly before she left him. "Google it," she'd shouted. And he did. Simply put, Landon tended to feel emotions more intensely than the average person, whatever normal meant. Especially emotions that involved Erin.

He took a deep breath and checked in with his body, which felt like an alien had invaded it and was stabbing him from the inside.

"Are you about finished?" Ed shook his head. "I have a pound of bacon to fry."

"You making pancakes too?"

"I wasn't planning to make pancakes, but you can if you want." Ed smiled and nudged his son on the shoulder, trying to knock him off balance.

Landon sensed this was coming; it was a dance they sometimes did when heated moments between them began to cool off. Friendly jostling, as it were. He planted his feet shoulder-width apart and crouched down at the knees to brace himself, pretending to get into his fighting stance. Landon didn't remember exactly when the tides had turned or when his father went from the stronger one to being careful to not hurt the weaker one. Even after Landon had gone through his growth spurt halfway through high school, he could not match feats with his father. But then something changed. Maybe it was right before he joined the Navy? Or was it when he returned from basic training? He supposed it didn't matter, except that he didn't like seeing his dad try to subtly mask a new pain here, the onset of frailty there.

He took a deep breath and let his dad mess with him for another few seconds before surrendering with roars of laughter and walking out of the workshop together.

Landon stood at the stove—one griddle sizzling with bacon, another dotted with lopsided pancakes. "Dad, I can't believe you still haven't leveled this stove."

"Your mother did fine with it just the way it is."

"She's not here any..." Landon stopped himself. "I'm sorry. I'll deal with it." He smiled but didn't turn around to look at his dad at the table, reading the comics with Willie. Despite his love of all things superhero, Willie's favorite character was Hammie from *The Baby Blues*. Landon listened with great admiration as his dad embraced the role of character actor and changed his voice as he read the comics out loud.

Landon flipped three pancakes and looked over his shoulder just as his dad acted out Snoopy trying to lick Lucy. Willie was in hysterics, and Landon regretted his decision to cut his leave short for a flash of a second. Not that he would have had a choice. Apparently, he was on his team's radar—they wouldn't have called him back unless necessary. And according to the watered-down, obfuscated details that Commander Diaz had sent in an email early this morning, it was essential. Why, then, was Landon unable to tell his dad? He was leaving in a few days; he needed to come clean soon.

"Spiderman Lady!" Willie tapped on Landon's leg. "Spiderman Lady is here!"

Landon's heart stopped. He flipped three more pancakes and slid them onto a tray piled high with at least a dozen oddly shaped flat blobs of cooked flour. He wiped his hands on his jeans and casually tore off a sheet of aluminum foil, smoothing it over his pancake mountain and popping the whole thing into the oven to keep warm. He allowed himself to turn around and look at Erin, crouched down at eye level with Willie saying something only a three-year-old boy would understand and find hysterically funny. He hadn't seen Willie laugh like that since before Taylor left.

Erin stood and acknowledged Landon with a nod. She was wearing a sundress—the same one with the big, swoopy flowers that flew out of her suitcase a few days ago when he discovered it was her —of all people—that he had been sent to tow. She looked beautiful, like Meg Ryan in *You've Got Mail*. He looked down at her prosthetic— Doris—and wondered how life would have evolved had he not blown her leg off. Maybe if he had just gotten the words out—*Erin, I love you, I've loved you since we were eight*—there would have been no need for the grand gesture of fireworks. He should have just gotten the damned words out. Now he wondered what he had been so afraid of.

He looked at Doris again and wondered why Willie hadn't yet asked about Erin's leg.

"Daddy, you're my best friend." Willie wrapped his arms around Landon's leg, then looked up at Erin. "But Spiderman Lady is my super best friend of the universe!" He let go of his "best friend" and ran back to his "super best friend of the universe" and firmly wrapped his arms around her legs. And, almost as if he had read his daddy's mind said: "She has a superpower metal leg so she could run the fastest of all the superheroes."

"Wait a minute, little man." Susan strutted into the kitchen and gave Landon a knowing glance as if to say *I'm here, I'm available, she's here, but she's not available*. She peeled Willie's arms away from Erin and lifted him up. In a voice thick with honey and sugar and teeming with butterflies and rainbows said, "I thought I was your super best friend of the universe." She pouted for Willie and winked at Landon. Willie wiggled his body, trying to get out of her grip. "We had a fun dinner last night, didn't we? You, me, your daddy. Remember?" She shot Erin a sideways glance. Willie continued wiggling, his concept of last night as remote and distant as last year.

"Put me down."

"Please," Landon said, correcting Willie. "You can ask Miss Susan nicely, and you can say, Miss Susan, please put me down. And you can also tell Miss Susan that we enjoyed dinner last night."

Susan planted Willie on the floor. "Well, if I'm not your super best friend of the universe, maybe I'm your super best friend of the galaxy?"

"You're just my friend." He ran to Landon. "I want pancakes!"

Landon pulled the pancakes out of the oven. He transferred one to Willie's Batman plate and cut it into bite-sized pieces. "Do you want your syrup on the pieces or in a little bowl on the side?" Recently, Landon made the dire mistake of pouring syrup directly over Willie's pancake. The way the little guy reacted, well, you would have thought Landon had abused him badly. And it wasn't that Landon never made pancakes; he made them often, weekly even, when he wasn't deployed. It was like some cosmic shift had taken place; suddenly and without warning, his son wanted to dip the individual pieces of pancake in a small bowl of syrup. Landon chuckled to himself, thinking about it.

"I'll do it how Spiderman Lady does it," Willie announced.

"Okay, Spiderman Lady. How do you take your pancakes?" Landon knew, or at least he had known a long time ago—Erin liked to drown her pancakes. He held his breath as he waited for her answer, hoping he was right, hoping to hold onto one tiny thing that hadn't changed.

Erin broke into a huge grin. "I think you know the answer to that." Her face turned red. Was she...blushing?

"Drenched it is." Landon bent down to muss Willie's hair, and in the split second his eyes were on his son and not on the scene unfolding in his father's kitchen, he had missed the segue from Act 1 to Act 2. He missed the ancillary characters' entrance and the leading lady's exit, too. Missed the change in the music's timbre—the orchestra changing from a light rom-com love song to a dirge. Where had Erin gone, and why was her mother now here? And the dweeb cardiologist? Landon glanced around the room, confused. His father had stepped out too. And so had Susan, apparently.

Wes wore khaki shorts, a short-sleeved button-down Hawaiian number, and a pair of Docksiders that he didn't seem all that comfortable in. He lunged at Landon, wearing a huge grin and an extended hand.

Landon set Willie's plate of drenched pancakes down on the table, got the kid settled into his chair, and took his time extending his hand to meet Wes's hand. But the dweeb cardiologist offered a closed fist instead of an open hand. Landon adjusted and gave it a little nudge.

"Fist bumps are the new handshakes," Wes said, the plastered grin fading into a straight line. "Sorry for the invasion. Erin insisted. She wanted to show me the boat."

"How thoughtful of her to invite you to my dad's house," Landon said, immediately regretful of his tone. "Welcome."

"Landon Shultz." Erin's mother stood behind Wes, her long skirt swaying as if to a secret song. "It's been a long time." She held out her arms for a hug.

Landon stepped away. "It's only been a long time because you—"

"You're right." She shrugged. "You're right."

Willie mumbled and grunted out a few words Landon couldn't quite make out. "Swallow your food, buddy. That's right. Now take a sip of your orange juice." He put on his best stern daddy face. "What did we talk about just the other day?"

"Don't talk with my mouth full."

"That's right. What were you trying to say with your mouth full of pancakes?" He winked. "Go ahead. I'm all ears."

"You're not all ears, Daddy." Willie laughed and shoved another piece of drenched pancake in his mouth. He chewed it carefully, then swallowed. "You have a head and arms and legs and a butt!" He laughed hysterically while the rest of the cast waited. "I said, Daddy, who are these people."

Landon pointed to Erin's mother first. "This is Miss Lydia. She is my friend Erin's mother."

"Mrs. Spiderman Lady!"

Next, Landon pointed to Wes. "And this is Erin's—"

"Fiancé." Wes didn't hesitate and repeated himself as if to drive home that point. "Fiancé."

LANDON'S CHEEK BURNED, like someone had slapped him. No, that was the easy part, and yes, his reaction to the word "fiancé" stunned him.

He recalled, in vivid detail, when he was "captured" during the survival portion of his SEAL training. Sitting in a dark cell, being asked inane questions such as whether he had a dog or cat and what were said pets' names. *Rover and Whiskers,* he had answered. And then, the interrogator asked if he had a girlfriend. *None of your damned business,* Landon remembered saying, barely audible. *I can't hear you, Maggot.* The interrogator lowered his face to within an inch of Landon's and spat out his question again. *Do. You. Have. A. Girlfriend?*

Landon repeated: *None. Of. Your. Damned. Business.* This time, at the top of his lungs. The force of the hand that met the side of his face gave him whiplash. And finally: *Erin. My girlfriend's name is Erin.* If only.

Landon slowly came back to the present. The pain from the face-slap subsided, and his eyes and ears focused on Erin's mother chatting happily about the big surprise. Willie had apparently finished his pancakes and was in the family room, plopped in front of *Sesame Street.*

"And that's why we need your boat," Lydia said to Landon's father. "Quiet, she's coming." She turned to Landon. "Please, don't say a word. Wes is going to propose tomorrow night."

"Congratulations," he managed to say to Wes before Erin and Susan entered the room, each carrying two folding chairs, which they proceeded to set up around the table.

LANDON, Susan, Erin, Wes, and, wonder of all wonders, the two arch enemies themselves, Ed Shultz and Lydia Conrad, ate breakfast together, chatting like they were old friends—like there hadn't been a Montague-Capulet-esqe feud for the past twenty years. If Landon wasn't screwed up in the head—for reasons he couldn't quite understand—he might even find the whole thing funny. But he wasn't in a funny mood. In fact, Landon wanted nothing more than to lunge across the table, grab the dweeb cardiologist by the throat, and pin him to the ground. He didn't want to hurt the guy, per se, but he wanted to make a point. But why?

Between bites of bacon, amid the casual chatter around the table, he managed to carry on a private side conversation with Susan, debating which actor was better at playing Frank Costanza in *Seinfeld*: the original John Randolph or the later season Jerry Stiller. *Jerry Stiller, hands down*, they both concluded. At the same time, he kept one eye on Erin and Wes, watching their interactions, trying to read the subtleties, cringing at the thought of the dweeb cardiologist on bended knee.

Landon's dad said something that made Erin laugh. She flung her head back and rested it on Wes's shoulder, closing her eyes, then opening them when her mother shot back with an even funnier word; this time, Wes flung his head back and laughed. Landon couldn't quite identify the words that had incited the raucous laughter. He looked at Susan, shrugged, and reached for a piece of bacon but met Erin's hand instead.

"Sorry!" They both said in unison. And like a pair of synchronized swimmers coming together and instantaneously retreating, their respective hands returned to their plates without bacon.

Landon watched as Wes lifted the bacon plate and waved it under Erin's nose. She took a piece, and Wes held the plate toward Landon in a posturing peace offering.

"No thanks," he said, faking a yawn. Strangely enough, he wasn't tired, even though he had been fixing most of the items on *Jolly Good Day's* punch list all night. Really, the only thing left to do was buff the road rash. He thought he remembered his father saying that Erin was coming over to do just that, so he supposed that was the reason for Erin's presence. Nah, not in her cute little sundress. And not with her entourage.

As a distraction technique, he put his arm around Susan and pulled her close. "It's good to see you," he said, low enough to not draw too much attention to himself but loud enough for Erin to hear. And apparently, her mother.

"How long have you two been seeing each other, dear?" Lydia stood, apparently not really interested in an answer. She brought the coffee pot to the table and refilled her mug. "Anyone need more? Ed?"

"Only if you have some of your magic coffee beans in your pocket." Landon's father laughed. "Truly, you make the best coffee, Lydia. I don't know how I lived without it all these years."

"That's it." Landon jumped out of his chair and paced the small kitchen. "I wish someone would explain to me what's going on here. I feel like I'm sitting in the middle of an improv comedy show."

"I'll go keep Willie company," Susan said to no one and everyone. "I'll be in front of the TV if anyone needs me." She disappeared into the family room, her bouncy energy a lingering vapor. Landon decided then and there that he would invite her to come to Coronado. He could learn to love her.

"Son, what's gotten into you?" Ed addressed his son, but looked at Erin. "He was up all night working on your boat."

Landon ignored his father and avoided making eye contact with Erin. Instead, he addressed Erin's mother. "Mrs. Conrad, with all due respect, you shunned my family for twenty years, and now you need a boat to ferry your little party, and so you're in my dad's kitchen sucking up to him?" The anger rising in his throat frightened him. And the silence around the table didn't help, either. If anything, he expected his dad to jump up and defend him...or at least agree with him that this whole scenario was strange.

"I have news for you, Son." Ed pressed his lips together and shook his head. He sighed. "When I heard that Doug died of Covid, my perspective changed."

"Your father and I talked yesterday, Landon," Erin's mother chimed in. "He has offered to help with repairs around the B&B. Painting. Gutters. Other little odd jobs."

"Mom, you never mentioned—"

"Never you mind." She swatted the air with the back of her hand. "Ed and I were friends a long time ago. We can be friends again."

Lydia's face softened in a way that made Landon uncomfortable. He imagined his mother, wherever she was, looking down on the scene and rolling her eyes. It made Landon smile, but really, he wanted to cry. He missed his mom and wished he had tried to visit more over the years, wished he had been better at telling her he loved her.

Erin got up and carried her plate to the sink. When she returned, she draped her arm over Wes's shoulder. "Deciding to become friends with your self-described mortal enemy is news, Mom." Erin's face was pink. Very pink. Pink rose, pink. Honey crisp apple pink. Landon swallowed and looked away. "Big news."

"What? I suddenly need your permission on who I call my friend?" Lydia mimicked her daughter's actions and carried her plate to the sink. "You're my daughter, and I love you, but some parts of my life are none of your business." She returned to the table and clapped her hands together, putting an end to any further discussion of the friends-to-enemies-to-friends-again trope. "So, Landon, sir, would you do us the honors of ferrying us to Oxford tomorrow night? We have a six o'clock reservation at Doc's, and you and Susan will join us for dinner too." She pressed her lips together, then opened her mouth to speak but said nothing. A wistful look washed over her. "It's what Doug would have wanted."

"Ma'am, I'd love to, but I'm heading back to Coronado the day after tomorrow. I'll be busy getting ready." He hadn't meant to blurt it out like that and was grateful Susan was in the other room. The silence that ensued hung in the air like smoke from a bomb. He looked at his father. "I'm sorry, Dad. I was going to tell you today. I spoke with Commander Diaz last night. Something is going down, and the team needs me back."

Ed stood, his hands pressed against the table for support. "We'll discuss this later."

Landon tried to read his father's face, but the pages were blank. He quickly glanced at Erin—also an empty page. Wait, was her face turning pink again? No. Red. Her face was red. Like she was going to cry. But why? His brain was unequipped to process anything.

Landon stood straight and saluted in a weak attempt to lighten the mood. Over the past two weeks, he'd gotten the feeling that his dad would love to have him retire from the Navy, return home, and help him run the business. Landon would never admit this to his dad, but on more than one occasion these past weeks, he had considered it too. It was never a serious consideration but a fleeting *what if*.

"Come on, Lydia." Ed extended his hand, and Erin's mom took it. "We've got planning to do." He looked at Wes. "You too, doctor."

Erin quietly got up and filled the sink with water while the three amigos sauntered outside. Landon shuffled toward the sink to help her with the dishes, then thought better of it. With her back toward him, he quietly slipped away.

27

Erin stood at the sink in Landon's dad's kitchen, arms up to her elbows in soapy water, her head spinning like clothes in a washing machine. Or lettuce in a salad spinner. Or, maybe most accurately, like the rotor at Happy Land. Her stomach—unsettled, bloated, and splashy—felt almost exactly like it did when she and Landon were about eleven years old, and their parents took them to the boardwalk, and Landon goaded her into riding the rotor. He called her a chicken, igniting tween competitiveness that made her want to prove that she wasn't a chicken. Plus, it wasn't so much that she was afraid to ride the rotor—she had ridden it before (but never with Landon as a witness to her misery); the issue was what happened to her after riding it. The dizziness. The low churning nausea. The rising bile. Her mouth filling with saliva. And finally, running for the nearest trash can. And yes, she had warned Landon. Still, he chided. And she wanted to impress him, so she waited in line with him, silently praying that this time would be different. Because she still wanted to go eat hot dogs at The Windmill afterward. She enjoyed eating at The Windmill even more than she enjoyed Happy Land for the sake of Happy Land.

Erin took a deep breath and thought about the boardwalk,

wondering why she had never considered taking Wes there. Maybe for his birthday. Perhaps they would even go to Happy Land and ride something mild, like the Ferris wheel or merry-go-round. That would be romantic, wouldn't it? It's been forever since she'd been to the boardwalk, let alone Happy Land, but she could still see the welcome sign and the mascot—the smiling clown with his jaunty little hat.

All those years ago, with nothin to prove, really, she stepped onto the rotor with Landon. First problem: there weren't two slots next to each other. Landon shrugged as the ride attendant ushered them in opposite directions. Erin's heart pounded as the attendant buckled her in. She pressed her back, legs, and arms against the wall and tried to look calm, cool, and collected. She dug her fingernails into her palms forcefully enough to leave little half-moon dents in her skin.

Second problem: she was wedged between an older girl and her boyfriend, both of whom reeked of cigarette smoke. They kept leaning over Erin to talk to each other, breathing on Erin's face, the smell of smoke and whatever food they had eaten threatening to choke her.

Landon's Cheshire Cat grin taunted from afar. The ride bucked, lifted, tilted, and starting spinning. It gradually gained speed until Erin knew the moment to escape was long behind her. She closed her eyes as tightly as possible. She chanted unintelligible words and syllables out loud amid the whoops and hollers of the idiots on the ride who were enjoying themselves. At some point during the two minutes of hell, she thought she heard Landon call her name.

Predictably, Erin staggered off the platform, angry that Landon could be in such a jolly mood. Jolly like that damned Happy Land clown. And predictably, she threw up in the nearest trash can and couldn't eat anything the rest of the day.

THE SOAPY WATER in the sink was no longer soapy and had cooled to barely lukewarm. The same three plates sat at the bottom of the water like sunken treasures, while the remaining dishes formed a line on the counter like Olympic swimmers on the starting blocks, awaiting the countdown.

Erin turned on the faucet and waited for the water to get hot, then extracted one plate at a time (nope, not a sunken treasure, just a plain, ordinary Corelle plate, industrial-looking green stripe surrounding its edge), rinsed it, then set it in the rack to dry. Why the hell was she washing Mr. Shultz's dishes, anyway? Where had everyone else gone?

Her mind had been so preoccupied that she hadn't bothered to look out the window above the sink until now, just in time to catch her mother throwing her head back in laughter at something Wes said. Or was her mother laughing at something Landon's father said? The three of them were plotting in the grass under the crepe myrtle. Of course they weren't plotting, per se, but that's certainly what it looked like.

Just then, Landon and Susan joined the group under the crepe myrtle, Willie perched on Landon's broad shoulders. Landon had changed his clothes since breakfast and was now sporting those damned booty shorts and a camouflage tee shirt that he had cut the sleeves out of.

Susan pulled Wes aside as Landon crouched down and let Willie jump to the ground. Wasn't that just like Landon to show off his huge quads and biceps? *Obviously, for Susan*, she thought. Landon was grinning. A big grin, like that day on the rotor. Like so many other times when she had made him smile or laugh.

The Happy Land mascot flashed through her mind for the millionth time this morning, bringing her back to the rotor. She turned off the faucet and stood, suddenly genuinely nauseous. She took a deep breath and put her hands on her throat, then quickly grasped for the faucet and turned it on. She let it run until the water was as cold as it was going to get, then bent toward down and splashed the frigid water all over her face, wondering why she suddenly felt so sick. Did seeing Landon with Susan have anything to do with it? No! Of course not! Landon didn't owe her anything. She swallowed the last bit of jealousy to join the contents of her churning stomach.

Jealousy. Is that really what this was about? How could she possibly be jealous of or upset by a relationship that Landon had every right to enjoy? Why, suddenly, did she feel even the tiniest bit possessive of something that had died twenty years ago?

She glanced out the window again. The happy couple (and Willie) had disappeared from her vision field. The rest of them were still talking and laughing (definitely plotting), and were now standing in front of the crepe myrtle instead of under it.

Feeling momentarily better, she leaned over the sink and inched her face closer to the window, wondering what was going on between her mother and Landon's dad. The wave of nausea returned. Perhaps she wasn't jealous of Landon and Susan at all. Maybe her mood and strange state of mind had nothing to do with Landon and everything to do with Ed Shultz seemingly hitting on her mother. A sudden, daughterly protective urge kicked in. She needed to intervene before her mother got entangled with a Shultz and ended up with a broken heart. She turned off the water and dried her hands on her dress.

ERIN FELT a presence behind her and slowly turned around. Landon was standing a little too close. She took a step backward, right into the counter. "Ouch. You could have at least tapped me on the shoulder, cleared your throat, anything to get my attention. You scared me half to death."

"You don't look scared."

She stood for a moment studying him. His eyes looked weary. "Is what your father said true? Did you really stay up the whole night fixing *Jolly Good Day*?"

"It wasn't such a jolly good night." He inched backward, just a little. "But it's done. I wouldn't exactly say it's as good as new, but at least you won't get blacklisted from ever renting a boat again." He smiled. "Not to mention the money I saved you."

"Thank you." Erin felt herself blush. "You didn't have to do that."

"I know I didn't. I couldn't sleep." He knit his brows and looked away. "You heard me say I have to go back to Coronado early." Erin nodded. "I didn't plan to blurt it out at the table like that. Susan was in the other room, so she doesn't know yet."

Erin decided to be brave. "So, you and Susan are—"

"I don't know what we are." Landon's tone was clipped. "I'm sorry. It's just that, well, I don't know. We've gotten to know each other better during the past few weeks." He looked at the floor. "She's great with Willie."

"He'll miss Susan when you leave," Erin said.

"He'll miss you too, Spiderman Lady." Landon busied himself, clearing the counter and gathering the breakfast detritus. He carried the jug of syrup to the refrigerator. "I'm thinking about seeing if Susan wants to come to visit for a while, or at least until school starts next month."

Erin shook her head and, despite her best effort not to, felt herself on the verge of tears. "I'm sure Susan would happily resign and find a new teaching job in Coronado." She swallowed. "Willie is quite a character."

"He is indeed." Landon closed the refrigerator door and stared at Erin, who grew uncomfortable, and looked away. "And you saved his life."

"Anyone would have." Erin was desperate to change the subject. Desperate to be away from Landon. Desperate to know what was going on outside with her mother, Ed, and Wes. Desperate. Desperate. Desperate. Suddenly and without warning, she was overcome by the aftertaste of Ed's coffee. Of course. Ed's coffee. The source of her nausea. "So, what's going on outside?" She nudged her head toward the window. "My mother, your father, and Wes look like they're plotting evil."

"They're plotting, alright." Landon laughed, then grew serious. "Not evil, though. Just trying to pin down logistics for your expedition to Oxford tomorrow evening."

"Sorry about that; I mean, my mother roping you and your dad into this." The nausea threatening to choke her now felt more like a lump in her throat. She willed herself not to cry. "This has been a hard year for my mom. She wants to make this family camp concept special, but it's not the same without my dad. Sandy and his family aren't coming either. I'm really pissed at him." She jammed a plate into the dish rack. "He knew how important this week was to my mom."

Landon shrugged. "It's a crazy world with Covid, and I don't blame him for not wanting to fly."

"It's not him. It's his wife who's paranoid."

"Don't be so hard on Sandy. He's your brother."

Erin squirted liquid dish soap into the sink and turned the water on full force. A mountain of bubbles rose out of the sink, an abominable soapy snowman in August. Or a friendly Frosty the Snowman putting on his magic hat and coming to life. *Merry Christmas*, Erin thought. She scooped up a load of bubbles and flung them at Landon, who didn't flinch.

"So, you're sticking up for Sandy now?" She scooped up more bubbles using both hands and launched them at him like a bona fide snowball. "You never really liked Sandy, so why are you suddenly sticking up for him?"

"Who said I'm sticking up for him?" He moved toward the sink. "He was always a pain in the ass." He nudged her out of the way, stuck his hand in the sink, and splashed bubbles into her face.

Erin squealed and put her hand to her mouth, embarrassed that she so quickly reverted to the behavior of a twelve-year-old.

"You're in for it now," she said amid raucous laughter. She pulled out the spray nozzle and held the handle down until it sprayed all over the kitchen, Landon ducking and bobbing, weaving like a cop in a raid. Or a SEAL in a combat mission, doing his level best to avoid being seen or heard, to avoid tripping a trigger. At least that's what Erin's mind conjured when she thought about the things Landon did in the field.

28

———

Landon caught a glimpse of the note as it plopped to the floor. He saw it before Erin was even aware that it had slipped out of her pocket during the bubble fight. He recognized it instantly—the way it was folded in half, then thirds, then half again, until it was the size of a travel-sized pack of tissues. The tape—yellow, old and brittle with age—that had dutifully held the pages together for twenty years was gone, indicating Erin had read his note.

Landon wondered when she had gone to the treehouse. When he snuck up there ten days ago, the note was still tucked deep within the *Scrabble* box. Dammit! He should have taken it with him. He imagined her laughing with the dweeb cardiologist, insisting on showing him all her childhood haunts. The more he imagined Erin with anyone other than him in that treehouse, the angrier he became. He felt it careening through his blood so fast that if Wes were to walk into the kitchen, Landon would see an enemy and not an innocent dweeb who just happened to be in love with the woman Landon had never quite gotten over.

How long had she been carrying around that note? Not long, he suspected. Two days? Three? An hour? Or two? One thing was certain, though—she obviously had the letter in her possession long enough to have read it. His entire body was awash in embarrassment. Complete and utter humiliation. He didn't remember exactly what he had written—it was mostly a series of words strung together in an attempt at groveling. You know, all the typical things you say to someone when you cause them to lose a limb. He babbled on and on for many pages. And then, on page eleven, he poured out his heart in a paragraph he remembered, almost verbatim—like he had penned it yesterday.

Let me in. Erin. Please. Let. Me. In. Talk to me. Please. Erin. Talk. To. Me. You're my best friend. I'm lost without you. I love you. There. I said it. I. Love. You. Not that it matters, but it's what I was trying to tell you the night of the accident. I love you, Erin Leigh. I love you.

Landon bent down and scooped up the note as quietly as possible, being careful not to be seen. Luckily, Erin was back at the sink, making more soap bubbles to hurl at him. He slipped the note into her pocket as stealthily as a magician about to perform a sleight-of-hand trick.

Erin was still laughing, oblivious. She turned around and pointed the sprayer at him, a gun to his heart. He looked her in the eye as he reached around her waist and turned off the water. Still holding her eyes (dammit, those eyes were dancing), he peeled the sprayer out of her hand and set it back in its cradle.

The magic of the bubble fight moment was over. She had obviously read the letter and acted like nothing significant had been written there. He knew her well enough to know that if she felt (back then, not now) an inkling of what he had felt for her, the note would have changed everything. And it didn't. His only regret was all the time he wasted quietly and secretly loving her.

29

Shocked at her bold playfulness—with a man she knew only as the boy he had once been—Erin felt giddy in a way that she hadn't in a long time. When he took the sprayer, his face was so close to hers that she could smell the intoxicating combination of syrup and coffee. As one instinctively knows these things, she was sure he wanted to kiss her. And the fact that she wouldn't have resisted scared her. She sighed with great relief when he backed away. They had been friends once—best friends—buddies, pals. Here, in his dad's kitchen, she experienced a glimpse of something missing in her life, something she regretted being too stubborn all those years ago to try and cultivate. Stubborn and pressured. Pressured by her mother, who apparently had her own recent awakening.

She wiped her hands on her dress and, without turning around, said: "There's something I want to show you." She watched as the past few minutes slid down the drain with the soapy water, but she wanted the light-hearted silliness to stay for a little while.

She hesitated for a split second, wondering what she was doing. She reminded herself that Landon had been her childhood friend for, well, basically her entire childhood. You can't just erase that or watch it slide down the drain. Or can you? Okay, true, anything could slide down a drain. Anything small enough. And their friendship was never small. It seemed larger than life, like close siblings, only better. Because you don't fall in love with your sibling. She supposed anything could slide down a drain if the drain was big enough.

Big things were harder to erase, though. Impossible, even. It was one thing to erase a word or two on her little dry-erase board at work. No big deal. Any ghost-like remnants on the board faded as if the original word hadn't been there too long. But what about the wall-sized dry erase board in the conference room? Scrawled across the top in fancy, purple letters were the titles of books and the names of her colleagues who had written a blurb for a book that hit the *New York Times* best-seller list (she had not yet reached that level of career prestige). Several of those titles graced the dry-erase board for years. One had been there for the length of time Erin had worked there. Erasing those long-standing scribbles would leave prominent imprints of what once had been—erasing them would not make them disappear.

She had tried to erase Landon. Tried to scrub him away with every cleaning product known to mankind. She even fooled herself into thinking she could bleach the imprint. But, in retrospect, it only made things worse—all it did was smear the past over the present in a smudgy, purple fog. No matter how hard she tried to erase Landon, the memories fought for space in her heart.

Erin took a deep breath and reminded herself that she was in love with Wes. She loved Landon too, but not in the same way, right? She loved Wes! She was in love with Wes. She would marry Wes without hesitation if he ever asked.

Surely Wes would understand her driving off with Landon for a few minutes. Just a few minutes. That's all she needed. She would never do anything to jeopardize her relationship with Wes. Never. She and Landon had unfinished business—a huge, pink elephant that needed to be slayed once and for all.

30

L andon kept his eyes straight ahead as he drove down the country road leading to Erin's old house. She said she had been to the tree house and wanted to show him something. No mention of the letter, of course. Just the tree house. Landon didn't want to go, didn't want to leave Susan to wonder. So, he didn't tell her. He simply told his dad he needed to run to the hardware store, and Erin was going with him.

Out of the corner of his eye (he was careful to not give Erin any indication that he was stealing glances), he watched her hair blowing around her face, her arm out the window, making dolphin dives with her hand.

He shook his head a few minutes earlier when she tried to turn on the radio. Careful to keep his little silent treatment going, he didn't offer an explanation or any kind of body language that might explain him not wanting music blaring like they used to do when they drove around in his truck so long ago. Luckily, today's music was not a part of their lexicon. Still, he couldn't risk an old song catapulting him back into a past he couldn't undo.

If silence was the absence of sound, how could you possibly give someone the silent treatment? Landon's father was infamous for giving people the silent treatment. He didn't do it often, but it was a doozy when he did. Days upon days until someone (usually not his dad) would crack and acquiesce that, yes, Ed Shultz had (still had) the upper hand.

And speaking of the upper hand, one thing that Landon never received was that hand coming down hard in anger. Ed Shultz was proud that he had never struck his child. Except for when a very young Landon tried to hug a German Shepherd wandering around the boatyard. Landon remembered getting yanked away from the dog and swatted. The dog got slapped too and never came back. Still, Ed Shultz's silence was anything but silent. He would grunt. And clear his throat. And sigh loudly.

When Landon announced that he had enlisted in the Navy, the silent/not silent treatment that ensued lasted a long time. Funny, but Landon thought his dad would support (and maybe even be proud of him) for enlisting.

"Nonsense!" Ed had been sanding a boat bottom on a sweltering mid-August afternoon. "You'll do no such thing."

Landon knew better than to bother his dad when he was sanding. But he had been walking around with his signed enlistment papers folded up in his pocket for days, trying to work up the courage to tell his parents. He wasn't sure who would take the news worse—his mom or his dad. It was a crapshoot, so Landon tossed a coin: heads mom, tails dad. It landed on heads the first time, but his mom was at work, and he needed to cough up the news soon. The little fact that he was due at Naval Station Great Lakes in less than two weeks might have had something to do with his sense of urgency.

"It's already done." Landon reached into his pocket and pulled out the copy of his contract. He unfolded it and handed it to his dad.

Ed turned off the sander, removed his safety goggles, then pulled the respirator below his chin. He skimmed the contract and handed it back. "So, you'll undo it." He repositioned his respirator, put his safety goggles back on, and resumed sanding.

At the dinner table that night, Ed leaned across the table and, with a voice barely a whisper, asked Landon if he had "undone" the thing.

"What thing," his mother said, a forkful of green beans suspended midair.

"I joined the Navy."

"I thought I told you to un-join." Landon's dad slammed his beer can on the table and looked at his wife. "He had a momentary lapse of judgment. He'll stay here and help me in the boatyard and the shop until he figures out what he's doing with his life."

"What do you mean you joined the Navy?" Landon's mother put her fork down, green beans untouched.

"We're changing the subject," Ed announced. "You son will take care of this mess first thing tomorrow."

Landon stood. "Dad, I'm not taking care of anything. Mom, I need a change of scenery, and I'm leaving for basic training a week from Thursday."

"He's just trying to escape his problems," Ed said. "He'll feel better in the morning and take care of this."

"It's done." Landon wanted to scream but kept his voice as even and calm as possible. "It's done, Dad. It's done. I'm not backing out." He glanced at his mom. "After basic training and A-School, I'm going to see if I could get into BUD/S Training."

"You're joking me." Ed shook his head. "Good luck with that."

"Ed!" Landon's mother shot her husband one of her looks, then turned to her son. "Your father always thought you would help him run the boatyard." She took a deep breath. "I understand why you want to leave. I wish you had talked to us before signing on the dotted line."

"He'll take care of this, Joelle."

"No, he won't, Edward." And then: "We can't stop him." Landon's mother left the table, leaving her plate of Olive Garden-inspired chicken untouched, the forkful of green beans perched neatly on top.

∾

LANDON PULLED onto the long gravel driveway, lost in the memory of his parents' reaction to his enlistment, wondering what the hell he was doing here with Erin. He still hadn't uttered any words since they hopped in his truck.

He remembered trying to out stubborn his father, who had stopped talking when his mother left the table that night. She sequestered herself in her room and only emerged to go to work, and at the end of the day, threw whatever happened to be in the fridge into a sorry semblance of dinner and ate in her room. Landon's dad took to eating in front of the local news, and Landon, well, Landon fended for himself, usually opting to skip dinner entirely.

On day five of Ed Shultz's so-called silent treatment, he cornered Landon down by the water and hissed, *you're killing your mother*. But later that day, which happened to be a Sunday, Joelle came out of her room and didn't go back in until bedtime. The next day, as she was getting ready to leave for work, she pulled Landon aside.

"I'm disappointed." She shook her head. "So disappointed you didn't trust us enough to talk about this before making such a big decision."

"I'm eighteen years old, Mom." He stiffened and puffed his chest out a little to make himself look more mature. "It's my life."

"Right. Eighteen. You can vote. You can join the military. Sure." She put her arm around him and gave him a little squeeze. "And yes, you're a lot bigger than me." She laughed, then grew serious. "You're not facing your problems. I'm worried about that. Trust me when I tell you that your problems will come back to haunt you if you don't face and deal with them." She looked him in the eye. "I guarantee your problems will find you again. Maybe not right away, but they will find you. Possibly when you least expect it and, at the most inopportune time."

She stepped out the door but lingered. "So, right, I'm disappointed. Your father is disappointed. But I understand, and I'll be supportive. Your father will come around. I promise." She stood on her toes and kissed his forehead. Landon stood at the door, watching her get into her car and back out of the driveway. She stopped halfway, rolled down the window, and hollered: "Your turn to make dinner tonight."

Landon remembered stepping onto the front stoop and sitting down, watching his mother back out of the driveway and disappear behind the crepe Myrtle trees at the edge of the property. He chewed on her words: *I guarantee your problems will find you again. Maybe not right away, but they will find you. Possibly when you least expect it and at the most inopportune time.* He didn't believe his mother. He would immerse himself in basic training and do everything he could to get selected for BUD/S training. And once a Navy SEAL, he wouldn't have time to think about Erin.

Later that night, Landon's dad broke the silence, mumbling praise about the dinner he had made—tacos from an Old El Paso kit. And finally, a loving punch on the arm and an unenthusiastic, *you'll make a fine SEAL, son.* Landon wasn't sure what his mother might have said to end the impasse, but it finally ended.

Silence. The absence of sound. Landon listened to the sound of his tires on the gravel. The sound of the wind rushing into the truck through the open windows. The sound of Erin, for whatever reason, respecting his need to not talk. His mother's words from so long ago bubbled up like too many jalapeños on a taco: *I guarantee your problems will find you again. Maybe not right away, but they will find you. Possibly when you least expect it and at the most inopportune time.*

His mother's prediction was spot-on. He calculated the time—twenty years ago, almost to the day, since he joined the Navy and his dad's silent treatment. He doubted his mother meant that it could take this long. But, dammit, she was right. *I guarantee your problems will find you again. Maybe not right away, but they will find you. Possibly when you least expect it and at the most inopportune time.* When you least expect it. The most inopportune time indeed.

∽

ERIN HOPPED out of the truck and stumbled to Landon's side, opening his door and tugging at his hand, which was still on the steering wheel. Was he going to continue his silence? The world around him was anything but silent. Baby ospreys screeching for daddy to bring a fish, finches darting around the trees, calling out in blissful song, a small wind chime hanging from the first branch of the tree whose outstretched arms held the treehouse.

Landon felt himself softening and getting sucked into her enthusiasm. He yielded to her pressure to exit the truck and wordlessly followed her to the ladder's base. *Wordlessly.* Perhaps that was a better way to describe a so-called silent treatment: a wordless treatment. Because if silence is truly the absence of sound, then there is no such thing as a silent treatment. The absence of words, though, was something he could get behind. As his father had demonstrated on multiple occasions, wordlessness worked except when it didn't. Ed Shultz's wordless treatment did nothing to stop Landon from boarding a plane to the Great Lakes for basic training. Erin ditched her prosthetic leg and started up the ladder, hopping from rung to rung with her real foot and pulling herself up the ladder with her arms. And with that, he broke his vow of wordlessness.

"Doris doesn't know what she did wrong, being left behind." He scrambled up the ladder behind her, suddenly wanting to see the treehouse with her, remembering it through Erin's eyes. Screw the letter he had written so long ago. Screw it. He was just a kid, then. If she never acknowledged the letter, well, so be it. It didn't matter. At least, that was what he told himself as he crossed the threshold into his past.

Erin plopped onto the floor where the loose board was and pried it open after Wes had unjammed it yesterday. "I couldn't get the board up yesterday when I was here with Wes. He fiddled with it, and poof, it popped open."

Landon's earlier suspicion was spot on—she had been here with Wes. His momentary elation following her up the ladder fell away and rolled across the floor until it came to the door, which hadn't entirely closed. It slipped out and crashed on the ground below.

"You were here?" He knew she had been, even without her admission. The letter that had fallen out of her pocket at the house was proof.

Erin shrugged. "I had to see the treehouse and see if the *Scrabble* set was still here."

"And?"

"Feast your eyes."

Landon stuck his hands into the well and pulled out the game, pretending he hadn't snuck in here himself several times over the years. "Wow. Amazing." He looked at her. "Like opening a time capsule."

"I took it home with me yesterday but returned this morning and put it back."

"Why?"

"I decided it was too painful to keep." She looked away, then gingerly back at Landon. "I found this yesterday too." She pulled the letter out of her pocket. "Does it look familiar?"

A wordless moment was about to transpire, not because Landon didn't want to say anything; he simply didn't know what to say. It was as if he was suddenly tongueless.

"I didn't read it yet." She pressed her lips together and shook her head. "Should I?"

Landon cleared his throat, which felt suspiciously like it was going to close and deem him unable to breathe. "Should you, what?"

"Should I read this? Or would you rather I didn't."

Landon suddenly became aware of himself and his surroundings. "Are you saying you didn't read it?"

"That's right."

"I taped it closed. The tape is gone."

"It flaked away when I touched it." She handed the letter to him. "It's okay, Landon. I don't need to read it. I'm not angry with you anymore."

Relieved and slightly disappointed, Landon shoved the note deep into his back pocket. He swallowed. Might as well take advantage of being here. "Wanna play *Scrabble*?"

"I thought you'd never ask."

THEY SET out the scrabble board and, Landon sitting cross-legged on the floor and Erin sitting with her back against the wall, silently played. Silently. There was that damned word again—silence. There was, of course, sound of the tiles hitting the board. The sound of Erin holding her breath when she selected a random letter from the velvet pouch. The sound of his heart beating through his shirt.

He could say they played wordlessly, except that many words were forming and morphing and growing across the Scrabble board. *Capture. Pudding. Lending. Shit* (this elicited a brief episode of laughter). *Storm* (built upon *shit*, inciting more laughter). *Clock. Salt.* The good words—the ones where you could rack up the points—seemed elusive, as if just being in the treehouse together required so much emotional energy that the brain power required to produce words such as *maximize, quixotic, equalize,* or *chutzpah* was just too much.

At one point, Landon had several tiles on his rack that, combined with other letters on the board could have formed the taboo words, words that might have caused him to blush. Was it even appropriate for a Navy SEAL to blush? There was no way in hell he would put down a tile to form *love.* Or *sweet.* Or *husband.* Or *wife.* Certainly not fiancée. He glanced at Erin, as he slowly came back to reality at the thought of that word. Fiancée. She was to become Wes's fiancée tomorrow. Thank God he would soon be gone.

Erin put down two tiles—W and I—using the I in *lending* as an anchor. *Wish.* Oh, how he wished his life had turned out differently.

"What do you wish for?" Erin said, blasting into his thoughts as if she could read his mind.

He was great at thinking on his feet when it was life or death out on a mission. But he sucked at it when it came to responding to a question he had no desire to answer. He grasped at straws and latched onto the only thought that popped into his mind. "Wish?"

Her eyes danced. "Wish."

It was now or never. Maybe he could say what he had tried to say so long ago—everything but the part about loving her. That was the bottom line—he wished he had just fucking told her he loved her, without trying to turn it into some grand gesture. He took a deep breath.

"I wish I could find a time portal to jump through. I'd go back to the Fourth of July twenty years ago. And when I concocted that stupid-ass plan to dip into your dad's fireworks and you said it wasn't such a good idea. Remember that?" He didn't wait for a response. Of course she remembered; how stupid of him to even ask. It changed her life. Ruined her life. "I would have listened to you." He rolled his eyes. "I wouldn't have been such a stupid, arrogant, clueless teenager." He held out his hands and, by a small miracle, she took them. "I would have—"

"There you are." Susan appeared in the small opening that was the treehouse's doorway. "Dammit, Landon. I've been calling and calling." She glared at Erin. "Hardware store?"

"It's not what you think," Erin said, retreating her hands. Her voice was steady and calm.

"Hell, it isn't." Susan's face turned stone cold.

"Susan, this really isn't what it looks like," Landon said. "I was in the middle of—"

"Don't even bother."

Landon's eyes met Erin's across the *Scrabble* board. He held her gaze for a split second, then looked away. And in that split second, Landon suddenly saw the scene through Susan's eyes. Whatever Erin had up her sleeve, he almost fell for it. How could he be so stupid? How? Had Susan not pierced the air with the sword of reality, he would have kissed Erin. He was certain of it. As if his whole life had been made up of a million little steppingstones leading to precisely this moment. He had almost felt the moment was ordained. Divinely orchestrated. Meant to be. *How could I have been so stupid?* Erin's lips were not his to kiss. They never were. They certainly were not now. The thought of almost kissing the (almost) fiancée of another man— a nice man, a good man, even if he was a dweeb—left him feeling dirty and cheap. He stood.

"It's truly not what you think, Susan." Landon reached out his hand to help Erin up. She swatted him away and in one graceful motion, pushed herself up using just her arms. Suddenly she was standing on one foot, balancing as steadily as if her leg had suddenly grown back.

"We don't have time for this," Susan said. "It's your dad."

31

By the time Landon and Erin—trailing in the truck behind Susan's Mini Cooper—reached the boatyard, the paramedics had already taken Landon's dad to the hospital in Easton. The new Urgent Care facility that had opened in Canvasback Cove a few years ago apparently couldn't deal with a sixty-seven-year-old man with a broken back.

"Puppy fell off the ladder," Willie said, surprisingly calm, sitting at the kitchen table with Erin's mother. "He's okay, daddy. There was no blood."

Of course. To a three-year-old, blood was the demarcation between life and death. A boo-boo with no blood was just a boo-boo, maybe eliciting a quiet whimper but no actual tears. On the other hand, the sight of even a drop of blood, no matter how tiny, had the uncanny ability to send Willie into a fit of despair, complete with massive, desperate wails. The fact that Ed had been transported to the hospital told Landon that blood or no blood, his dad was severely injured.

In the truck, Erin's mother was on speaker, trying to explain what had happened. According to Lydia, she and Willie had been walking around in the boatyard, collecting rocks and oyster shells. She heard a shout, then a crash.

"He had the ladder against that damned sailboat," she'd said to Erin. "You couldn't just drive home, Erin? You had to make a grand gesture with that damned boat?" She clicked her tongue, and Landon could picture her shaking her head.

"Mrs. Conrad, this isn't helpful," Landon yelled from the driver's seat.

"I can hear you perfectly fine. You don't need to yell."

"Stop it, Mom. Where's Wes?"

"Talking to the paramedics."

WHEN LANDON, Susan, and Erin arrived at the house, the paramedics had already whisked Ed away. Logistical issues suddenly surfaced; Landon didn't know what to do with Willie. Worst case, he would just have to bring him along to the hospital, maybe promise him ice cream on the way home.

"I'll stay here with him," Susan said, reading his mind. "Lydia, you go with Landon and Erin and Wes."

"Wes rode in the ambulance with him," Lydia said.

"Was Dad conscious?" Despite his blatant dislike of the dweeb cardiologist, Landon thought it was big of Wes to stay with his dad. He hated to admit it, but he was grateful and relieved to have an advocate—a cardiologist!—in the mix.

"Yes. Yes, your father was conscious," Lydia said. "In a lot of pain, though." She shrugged. "Thank God, he doesn't seem to have any paralysis."

"Thank God," Landon repeated.

Landon felt tender toward Susan, suddenly, and hugged her. "Thanks for offering to stay with Willie, babe." He wished he could take the term of endearment back. He couldn't. So, there it was. Out there for all to hear. He supposed since it tumbled out of his mouth without his knowledge or consent, it must mean something.

32

E rin wanted to crawl into a hole. In fact, there was a perfectly good, four-foot hole just outside the door, practically. She would have to walk a few hundred yards, but it was there. She doubted anyone had filled it in yet. And what was Landon's dad doing up on a ladder anyway? If Landon was up all night repairing the boat, what business did his father have up there? Was this some sort of karmic episode? Tragedy befalling the Shultz family for what Landon had done to her all those years ago? God, she hoped not. And now, her mother's words would forever haunt her. *You couldn't just drive home, Erin? You had to make a grand gesture with that damned boat?*

She replayed what she had just heard Landon say: *Babe.* Landon called Susan *Babe.* Babe. Babe. Babe. Babe. Erin wanted to crawl into the hole, and she wanted someone to cover her with dirt. She couldn't believe she had almost thrown away six months with Wes less than an hour before. Erin cringed at how close she came to pouring her heart out to Landon. She almost picked up the Scrabble game with both hands. She almost flung it behind her, leaving a nice, empty path toward Landon. She wouldn't have had to travel very far—a foot, at most—before she was in Landon's arms, which she now realized, was exactly where she wanted to be. It didn't matter what he had written on that notebook paper so long ago. She loved him then, and she loves him now—twenty years too late.

She glanced at the two of them, huddled near the sink, talking in hushed tones. Erin felt like an outsider in Landon's house. A stranger who had walked in off the street. She imagined Landon and Susan floating away in a hot air balloon into the sunset, Willie standing at the edge of the basket waving and yelling, "Look, Spiderman Lady! I'm flying!" She watched as the balloon grew smaller and Willie's voice grew fainter, Landon's arm pulling Susan close. Hopefully, the mental image would make it easier for her to bury Landon once and for all. She was in love with Wes, wasn't she? *He makes me laugh. We have fun together. He's a cardiologist!* And he rode in the ambulance with a man he barely knew and probably didn't even like. As much as she wanted to rush to the hospital to be with Wes, she knew what she needed to do.

"I'll stay here with Willie." She looked at the floor but addressed the happy couple. "You go. I'm the outlier here. I'll keep Willie company."

"I don't know." Landon broke away from Susan and took a step toward his son, who was coloring with Erin's mother at the table. "I don't think I could deal with another incident."

"She won't let him feed the bird," Susan said. "Let's go, sweetie. Your dad is probably wondering where you are." She glared at Erin, then turned back to Landon. "Come on, let's go."

"Another incident?" Erin lit into Landon. Apparently, burying him would be easier than she thought. She stopped talking and turned away, hot tears streaming down her cheeks.

"I'll stay," Lydia said, her eyes never leaving the coloring book, the blue crayon in her hand making mindless, swooping maneuvers on the page. "You kids go. Erin, I know Wes will want to see you."

"Does she have to ride with us?" Susan put her arm around Landon's waist.

Erin didn't want to hear Landon's response. "Mom, could I take your car, please?"

"Don't be silly," Landon said. "You'll ride with us. There's plenty of room in my truck."

Susan shot him a look.

"She'll ride with us," Landon shot back. He looked at Erin. "You'll ride with us."

33

"I wanted to check the running lights, make sure they worked," Ed Shultz told the emergency room doctor just as Landon walked in. He looked up at Landon and winced. "Would you believe it, Son? The damned ladder started to slide, and I didn't realize what was happening until it was too late." He touched his head. "Didn't bump the old noggin, thank God."

The ER doctor stepped outside the confines of the curtain.

"He's fortunate," the dweeb cardiologist chimed in. Landon didn't realize he was even in the room until now, and he felt terrible for silently referring to him as a dweeb these past few days. The good cardiologist helped his dad; he was anything but a dweeb.

"Thank you, Wes, for riding in the ambulance with him."

"This guy tells the best jokes," Ed said. He looked at Wes, who nodded. "Why did the doctor tiptoe past the medicine cabinet?"

"So he wouldn't wake the sleeping pills." Erin walked into the cubby hole and hugged Wes, then winked at Ed. "He told me that joke on our first date."

Landon squashed the image of Erin and Wes staring at each other across a corner table in a quiet little bistro and reached for Susan's hand. "Dad, tell us what happened?"

"I already told you, the ladder started to slide." He shook his head. "I knew I was hurt the second I landed." The curtain parted, and the ER doctor returned.

"I'm his son." Landon extended his hand. "Landon Shultz."

"Navy SEAL," Ed added. "About to go on an important mission. Tomorrow, I think."

The doctor seemed unimpressed with Landon's job title and uninterested in his "important mission." He moved on from the introductions and pointed at the X-ray in his tablet: a jagged, white line crossed two of Ed's lumbar vertebrae. "Your father also shattered his right heel and broke his left wrist."

Susan and Erin gasped while Wes stood by, stoic and detached. Landon fixed his eyes on the doctor's screen and wondered how the hell he could possibly leave tomorrow. How? It wasn't like he had a choice—not this time. As the Chief Petty Officer of his unit, he had to be on that plane. Had to lead the mission to South America that Commander Diaz had cryptically described. Landon knew enough to fill in the blanks to understand that he needed to be there. Now that he knew his father's condition wasn't life-threatening, the gravity of this logistical nightmare came at him like a freight train.

Landon slowly tuned his ears so that they were in synch with the ER doctor's words. "Your father's choices are surgery to implant screws or four to six months in an orthotic brace."

"That's simple," Ed said. "The brace." He looked at Landon. "No way anyone is cutting this guy open." He jabbed at his chest with his finger. "No way in hell."

Problems at home, Landon texted to his Commanding Officer. His father was out of the ER and settled into a private room, his foot and wrist wrapped in plaster. *Long story, but my father fell off a ladder this morning. In hospital now. I'm still flying back tomorrow but may have to take more leave after the mission.*

He pressed the send button, relieved that his father would at least be in a rehab facility for a few weeks—long enough that Landon wouldn't need to worry about him while he was out of the country. He figured he could ask Lydia Conrad to check in on him a few times a week now that she and his dad were chummy. Landon still couldn't believe the Hatfield's and McCoy's were again on speaking terms. He glanced upward, wondering if his mother somehow intervened, knowing that her beloved husband would one day need help.

A roar of whooping and hollering, punctuated by laughter and clapping, slid into the room from under the closed door. Landon looked at his father, pumped full of painkillers and sleeping heavily. He squeezed his dad's hand and shuffled toward the revelry in the hallway.

LANDON MET Susan's eyes across the hallway. She was standing near the nurse's station, holding a cardboard tray containing four plastic coffee cups. She gestured with her head toward the source of the happy commotion.

He walked toward her, glancing sideways at the two people in the center of a circle of random doctors, nurses, and other hospital staff who must have just happened to be walking by. Could anyone resist the sight of a dweeb on bended knee, holding out a shiny diamond toward the woman he loved? It was too much. Too, too much.

"Wes proposed," Susan said when Landon reached her, the relief in her voice palpable. "She said yes. We'll have to plan a party, you know, once your dad is better."

"Right." He locked eyes with Susan and imagined a similar scene where he proposed to her. He couldn't do it. He simply couldn't conjure the mental picture of him and Susan living happily ever after. He knew such a concept didn't exist. His dad had lost the love of his life. And now, it felt like he had lost the love of his life too. "Susan, we need to talk." The buzz of his cell phone startled him. Probably Commander Diaz, he thought. He looked at Susan. "I need to take this," he said, stepping aside and reading the text, putting his melancholy on hold.

SECDEF told us to stand down. Situation resolved itself. You'll read about it in the paper tomorrow. Anyway, stay as long as you need to. When you return, we'll start discussing your test for promotion to Senior Chief. Landon smiled as he read the text. Again, he wondered if his mother was sitting on a cloud, orchestrating his movements here on Earth.

Landon texted back, surer of his next move than he had ever been about anything in his life. *Actually, Sir, I've decided to submit my papers.* Landon didn't need to elaborate—Commander Diaz would know... and would know not to try and talk him out of it.

The response came several seconds later: *Retirement! Holy cow! God help us! The civilian world is in for it! Congratulations!*

34

———

Erin heard the sound of tires on gravel, distinguishing between the truck approaching Landon's house from Wes's softer Acura tires that had pulled away from the house a short time ago. Erin went to the door and watched Landon's truck rattling up the driveway.

She and her mother had been chatting quietly in the family room while Willie snored on the couch. He had fallen asleep watching *Toy Story* when Woody accidentally knocked Buzz Lightyear out the window.

"But he seemed so good for you," Lydia said. "I don't understand. I really don't." She studied her daughter. "He was so sure you would say yes."

"I did say yes."

"Semantics, sweetie, semantics." She grasped Erin's hands. "It's not yes if the no comes five minutes later."

"I love Wes. Or at least I thought I loved him." Erin looked at her left hand, absent the beautiful ring Wes had slid on her finger. Wes said it was his grandmother's ring. And a lovely ring it was, dainty with tiny diamonds flanking a brilliant sapphire. It fit perfectly. And she hated pulling it off her finger; marrying Wes was something she thought she had wanted. Not surprisingly, he took it back without a fight. She wiggled her bare fingers, shaking them as if swatting imaginary gnats. She felt the tears sting her eyes just as she heard the tires. She was still wiping them away when Landon climbed out of his truck.

"How's your dad," she said as Landon walked into the house.

"Stubborn. Stable. Sleeping."

"Someone else is sleeping, too." She nodded her head toward the family room and searched for something to say. "So, you're leaving tomorrow?" And then: "Where's Susan?"

"I dropped her off at her house." Landon started moving toward the family room, then turned to face Erin. "Congratulations, by the way."

"For what?"

"Your engagement."

"How did you know about that?"

"How could I not?"

He stepped closer to the family room, did an about-face, and went down the hall instead.

ERIN FOLLOWED Landon down the hall, taking great care to not be noticed. She stood several inches away from the door, watching him opening dresser drawers, flinging clothes into the open waiting mouth of his hungry duffle bag sitting in the middle of the bed.

"I never thanked you for fixing *Jolly Good Day*," she said. "I don't know how I'll ever repay you."

"No worries," he said, his back toward her, waving her away from behind.

"I said no." Erin waited. He closed the drawer and opened the one below it, pulling out several socks rolled into neat little balls. "Landon, I told him no."

He turned around slowly. Erin stepped into the room and wiggled her fingers in front of him. "See? No ring."

"I don't understand. It was like New Year's Eve in the hospital." He knit his brow. "I saw you say yes and watched him put the ring on your finger."

"What difference does it make?" She took a deep breath. "I wasn't honest with you yesterday." She shrugged. "I read your note."

He blushed. "I know." He inched his way closer to her. "I went to the tree house more than once since I've been home. The tape never disintegrated when I touched it."

She nudged him back. "So, is Susan planning to meet you in Coronado after your mission?"

Landon's eyes grew big. He shook his head. "Why would she?"

"I thought you were together."

"Why would you think that?"

"You called her 'Babe' this morning."

Landon sat down on the bed. He rested his elbows on his knees and cradled his head. "I tried to make something, anything, work with her." He reached for Erin's hand and pulled her onto the bed beside him. "We talked this afternoon. I told her I wasn't in love with her. I told her I never got over my first love." He brushed a lock of hair out of Erin's tear-filled eyes.

"We have spectacular timing, don't we?" She laughed through her tears. "You're leaving tomorrow."

"Only to submit my retirement papers." He smiled his crooked smile. "I'll be back next Thursday." He kissed her. "This time, for good." He kissed her again, more urgently. He stopped long enough to add: "I figure my dad needs help, especially now."

"Shut up, Landon." Erin's voice wavered, caught between a laugh and a sob. She pulled him into a hug, holding on as if she could keep him there forever. As his heartbeat echoed against hers, she whispered into his neck, "I'm not letting you go again. Not ever."

～

AFTERWORD

I'm delighted that you decided to pick up *Canvasback Cove*. These days, an author's success depends quite a bit on reviews: the good, the bad, and the ugly. I would be hugely grateful if you could take a few minutes and post a review. Whether you liked the book, felt lukewarm about it, or absolutely hated it, potential readers want to know what you think. Feel free to post a review on Goodreads, the retailer of your choice, your own blog, wherever you desire.

JOIN MY ONLINE FAMILY

One of the things I enjoy most about writing is building a relationship with my readers. I occasionally send newsletters with details on new releases, special offers, and other surprises.

I would love to stay in touch. Join my online family to receive updates on future books. You can sign up at https://substack.com/@ lynnstewart.

ACKNOWLEDGMENTS

This book began with deciding whether to set the story in an actual Eastern Shore town or create a fictional one. Ultimately, the fictional town of Canvasback Cove won out, allowing me to shape the community and geography to fit the story. Still, the beauty and charm of the real Eastern Shore, a place that will always hold a special place in my heart, remain ever-present in my writing.

I wrote the first draft of this book in early 2022 in Kathryn Johnson's (https://writer.org/organizer/kathryn-johnson/) The Extreme Novelist class. I later put it aside to work on another project in Diane Zinna's (https://dianezinna.com) Novel in a Year class. After struggling with my current work-in-progress (a story about grief, which is draining to write about), I decided to take a break from Muddle Toe and resurrect Canvasback Cove.

I would like to extend my deepest thanks to Kathryn Johnson for her invaluable insights and to Diane Zinna for her inspiring guidance and mentorship.

The pandemic impacted us all in countless ways, and I want to acknowledge the immeasurable loss of life and the resilience of those who navigated through such difficult times. Writing during Covid was both a challenge and a balm, and I'm deeply grateful for the creative outlet it provided, a source of relief and joy amid uncertainty.

Finally, my heartfelt thanks go to my husband, Mike (Sweet Petunia), for his unwavering love and support. Your feedback, wine-fueled plot discussions, and countless read-throughs kept me grounded—and laughing—throughout the process.

BOOK GROUP QUESTIONS

Grab a beer, a crab cake, some fries, and friends!

1. **Landon's Relationship with His Father:** Landon's father runs the family boatyard and is still very much present in his life. How does the relationship between Landon and his father impact Landon's decisions, particularly regarding his career and parenting? What role does Landon's father play in grounding him during moments of doubt?

2. **Erin's Struggle with Identity:** Erin grapples with the loss of her leg and the impact it had on her future dreams. How does her physical injury symbolize her emotional wounds? How does it affect her relationship with Wes and her reconciliation with Landon?

3. **Landon's Guilt and Redemption:** How does Landon's guilt over the accident and his feelings for Erin shape his actions throughout the story? Do you believe he finds redemption by the end of the novel?

4. **The Absence of Landon's Mother:** Landon's mother passed away, yet her memory lingers over his life. How do you think her absence affects Landon's emotional state and his relationship with Erin? In what ways does her death contribute to his guilt and his search for redemption?

5. **Susan's Role in the Love Triangle:** Susan clearly wants to be with Landon, but he is hesitant. How do you think Susan's feelings for Landon complicate his emotions? Do you believe her presence ultimately helps or hinders his growth?

6. **The Impact of Parenthood:** Both Erin and Landon face challenges related to parenting. How do you think being a parent has changed Landon, and how does Erin view her role in his and Willie's lives? What do you think about the idea of Landon trying to convince himself a relationship with Susan might be good for Willie?

7. **Themes of Forgiveness:** The novel explores the need for forgiveness, both from others and within oneself. Do you think Erin has truly forgiven Landon for the accident that changed her life? How important is forgiveness for the characters' growth?

8. **The Influence of Erin's Father:** Erin's father plays a significant role in shaping her love for sailing and her identity. How does his memory influence Erin's decisions and emotional journey throughout the novel? In what ways does Erin continue to seek his approval or guidance even after his death?

9. **The Significance of Canvasback Cove:** The town serves as more than just a setting. How does the location of Canvasback Cove influence the characters' relationships and personal journeys? How does returning home affect both Erin and Landon?

10. **Parental Expectations:** Both Erin and Landon grew up with strong parental figures who had expectations for them. How do these expectations (both spoken and unspoken) shape Erin and Landon's personalities, choices, and conflicts? In what ways are they still influenced by their parents' ideals, even after their parents have passed or grown older?

11. **Wes as a Foil:** Wes, Erin's current boyfriend, seems like the opposite of Landon in many ways. What does Wes represent for Erin, and how does his presence affect her ability to reconnect with Landon? What does his reaction to sailing tell us about his character?

12. **Erin's Relationship with Her Mother:** Erin's mother is still a strong presence, particularly through her B&B and the concept of 'family camp.' How does Erin's relationship with her mother reflect Erin's own struggles with identity and moving forward? Do you think her mother supports Erin's choices, or does she complicate Erin's path?

13. **Landon's Transformation:** Throughout the novel, we see how Landon has changed since his youth, especially following his Navy SEAL career and the incident with Erin. How do you think his career shaped his personality and his relationships, particularly with his son and Erin?

14. **Landon and Erin's History:** Landon and Erin have a complicated past, tied together by a tragic accident. How does their shared history affect their ability to move forward? Is their reconnection inevitable, or do you think the past is too much to overcome?

15. **The Role of Sailing as Metaphor:** Sailing plays a central role in the novel. How does sailing serve as a metaphor for control, freedom, or the unpredictability of life in the characters' journeys?

ABOUT THE AUTHOR

Lynn Stewart writes contemporary women's fiction that explores the complexities of relationships, family, and personal growth. Living on Maryland's Eastern Shore, Lynn draws inspiration from the coastal life around her, infusing her stories with themes of second chances and healing. In addition to writing, she is an avid triathlete and enjoys sailing with her husband. When she's not crafting her next novel, Lynn shares her thoughts on life and creativity through her Substack, *Colorful Chaos* (https://lynnstewart.substack.com/).

ALSO BY LYNN STEWART

Stay Back! Trilogy

Book 1: Stay Back!

Book 2: Back And Forth

Book 3: Stay Here

Follow retired cop John Butterfield's story as he navigates the aftermath of his wife's brutal rape in *Stay Back!*, is thrown into an unconventional mission during the 9/11 attacks in *Back And Forth* and finds himself face-to-face with the kid he walked away from six years before in *Stay Here*.

Over the Rail Series

Book 1: Over the Rail

She's afraid to let go. He can't say goodbye. Will Fate pair two broken hearts?

Book 2: Second Saturday

A brew that could kill. A retiree crew ready to sip. Can she keep her relationship and the feisty seniors alive?